PASSION'S DESTINY

Jakarta grew angrier and angrier as she stewed over the feature. *How could he allow this to happen? I don't see how this has any political benefit at all.* She started walking back to the apartment, hoping the exercise would help her work off some of her anger.

When she arrived at the apartment, she saw Zane's car parked out front. Any anger she had managed to walk off on the way back flared up again with a vengeance. She stormed up the stairs to the apartment and flung open the door.

"Oh, so is this what you are now, an eligible bachelor?" Jakarta slapped him in the chest with the copy of *Ebony* magazine she'd opened to his picture. "So what exactly am I doing here, Mr. 'eligible bachelor'?"

Zane was dumbfounded by her attack. "Wait, wait, wait. Hold up!" he said, holding his hands out in front of him. "It's not like that and you know it. This was just a campaign thing. We thought it would be good exposure."

"This is the kind of exposure you want?" Jakarta demanded. "'Zane is looking for a woman who is politically minded and committed to improving our society.'" She sneered the words. "Did you notice in here"—she pulled the magazine back and pointed to blurb copy toward the end—"the magazine has instructions on how women can contact the bachelor of their choice? So is that what you're after?"

"It's just politics, baby. You know that."

"Uh-huh. That's what it is today. Who knows what it'll be six weeks from now when the letters start pouring in?"

"I swear to you, Jakarta, it's not like that. I'm not looking for anybody else. I want to be with you."

"Uh-huh."

"It's true. I am your eligible bachelor and that's it."

Jakarta tossed the magazine on the bedroom dresser and turned to him. "My eligible bachelor?"

"All yours," he said.

PASSION'S DESTINY

Crystal Wilson-Harris

ARABESQUE

BET BOOKS

BET Publications, LLC
http://www.bet.com
http://www.arabesquebooks.com

ARABESQUE BOOKS are published by

BET Publications, LLC
c/o BET BOOKS
One BET Plaza
1900 W Place NE
Washington, DC 20018-1211

All Kensington Titles, Imprints, and Distributed Lines are available at special quantity discounts for bulk purchases for sales promotions, premiums, fund-raising, and educational or institutional use. Special book excerpts or customized printings can also be created to fit specific needs. For details, write or phone the office of the Kensington special sales manager: Kensington Publishing Corp., 850 Third Avenue, New York, NY 10022, attn: Special Sales Department, Phone: 1-800-221-2647.

First Printing: October 2003
10 9 8 7 6 5 4 3 2 1

Printed in the United States of America

For my family
Reafeal, Lindsay, and Jay
Who so willingly went above and beyond to help me
see it through

Chapter 1

She could feel it beginning. It had taken longer than usual this time, but Jakarta Raven had no doubt it was beginning again. As she stood in her sister Savannah's kitchen, cupping a mug of cooling coffee and looking out the window at the gently falling leaves, Jakarta knew the time had come.

How are they going to react? she wondered idly, thinking about her sisters. *We've rebuilt a strong relationship over these last months, but is it strong enough to handle this?* Shrugging, she turned from the window and poured the now-cold coffee down the drain. "I can't take it anymore." She finally said the words aloud that had been scratching at the edges of her mind for a while now. "It's time for me to move on."

She went to the refrigerator and pulled out the chicken Savannah had asked her to roast for the weekly family gathering. Once Savannah's drama was behind them and life started returning to normal, Paris, the self-appointed overseer of the family, had insisted they all make time in their schedules for weekly Wednesday dinners. So every Wednesday, like clockwork, the Raven

sisters converged on Savannah's house for dinner.
Sydney, their corporate mover and shaker, had initially
balked, saying that on some Wednesdays she had to go
to her sorority meeting. "It's important for me to be
there," Sydney had said to a stern-faced Paris. "It's not
just sorority business that goes on at those meetings."

But Paris was having none of it. "If we learned nothing else over this last year, we've learned that family is
everything. Don't even try to act like it's a tough call
between your blood sisters and your sorority sisters."

Even D.J. and Stephanie, Savannah's teenaged children, understood that Wednesday dinner was a command appearance. As she seasoned the chicken, Jakarta
smiled, thinking about how willingly they had made
room at the table for one additional plate.

Anthony Martin, the handsome young detective who
had helped secure Savannah's freedom, now had become
an integral part of all their lives. Watching the happiness
Savannah had found with Anthony only served to further cement Jakarta's resolve to move on. *I'll tell them
all tonight,* she decided. *And let the chips fall where
they may.*

Jakarta slid the chicken into the oven and washed
her hands over the sink. After making sure she'd cleaned
up her mess in the kitchen, she headed to the computer
room to check her e-mail. A shiver of anticipation shim-
mied down her spine. "Wonder if he wrote me back."

As she settled in front of the computer and powered
up the machine, Jakarta pushed a stray lock out of her
eye. Catching a glimpse of her reflection in the screen,
she found further confirmation of her conviction that it
was time for her to go. She had begun to measure time
by the length of her locks. When she had first come back
into the bosom of her family nearly eighteen months ago,
her sister Savannah was dealing with abandonment and
then murder charges. At her sister's request, Jakarta

had cut Savannah's hair into a close-cropped Afro that had been widely admired. Savannah had kept the short do, often commenting on how low-maintenance it was compared to the weave she'd worn before her husband disappeared. Feeling a little envious, Jakarta had decided it was time for her own makeover. So, shortly after she trimmed Savannah's locks, Jakarta cut all the chemical relaxer out of her own hair and began the process of locking it.

It was torturous at first, and many times she thought about cutting the locks out and going back to the relaxed style, but someone had once told her that locks were a lifestyle commitment, not just a fashion statement, so Jakarta had decided to see it through. Now as she ran her fingers through her hair, fluffing the locks, she was glad she had stayed with it. Eighteen months of growth had yielded a chin-length head of healthy, well-maintained locks, which she had adorned with a few cowrie shells tied in. Their auburn color was lighter in some places because Jakarta had periodically spritzed her hair with strong brewed tea, knowing the tea would serve as a natural hair lightener.

The auburn locks were a perfect complement to her pecan-colored skin. There was a slight sprinkling of freckles across the bridge of her nose and on her cheeks. Jakarta had hated her freckles as a kid, and she'd tried every home remedy she'd ever read about—from lemons to fade cream—to try to get rid of them. Eventually, she had come to accept and now enjoy her freckles.

"You've got mail." The familiar voice spoke the words she hoped to hear. With a huge smile on her face, Jakarta clicked on the appropriate icon and leaned forward to read her mail.

* * *

Dinner that night was the normal raucous affair. D.J. was regaling the family with stories from football practice, barely containing his enthusiasm at the turn of events that had him moving into the starting running back slot after the usual starter had been injured.

Reactions to D.J.'s news were fairly predictable, ranging from Savannah expressing concern to Anthony giving the teen a high five. Jakarta, however, sat quietly through the meal, toying aimlessly with the roast chicken and scalloped potatoes on her plate.

"What do you think, Jakarta?" Savannah asked. "Should D.J. start for the varsity team?"

"Mm-hm," Jakarta said noncommittally.

"What's up, J?" Paris asked. "You don't really seem to be here with us tonight."

Jakarta looked around the table and found herself under the scrutiny of six pairs of eyes. *Here goes nothing,* she thought.

"It's going to sound foolish and selfish," she said tentatively.

"That's not that big a surprise," Sydney said dryly.

"Hush, Syd," Savannah ordered. "What's going to sound foolish and selfish?" she asked Jakarta. "What are you talking about?"

"It's been a helluva last year for us," Jakarta began.

"Who you telling?" Savannah laughed. "But everything worked out in the end." She reached for Anthony's hand across the table.

"Yes, it did," Jakarta agreed. "And I'm so happy for you and Anthony, but . . ."

"But what?" Paris prompted.

Jakarta took a deep breath. "I'm feeling like I've been home too long."

Sydney's eyes widened with shock. "Home too long? It's barely been a year. Are you saying you can't spend a year with your family?"

"It's been eighteen months," Jakarta pointed out. "And it's just that I need more."

"More than what?" Savannah asked.

"More than this," Jakarta said, gesturing around the table. "I love you all, and I've loved spending time with you, but I'm not cut out to be stay-at-home help. I need more than I'm getting now."

"I have offered you a job at Dailey Plumbing," Savannah reminded her. "You turned me down."

"No offense, Savannah, but I'm not meant to be in the plumbing business either."

After a few silent moments, Savannah shrugged. "Well, I suppose I knew that all along. I suppose I knew your wanderlust wouldn't let you stay here for too long."

"I thought you were putting your vagabond nature behind you," Sydney said. "I thought you had come to realize there's no place like home."

"Actually, *Dorothy*," Jakarta said, emphasizing the name, "I think it's time for me to follow the yellow brick road."

"So you're leaving us again." Paris's tone revealed her disappointment. "Where are you going to go?"

"I don't know for sure," Jakarta said.

"Is that right?" Savannah folded her arms across her chest and leaned back in her chair. "I thought you might be heading toward New Orleans."

In spite of herself, Jakarta smiled. "Umm, I don't know about that. . . ."

"Don't try to be coy," Savannah said. "Everybody knows. Do you think I haven't noticed that you've been getting calls and cards from New Orleans?"

Jakarta looked away. "It's just all a little embarrassing."

"You do realize this was the man that tried to put Savannah in jail for the rest of her natural life," Paris demanded, always fiercely loyal to the family. "Of all the men in the world that you could develop a relationship with, you would pick the one that tried to destroy our family."

Jakarta was quick to defend him. "He was not trying to destroy our family, he was trying to do his job. Anthony told us that Zane set him on the right path to getting the information he needed to free Savannah. How can you just ignore that?"

Unconvinced, Paris sucked her teeth and turned away.

"Does he know that you don't really do anything for a living?" Sydney asked. "I mean, he's the assistant prosecutor of a huge, nationally prominent city. That's pretty prestigious. Is he aware that you are just kind of a drifter?"

"I'm not sure why you think that would make any difference," Jakarta said defensively.

"Oh, please, don't kid yourself. You and these romantic notions about love." Sydney wagged her finger at her baby sister. "There's a reality at work here, and the reality is that he's going to have social and political obligations and responsibilities to his constituency that you are not equipped to help him meet."

The words stung Jakarta more than she had expected them to. But she shook her sister's declaration off. "Whatever. I'm only going for a visit. Just a week, Syd. No permanent commitments or long-term decisions." A wicked grin had appeared on Jakarta's face. "We'll probably just have sex the whole time," she teased her older sister. "I don't think we'll have to worry about his 'constituents' for the next week or so."

Sydney, too, sucked her teeth, rolled her eyes, and turned away.

Savannah, the sister Jakarta had expected to have the most strenuous objection, was serene.

"Sweetheart," Savannah said, "if you like this young man and you want to spend some time with him to get to know him, I say go for it. Life is just too short to deny yourself the things that you want."

Jakarta smiled then, knowing that it wasn't simply Savannah's altruism and love of humanity that led her to that position.

"Life's just too short," Savannah repeated as she looked across the table at Anthony. For his part, Anthony smiled slightly at Savannah and nodded. "Zane Reeves is a good man. He didn't have to help me, but he did. And he bent several rules to do it." Anthony squeezed Savannah's hand. "Reeves knew Savannah was innocent, and he went above and beyond the call to make sure an innocent woman didn't go to jail."

Paris, apparently not ready to concede the point, chimed in. "That's Zane Reeves the prosecutor. What do you know about Zane Reeves the man? You're talking about leaving your family to go off to be with this man you don't really know. Honestly, Jakarta, is being home *that* bad?"

"Look, Paris," Jakarta said shortly, "I'm not talking about moving to New Orleans. I'm going for a visit. Zane and I have been talking and e-mailing each other for months now. I know a little bit about him. . . . He's certainly intriguing, and I'd like to get to know him better." Jakarta glared at Paris. "I'm only going to be in New Orleans for about a week. I'm not abandoning the family homestead; I'm not turning on my sister—I'm just going for a vacation. I need a diversion and this is it. Now if you can't accept that, I'm sorry, but I need to do this for me."

Jakarta pushed away from the table and stood. "Anybody else got anything else to say before I go?" She looked at each face closely. "Well, then, hearing nothing further," she said, "if you'll excuse me, I'm going to my room to pack."

"Pack?" Paris said. "Are you leaving soon?"

"I'm leaving Friday," Jakarta said. "I'll be gone for a week, and I don't anticipate any problems." She turned to go.

"People never do," Paris said to her retreating back.

Chapter 2

Zane Reeves felt an anticipation that he could neither explain nor deny. As he stood in the airport awaiting flight 1832 from Detroit, he couldn't keep the foolish grin off his face. "You are building this up too much in your mind," he tried to tell himself. "It's just a week, just a visit. Nothing may come of it." All his constant admonitions did nothing to quell the small flutter of anticipation that twisted in his belly.

When finally the announcement blared over the airport speaker that the flight was at the gate, Zane took a deep breath and consciously tried to steady his nerves. *Just a woman . . . no big deal,* he repeated again to himself. He stood at the gate, carefully scanning the faces of the passengers as they deboarded, watching reunions happen around him. It seemed to be taking an inordinate amount of time. *Did she miss the flight? Did she change her mind?* Insecurities rattled through his mind. And then, there she was. And the goofy smile Zane feared was going to spread across his face surely did.

"Jakarta," he breathed. "You made it."

"I made it," she agreed. "But it was more than a notion. I swear I hate to fly."

He watched as a slow smile replaced the travel weariness on her face. *Just as beautiful as I remembered,* he thought. Zane's slow gaze absorbed every detail of Jakarta, refreshing his memory on some details, and adding new information on others. Petite was the first word that came to mind when he saw Jakarta. The top of her head barely reached his shoulder, surprising him because Zane had always been drawn to the tall, willowy type. Her skin was the color of the pecan pralines that had helped make New Orleans one of the food capitals of the world. *Her locks are longer than the last time I saw her,* Zane thought, noting yet another feature that separated Jakarta from the type of woman he usually liked.

"Aw, flying's not so bad," Zane said.

"Tell that to my stomach—once it catches up with me." Jakarta feigned nausea.

Zane had to laugh at that. "Well, at least you're here." He took her in his arms and embraced her, a tentative hug, because this was new territory for both of them.

"Did you check your bags?" he said inanely, knowing it was not what he wanted to say to her, but accepting that it was all he could manage to say right then.

"Yeah." She nodded. "Hope that's not a decision I live to regret. If my suitcase gets lost, I'm screwed."

"There's only one way to find out," he said and took her hand and led her to the baggage claim.

As they made their way through the crowded airport, Zane worked up his nerve to say what was on his heart.

"I'm really glad you came," he said after clearing his throat. "I felt like you got a bad impression of my city the last time you were here."

Jakarta had to laugh. "Last time I was here, my sister was wrongfully imprisoned for murdering the husband who had abandoned her. You have to figure that would color my opinion a bit."

"Yes, well," Zane said, fidgeting uncomfortably, "but New Orleans is such a beautiful, vibrant city, and I'm glad you're going to give me a chance to show you more of it."

Jakarta smiled at him, a private, wicked thought passing through her mind. *I'm glad I'm going to get a chance to explore more of you.*

At thirty-two, Zane Reeves looked boyishly youthful. That was one of the first things Jakarta had noticed about him—that and the smooth almond color of his skin. The almond color, combined with his almost jet-black wavy hair and darkly intense eyes, had led many a person—at least those not familiar with New Orleans's unique culture—to question Zane's ethnicity. He had been mistaken for Indian, Arab, Egyptian, and even Palestinian. But those from the N'awlins area had no doubt that Zane Reeves was Creole. At least on his mother's side. His mother had married a non-Creole, a choice that had gifted her children with slightly fuller features than the traditional Creole, but one glance at Zane made his heritage clear.

He was tall, but not nearly as imposing as Jakarta thought she remembered him to be. Thinking back to her first encounter with Zane Reeves, she realized he probably seemed taller and more threatening because his mission had been to prosecute, convict, and incarcerate her beloved oldest sister. *That must have made him seem much more menacing,* she acknowledged to herself. Now, as she considered him in a different light and for a different reason, she put his height at just under six feet. He was stocky, but not overweight—just firmly and solidly built. He looked as though he could have played football in college. Jakarta made a mental note to ask him about that, thinking if he had, that would be a very interesting insight into his character.

Unlike the other times she had seen him, when he was dressed professionally in a well-made suit and carefully color-coordinated tie, today to meet her at the airport Zane was wearing jeans and a colorful print shirt.

"My, don't you look different than I remembered." Jakarta grinned.

"Well, when they let me out of the office, I tend to bust completely out of the office."

Jakarta laughed. "I'll say. You know, you would not have been nearly as intimidating to me if I had seen you in this wild Hawaiian shirt when we met before."

"Oh, there are so many things going on in that sentence, I don't even know where to start responding," Zane said with a grin. " 'Intimidating'? 'Hawaiian shirt'? Back up for just a moment. First of all, I'll have you know, Ms. Raven, that the batik print on this shirt was created by local artisans."

"Wow." Jakarta tilted her head to study him more closely. "Batik print? Local artisans? What do you know about that kind of thing?"

"I am a connoisseur of the arts; I make it my business to know that kind of thing. And furthermore, I was not intimidating—I was just doing my job."

"Uh-huh. And your job was to persecute my sister."

"Prosecute. My job was to prosecute your sister."

"You say tomayto; I say tomahto," Jakarta responded.

"Look, are you going to keep holding that against me?" Zane asked. "It all worked out . . . your sister is free and home with her family—doing quite well according to what you've told me. Do I have to stay in the doghouse?"

Jakarta shook her head. "No, you're right. I just had to jerk your chain a little one last time. Really, I should be thanking you instead of picking on you. Anthony told us all your part in helping him to get the information he needed to free her. You'll never know how much that means to me." She reached for his hand and squeezed it firmly, all the while locking her eyes with his in an intense stare. "Honestly, Zane, you saved my family, and that's something I'll never forget. Thank you."

Zane returned her stare with an intensity of his own. "It was my pleasure," he said. "All I ever really want is to see justice done."

For months, ever since Savannah had been cleared of the charge of murdering her husband, Jakarta and Zane had maintained a long-distance contact. E-mail and the phone had become her best friends. It was good to get to know him that way, because it provided her with a buffer zone. It was so much easier to be real and honest to a computer monitor and keyboard than it was to a person face-to-face. And now, after months of intimate but distant exchanges, Zane had suggested— and she had agreed—that it was time they were in the same place at the same time.

All the way to New Orleans, Jakarta had found herself questioning the sanity of this decision. *You hear these kinds of things all the time,* she thought. *A woman goes to a different city to meet a man and then she's never heard from again.* Intellectually, she knew that was not a realistic concern, but of all the things that she worried about as far as Zane concerned, some sort of foul play involving him was at the bottom of that list. Yet it was the easiest thing to latch on to, she realized somewhere deep in her psyche. It was the easiest thing to put a voice to, the easiest concern to focus on. Because if she didn't focus on that, she would be forced to admit she was just plain scared. She had agreed to come to New Orleans to spend time with this man to see if they could have more than just a casual relationship, and she was just downright scared.

However, by the time they stood next to each other at the baggage claim area, Jakarta was at peace with her decision to make this trip. *Whatever will be will be,* she thought philosophically.

They stood silently, watching the parade of luggage slide down the ramp to the steel carousel below. Jakarta watched with growing trepidation as one after another of her fellow passengers claimed bags and disappeared. Finally, the only thing left spinning around on the carousel was a collapsible stroller, neatly folded with a tag dangling from its handle.

"Where is my bag?" Jakarta hissed. "I knew it! I just knew it!" She stomped her foot in frustration.

"I'm guessing that stroller doesn't somehow convert into a suitcase," Zane said wryly.

"Uh, no. And I have no clothes," Jakarta said. "You're the assistant prosecutor of the fine parish of New Orleans—do something! Prosecute somebody . . . make 'em bring my bag!"

Zane laughed. "Sadly, that's kinda out of the realm of my authority. Otherwise I'd haul all those baggage handlers into court for you."

"What are we going to do?"

"I think the first thing we have to do is file a claim, so they can track your luggage down."

Together, they crossed the baggage claim area to go to the airline's lost luggage office. They took their place in line behind a few other travelers whose baggage had taken a detour.

When their turn came, Jakarta's already worn patience stretched even thinner as they gave the clerk a detailed description of her bag and waited while the claim number was recorded in the computer. By the time Zane had given the clerk his address and phone number so the airline could deliver the bag when it arrived, Jakarta was ready to scream.

"See? This is why I don't get on planes," Jakarta declared as they were leaving the terminal, heading to the parking garage. "Give me a bus or a car and I don't have to worry about this, 'cause I have my suitcase with me. But every time I get on a plane, something like this happens."

"You should count your blessings that the biggest 'something' that happened to you was lost luggage."

Jakarta sighed. "Whatever you say, *Annie*. The sun will come out tomorrow—right?"

Zane's easy laugh lightened the mood. "Don't worry, be happy."

"You know, that optimist stuff is pretty damn annoying." Jakarta couldn't help smiling back at him. "Well, I hope you like this little ensemble I'm wearing." Jakarta gestured at her capri pants and sleeveless tank. "Because it looks like this is it for me for the week."

"Don't be ridiculous." Zane shook his head. "You're in New Orleans, one of the most cosmopolitan cities in the country. You haven't flown into some backward bush country. Let's go shopping."

Jakarta paused for a moment, mentally calculating the funds she had in her purse. "Um, I don't think I'm prepared to go shopping for a whole new wardrobe," she said. "Let's just hold out hope that the airline will find my bag and send it on."

"Okay," Zane said slowly, "but if your things aren't here by the morning, we're going shopping."

Jakarta nodded indulgently. "Whatever you say."

When they reached his car in the parking lot, Jakarta couldn't help commenting on his choice of vehicle. "Buick Regal . . . steady and reliable. Not exactly what I would have figured you for."

"What do you mean? You've ridden in my car before, remember?" Zane held the door open for her.

Jakarta nodded briefly. "I remember—you came to my hotel to take me to the jailhouse to see my sister." She climbed into the car and settled in the seat.

"Who was about to be released," Zane interjected quickly. He closed the door and crossed to the driver's side. "Don't forget that part," he said as he eased into the seat next to her.

"No, I remember some things. I remember how excited and happy I was. I remember thinking it was taking forever to get to the jail." Jakarta glanced over at him and smiled. "But I don't really remember your car. Guess my focus was elsewhere. But now that I see it again, I suppose I would have figured you for something flashier or sportier."

Zane shook his head vigorously as he started the car. "I'm a public servant who serves at the pleasure of the taxpayers. What kind of image would that project for me to drive a red Corvette or something? It would be irresponsible."

"Oh, yes, I keep forgetting that you are beholden to the good people of New Orleans."

"Yes, well, I never do," Zane assured her.

Jakarta studied his profile as he piloted the car out of the parking lot and into the traffic. "I'm sure you don't," she mumbled softly. She turned her attention to the scenery they passed as they wound their way through the traffic to his home.

Chapter 3

Soon, they reached a picturesque side street on the edge of the French Quarter where there were mostly stately old houses. Zane came to a stop in front of a lovely redbrick building surrounded by blooming magnolia trees. Jakarta followed as he helped her out of the car and led the way through a courtyard, past a fountain, to an apartment in the back.

"This is beautiful," she said.

"Thanks." Zane smiled. "The building itself dates back to around the time of the Civil War. It's been updated. It used to be one huge house, but it's been renovated and divided into four nice-sized apartments. But it still has a lot of its classic old charm."

Zane's unit was the farthest back in the courtyard on the second level of the building. He opened the door with a flourish.

"Welcome to my humble abode," he said.

Jakarta stepped in and got her first look at his private sanctuary. Zane's apartment consisted of a large main room that was used as both a living room and a dining room. Directly across from the front door, there were French doors dressed with sheer panels. The room was furnished very masculinely with leather club chairs and a sofa grouped around a glass and marble coffee table. There was no TV in the room, and Jakarta wondered about that since she figured that all men were TV nuts.

The dining area featured a dinette set with a round table and four chairs, the table and chairs each constructed with wood tops and wrought-iron bases. Beyond the dining room area, there was a swinging door that led to what Jakarta assumed to be the kitchen.

Down a hallway, Jakarta could see three other doors. Bedrooms and bathroom, she assumed.

She wandered toward the French doors, opened them, and stepped out onto his balcony.

"You've got a beautiful view of the courtyard," she observed.

"What I really like about it is that even though it's in the Quarter, it's on the fringes, so it's never really too loud. Except of course during Mardi Gras."

"I have always wanted to go to a Mardi Gras," Jakarta said.

"Well, we'll have to see if we can arrange that," Zane replied easily. "Come on, let me show you to your room. It's a two-bedroom apartment, and I didn't want you to feel like I was putting any pressure on you, so I'm going to set you up in the guest room."

Jakarta's soft smile was her only response.

The room he led her to was furnished with a wooden, mission-style futon and an array of electronic equipment, including a TV, DVD player, and a stereo component system with several speakers.

"I don't get much company," Zane said by way of apology, "so this is actually my den. The futon lets out to a bed." He walked over to the wooden couch, lifted and pulled, and laid out a double-sized bed.

"Aren't you the courtly gentleman," Jakarta joked. "How do you know I wanted to sleep on the futon? You should let me have your bed and you sleep on the futon."

Zane looked stricken. "I am so sorry—you're exactly right. Of course you can have my bed and I'll sleep in here."

"Oh, Zane, I was just teasing," Jakarta was quick to assure him. "This is going to be fine."

"Are you sure? Because I can sleep in here, no problem."

"Zane, relax. I'll be fine," Jakarta said firmly. *Besides,* the thought entered her mind, *before this week is out I'll be sleeping in your bed anyway.* She chose to keep that prediction to herself, not sure how the very proper Mr. Reeves would react.

Zane rubbed his hands together in anticipation. "So, what should we do first?"

"Actually, I don't really want to go anywhere until we hear from the airline. You gave them this number and address, so if my bag ever shows up, this is where they'll bring it." Jakarta settled on the edge of the futon. "So if you don't mind, I'd kinda like to stick close by until we hear from them."

"No problem," Zane said. "I'll just whip us up some dinner."

"You cook?" Jakarta didn't even attempt to conceal her surprise.

"All self-respecting New Orleans men cook," Zane stated. "My mama wouldn't have it any other way."

"Your mama?" Jakarta looked at him curiously. "I've never heard you mention your mama. Does she live in New Orleans?"

"Actually, no. Mama and her sister, my aunt Nita, live together in Hammond. That's about an hour north of here." A slight chuckle rocked his shoulders.

"What's so funny?" Jakarta asked.

"Oh, I was just thinking about Mom and her sister. Nazimoba and Juanita are the grande dames of Hammond. Everybody calls them Miss Naz and Miss Nita. They know how everybody should do everything, and they are not the least bit shy about telling folks what to do. The funny thing is, they're usually right." Zane nodded.

"Nazimoba and Juanita? Now there's a pair of names for you." Jakarta laughed.

Zane shook his head. "Oh, I know you—Jakarta, sister of Savannah, Sydney, and Paris—could not be talking about anybody's name."

Jakarta laughed good-naturedly. "Touché. So what have Nazimoba and Juanita taught you about cooking?"

"How about . . ." His voice trailed off as he stared briefly off into space trying to decide what to cook. "A little crawfish étouffée? How do you feel about that?"

Jakarta shrugged. "Well, since I don't even know what that is . . ."

"You'll love it," he assured her. "I'm going to go on out to the kitchen and get it started."

Jakarta followed him into his small, well-appointed kitchen, enjoying the view of his backside along the way. "Can I help?" she asked.

"Well, I don't know. Can you cook?"

"Just because I don't know what crawfish étouffée is doesn't mean I can't cook."

"Then sure, I'd love to have your help."

Jakarta nodded triumphantly. "Uh, what is crawfish étouffée, by the way?"

Zane laughed. "It's going to be easier to show you than it would be to tell you. But it's basically a rice dish, so we're going to need a lot of rice. Suppose I put you in charge of that?"

"Rice? That's the best you think I can do? You want me to cook the rice?" Jakarta was indignant.

"Okay, no then. Just remember, *Ms.* Raven, you asked for it." Zane moved to the refrigerator and pulled out an onion, a pack of celery, a pair of green peppers, and a couple of green onions. "I need some vegetables diced."

"I can do that," Jakarta said as she walked to the sink to wash her hands. "I'll need a knife and a cutting board."

"Your wish is my command." Zane produced the desired implements.

"And what are you going to do while I'm over here crying over these onions?"

"Crawfish étouffée requires crawfish. And crawfish tails have to be peeled."

"Crawfish tails . . ." Jakarta shook her head. "Don't get much of them in Detroit."

"That's what I figured. So I'll take care of that part." Zane reached back into the refrigerator and pulled out a plastic bag filled with what looked like miniature lobster tails.

"You just happen to have crawfish tails on hand?" Jakarta asked. "Is this some kind of staple in New Orleans?"

"Well, actually, it is, but I don't usually have any." Zane had dumped the shellfish in a colander and was rinsing them. "I'll be honest, I went out and stocked up in preparation for your visit. I knew I was going to want to show off my cooking skills a little. Normally, I would not have any of this stuff on hand," he admitted. "Normally, I eat out."

"But I thought you said you could cook?"

"I can," Zane said. "I usually don't have time to. Besides, it's really hard to cook for one. I usually wind up cooking too much. I cook like my mom; she always cooked for an army. It's just no fun when you're only cooking for one."

Jakarta considered letting the obvious question slide, but then decided that she couldn't. "And why are you only cooking for one, Zane?" she asked as she diced the pepper. "Surely there's some woman around here who would appreciate your culinary skills."

Zane shrugged. "Maybe. But that's not something I usually have time for either."

"And yet, here I am in your kitchen," Jakarta pointed out.

"Well, I guess I decided I'd make the time."

Jakarta looked up from the cutting board and smiled at him. "Well, I guess I'm glad you did."

They worked side by side in a companionable silence for a few minutes, Zane peeling and Jakarta dicing, until all the ingredients were ready.

"Now," Zane said, pulling a large sauté pan out of a cabinet under the counter, "we put it all together." He put the pan on the stove and started the fire under it. He adjusted the knobs until he was satisfied with the height of the flame, and then tossed a stick of butter into the pan. Next he swept the vegetables she had chopped into the melting butter. The sizzle of sautéing vegetables filled the room.

"Hand me that spoon." Zane pointed toward the counter at a jar with numerous utensils. "The wooden one." Jakarta passed him the spoon.

He stirred the vegetables quickly. Then he grabbed the handle of the pan and, with a flick of his wrist, flipped the entire mixture.

"That was very smooth," Jakarta said. "If I had tried that, there would be vegetables all over the floor."

"Believe me, the first few times I did it, that was exactly what happened. But you get better." He pointed at the sink where he'd left the colander of peeled tails.

"Now the crawfish." He tossed in the tails, some chopped garlic and bay leaves, and then stirred the whole mixture thoroughly.

"That smells fabulous," Jakarta said.

"You'll love it, I promise. Tell me, do you like your food spicy?"

She nodded. "The spicier the better."

"Excellent!" He nodded his approval. "It really would help now if you'd go on and measure out the rice."

"Oh, of course," Jakarta agreed.

"There's a box of instant rice in the cabinet above your head."

She opened the door and was impressed by the neat array of staples in his cabinet. "You really did stock up, didn't you?"

"Better to have it and not need it, my mother always says, than need it and not have it." Zane continued his stirring.

She pulled down the box of instant rice. "Measuring cup?"

"Behind you, second door on the left."

She went to the designated cabinet and retrieved the measuring cup. "Two servings enough?"

Zane smiled confidently. "You might want to cook up more than that. . . . You're really going to like this. Besides, crawfish étouffée is actually better the next day—for breakfast."

In short order, the meal was completed. They dished up two plates of rice and spooned the crawfish mixture over it.

"It looks like gravy," Jakarta observed.

"Okay, if that makes it easier for you—think of it as crawfish gravy then," he said agreeably.

He picked up the plates and started out of the kitchen. "Grab that bottle of wine from the refrigerator. The glasses are in there, and the corkscrew is in that second drawer." He gestured toward a cabinet door with a nod of his head. "Come on, let's eat."

Jakarta did as she was instructed and followed him to the corner of the apartment's great room that had been designated as the dining room.

"Now, Ms. Jakarta," he said as he set the plates on the table, "you're going to get a taste of my cooking."

Jakarta's first bite of the rich dish was heavenly. "Oh, my goodness," she said, "this is delicious!"

"Thank you, and stop sounding surprised." Zane looked pleased.

"I really am surprised; this is fabulous!" Jakarta slid another forkful in her mouth.

"Trust me, I've got skills."

"Is that right?" Jakarta cocked her head to one side. "What other skills do you have?"

A sultry smile spread across Zane's almond-colored face. "Play your cards right and I'll show you." The look he gave her was intimate and intense. Jakarta felt a tingle begin in her belly as she returned the intense gaze.

The shrill of the telephone shattered the moment. With an apologetic shrug, Zane rose from the table and grabbed the phone from a nearby wall.

"Zane Reeves," he answered. "Uh-huh . . . yes, Ms. Raven is here."

Jakarta's ears perked up when she heard her name.

"Is that right?" There was a pause as Zane listened to the response. "Well, I'll let her know, but she won't be very happy. Yes, we appreciate your doing all that you can. Thank you for calling." He hung up and turned back to her.

"I can tell by the look on your face that that wasn't good news." Jakarta sat back in her chair.

"It was the airline. It's sort of good news, bad news."

"Oh?"

"The good news is they think they've located your bag."

Jakarta smiled. "That is good news."

"The bad news is they think it's in Barcelona."

"What?"

"I don't know how it happened either, and they don't have an explanation, but they think they've tracked it down. However, they won't be able to get it here to you before sometime tomorrow night at the earliest." Zane gave her an apologetic smile.

"Oh, this is just rich!" Jakarta said, annoyed.

"Don't worry, we'll go shopping in the morning. Since your bag's coming tomorrow, we won't get a whole wardrobe . . . we'll just go out first thing in the morning and get you what you need."

Jakarta sighed heavily. "Well, there are a couple of things I'm going to need tonight."

"Like what?"

"I don't have anything to sleep in. . . . I don't even have a toothbrush."

"Oh." Zane nodded. "I hadn't thought of that. Just a second." He disappeared down the hallway and emerged a few minutes later carrying an oversize New Orleans Saints T-shirt and a new toothbrush. "You can sleep in this if you don't mind."

Jakarta jumped out of her chair and reached for the T-shirt. "This is perfect." She held the shirt up to her chest. It was easily the length of a minidress on her. "And how is it that you just happened to have a new toothbrush handy?" she asked as she took the package from his outstretched hand.

"I always have an extra toothbrush." He shrugged. "Some people have spare tires, I have spare toothbrushes."

"You are Mr. Johnny-on-the-spot. This is just perfect." She beamed at him.

"So tomorrow we shop, and tomorrow night your luggage will be here and everything will be fine." Zane shook his head. "This visit is getting off to an auspicious start."

Chapter 4

The next morning, Jakarta was awakened by the delicious smell of coffee wafting through the apartment. She rolled out of the futon and made her way down the hall to the kitchen.

"Good morning, sleepyhead," Zane said cheerfully. "I wasn't sure how you liked your coffee, so I didn't fix you a cup. But the pot is still hot, so if you tell me what you like in your coffee, I'll be happy to make it for you."

"What are you doing up already?" Jakarta rubbed her eyes sleepily.

"Already?" Zane shook his head. "It's nine o'clock. If I hadn't taken off work, I'd have been at my desk for at least an hour and a half by now."

"Oh, that's just wrong," Jakarta said.

Zane chuckled. "Coffee?"

"Absolutely. Cream and two sugars please."

"What? No sweetener for you?"

"Oh, I hate that artificial stuff," she said. "Ruins a perfectly good cup of coffee."

Zane laughed and nodded. "I couldn't agree more—

chalk that up as something else we have in common."
He prepared the coffee and set the cup in front of her,
along with a plate of pastry. "These are beignets," he
said, "and they are not nearly as good as the ones we'll
get later on in the Quarter from Café Du Monde, but
these are pretty good."

"Beignets?" Jakarta looked at him quizzically.

"They're sort of like a donut. You should try one."

She took a bite of the sweet pastry and smiled. "This
is delicious."

"Just wait until you taste the ones that come fresh
from the café. You will never eat a regular donut again."

She smiled and sipped her coffee.

"So you need to get dressed," he said. "We've got
shopping to do."

"Zane, that's not really necessary," she said. "The airline promised the luggage would be here tonight."

"Well, tonight's a long time from now, and besides,
you're in New Orleans—shopping is a moral impera-
tive. We'll just go out and get you a couple of things so
you'll be comfortable."

She stood and modeled the gigantic New Orleans
Saints T-shirt she had borrowed from him. "But I am
comfortable."

"And you look lovely. But we're probably not going
to want to go out with you dressed in my T-shirt. So
come on, let's go."

"Okay, let me finish my coffee," she groused as she
plopped back into the chair.

"Not a morning person." He pretended to make a
note on a checklist. "I'll have to file that away for future reference."

She glared at him with mock severity, and munched
on her beignets. Within the hour, she was dressed and
ready to go.

"I seriously hope I don't run into anyone who saw

me yesterday. Look at me, wearing the same clothes two days in a row," she complained. "It's so embarrassing."

"Well, you should be embarrassed," he teased. "I just hope nobody sees me with you. Think of my reputation."

"Okay, that does it." Jakarta turned from the door and went to sit on the couch. "I'm not leaving this apartment until my clothes show up." She crossed her arms and pouted.

"Relax, you look fine, stop worrying," he assured her. "I was just playing with you." He held out his hand to help her up. "Come on, let's go get you some new clothes."

Jakarta's face melted into a smile as she reached out to take his hand.

"Okay, where to?" she asked.

"Let's walk."

From his apartment on the outskirts of the Quarter, they walked together through New Orleans's historic French Quarter. They passed several boutiques during their stroll, but Jakarta refused to even enter them.

"I can tell from here that stuff is too expensive," she said at each shop.

"Why won't you let me buy you something nice?" he asked, frustrated.

"Why do you want to?"

Zane looked sheepish. "I feel so bad about your luggage being lost."

"Zane, you didn't have anything to do with that. That was the airline's fault. Now, I don't want one of these dresses from these chic-chic boutiques."

He paused for a moment, thinking. "Okay, then I know the perfect place. Come with me. We're going to the French Market." He switched directions and led her toward the far side of the Quarter.

Jakarta wrinkled her nose. "It sounds like another chic-chic place."

"Not at all, wait till you get there. It's like a big open-air bazaar, and they sell all sorts of things. It's real touristy," he warned, "which means they've got a lot of T-shirts and things like that, but I'm sure we can find something that you'll like there."

A few moments later, they arrived at the French Market. As he had promised it was very much the way the open-air marketplace might be in Morocco or Marrakech. Vendors were selling all manner of things from food to clothing to cheesy souvenir snow globes.

"This is perfect," Jakarta exclaimed.

They walked through the market, stopping at several T-shirt stands. She saw one displayed that said *Suck their heads and Eat their tails.*

"What on earth is that all about?" she asked.

Zane laughed heartily. "It's about crawfish—that's how you eat them . . . you suck the stuff out of their heads, and you eat their tails."

"That's a little suggestive."

"Intentionally so," he said.

"Well, then, I simply have to have one of those." Jakarta reached for a bright yellow shirt with the provocative slogan emblazoned across the chest. Laughing, Zane handed the vendor the money for the shirt. They continued their stroll through the market and came upon a vendor selling dresses made from T-shirt jersey material. The dresses were sleeveless tanks with scoop necks and each one had a different, vibrantly colorful tie-dyed pattern.

"All handmade, miss," the vendor said. "We make 'em at night, and sell 'em here during the day."

"These are beautiful," Jakarta breathed, looking through the selection.

"Which one you like?" the vendor asked.

She went through them until she found one that was a blue-green tie-dyed pattern. The vendor pulled it down and handed it to her. She held the dress up to her body. The dress ended about midcalf.

"It's a little longer than I wanted," she said.

"Let me see if I've got another one." The vendor sorted through his inventory and found a dress with a similar color and slightly different pattern variations. When she held this dress up to her body, it fell to just above her knee.

"This is it," she said, turning to Zane. "What do you think?"

"I think you look beautiful," he said in a low voice.

"Good. This is the one I want." She reached for her purse and started to pay, but Zane wouldn't hear of it.

"My treat," he insisted.

"Zane, you already bought me a T-shirt, you don't have to buy me a dress."

"I know I don't have to," he said as he handed the vendor a bill. "I want to."

Jakarta bowed her head slightly. "In that case, thank you again," she said.

"Okay, I'm all set," she added.

"No, you have a T-shirt and a dress. You need some shorts to go with that T-shirt, don't you think?"

"Shorts?" the vendor said. "I've got shorts right here, right here." He grabbed Jakarta's hand and led her to a corner of his stall where there were piles of brightly colored shorts neatly folded. "What color you want?"

She picked a pair of hot-pink shorts and the vendor added those to the total.

"I'll throw in a hat if you want," he offered, "no charge." He pointed at his selection of straw hats.

Zane pulled down a hat with a wide floppy brim and playfully placed it on her head. "Oh, that's perfect," he teased.

She took a mirror from the vendor to see for herself and burst out into uncontrollable giggles at the sight of herself in the oversize hat.

"Ah, maybe not," she said. She reached for another one, this brim not quite so wide, with flowers on the band. "I think I'll like this one with my dress," she decided as she tried it on.

Zane shrugged. "It looks okay."

"Just okay?" she asked.

"I liked the first one." He smiled.

"So clearly your opinion isn't going to count here." She turned to the vendor. "I'll take this one, sir." She took the hat off her head and handed it to him. The vendor nodded and put the hat in a plastic bag with the dress and the shorts. "Thank you," he said as he handed Jakarta the bag and turned his attention to the next customer.

Jakarta and Zane headed out of the French Market. "Now I am fully outfitted and ready for New Orleans," she said. "A 'Suck their heads' T-shirt, bright pink shorts, a straw hat, and a tie-dyed dress—what else could anybody need?"

Zane had to laugh. "You're right, you're ready for my town. Now, how 'bout some lunch?"

"What do you recommend?" she asked.

"Let's go to the Central Grocery," he suggested.

"We're going to a grocery store for lunch?" She sounded skeptical.

"It's not really a grocery store. You'll see when we get there."

He led the way, and they came upon the store in the center of the bustling French Quarter. Central Grocery actually was a deli, doing a huge business when they walked up.

"Try the muffaletta," he said, "you'll love it."

Jakarta shrugged. "I've given up trying to understand what I'm eating here. I'm just going to put myself in your hands."

A sultry smile spread across Zane's face. "I hope you mean that."

Jakarta paused, trapped in the allure of his dark eyes. "In every way possible," she murmured.

Zane nodded. "But the muffaletta for now." He went to the counter and ordered the sandwich. A few moments later, he emerged from the deli with a tray weighted down by two gigantic sandwiches and two cups of soda.

"This muffaletta thing is huge," she exclaimed. "I don't see myself being able to eat this whole thing." She looked at the sandwich in amazement.

"Well, that's the beauty of the muffaletta," Zane said. "It'll keep. We can wrap it up, and have it again later. It'll be even better the second time around."

He led her to one of the many tables set up on the sidewalk. "Here's to your further taste of New Orleans." He lifted the sandwich. Smiling, she did the same.

Much later that day, after they had strolled through most of the French Quarter, Jakarta and Zane arrived back at his apartment. She struggled to hide a yawn as they entered.

"Tired?" he asked.

"A little," she admitted. "I did get up much earlier today than I usually do."

"I hope you had a good day." He seemed anxious to hear her answer.

"It was a wonderful day. Thank you for everything."

She moved close to him, intending to kiss his cheek. Boldly, Zane turned his head and surprised her by meeting her mouth with his. She started for a moment.

"I'm not being too forward, am I?" he asked.

Jakarta stepped back and studied him carefully. It surprised her how much this man had consumed her thoughts since they'd met and begun corresponding. She felt as though she knew more about him than any other man she'd ever been involved with. Even though most of their interactions up until now had been long-distance, she felt close to him.

"Forward?" She considered the word. "I think it's time we did move forward, don't you?"

Zane needed no further encouragement. He pulled her into his arms and they kissed long and slow. Their breaths and their tongues mingled until it would have been difficult to say where one ended and the other began. Soon, the ardent kiss and the fervent embrace were not enough. With one smooth movement he lifted the petite Jakarta into his arms and carried her the few steps down the hall to his bedroom. Kissing her all the while, he laid her gently in the center of the bed.

"You are truly beautiful," he breathed. He reached for the hem of the sleeveless tank top she had traveled in and eased it up her body, running his hand up her sides and a feathery touch past her breasts as he pulled the top up and over her head. He turned his attention next to the capri pants, sliding them past her waist, down her legs. His hands fairly burned from the heat his touch generated. She lay there before him with only her lacy bra and panties. Zane hovered over her a moment as if trying to brand the image of her in his mind forever. After a few moments, Jakarta sat up and reached for the buttons of his shirt. Slowly, deliberately, she released each button until the shirt hung away, exposing his solid chest. Climbing onto her knees in the bed, she slid her hands across his chest as he shrugged out of the shirt and it fell to the floor. He pulled her to him, their warm flesh touching from shoulder to waist, and they kissed slowly, allowing passion and yearning to build. Jakarta slipped her hands between their bodies and deftly released the buckle of his belt and the button at his waist. Zane felt her hands at his hips and then sucked air through his teeth as her hands found his erection. Zane pulled back far enough to gently cradle her head between his hands. He marveled at how soft her locks felt between his fingers. As she caressed his already throbbing erection, he felt a flame build from his groin, growing hotter and more intense with each caress of her soft hand. She released her hand long enough for him to slide completely out of his pants and briefs until he stood naked before her.

Jakarta kissed his neck and with her tongue traced a hot, wet line from his neck, down his chest, past his firm, flat stomach, until she nuzzled the coarse hair at the base of his shaft. Zane struggled to maintain his balance as he felt his knees threaten to buckle under him. He reached out and grabbed her shoulders as much for support as he did for the sensation of feeling her silken skin in his hands. Jakarta's wicked tongue traced a fiery path along his erection, teasing and tantalizing and torturing him until Zane was sure he would explode. With a guttural groan building in his throat, he gently eased Jakarta away from him. Cupping the sides of her face with his hands, he guided her up to his mouth where he kissed her deeply, his tongue probing her mouth. He felt as much as heard her sigh as their kiss consumed them both.

He reached around and unhooked the lace bra and slid his hands under the loosened cups. Running his thumbs across her nipples, he felt the hot flesh pebble beneath his touch. Jakarta was pressed fully against him now, signaling her need clearly. Zane removed the last barrier between them as he slipped his fingers underneath the waistband of her lace panties and slid them over her hips and down her legs. Jakarta stepped out of her undergarment and it, too, joined the pile of clothing on the floor.

They faced each other naked, and her beauty overwhelmed Zane. The rich pecan color of her skin fairly glowed from the heat that suffused them. He allowed his gaze to travel the length of her, starting at the healthy locks of hair that were disarrayed around her head, moving past her soft shoulders, drinking in the firm roundness of her breasts, moving farther to rove over her taut, flat belly, and farther still to the triangle of dark, curly hair at the juncture of her thighs. Soon looking was not enough. His hands followed the path already blazed by his eyes. The sound of Jakarta's soft moans was music to his ears. He wrapped her in his arms and held her against his chest, reveling in the sensation of her naked flesh against his. Then he eased her back onto the bed and she lay still, gazing at him. He was moved by her show of trust and confidence. She made no move to cover or protect herself from his wandering gaze.

He reached into the drawer of the nightstand next to his bed and retrieved a small foil pack. As she watched his every movement, Zane opened the condom and slid it on. He eased onto the bed next to her and lowered his head to kiss her, deeply, fully. Her hands wrapped around his neck, and he felt her gentle massage on the corded muscles of his shoulders. He dipped his head lower and kissed the hollow at the base of her throat, then lower until he suckled first one nipple and then the other, savoring the feel of the taut flesh. Jakarta arched her back as a moan of pleasure slipped from her lips. Zane needed no further encouragement.

His hands caressed every inch of her body, moving with great patience, down her hips, to her thighs, to her inner thighs. With his thumbs he drew ever-widening circles on the tender flesh of her inner thigh. Her legs eased farther open, allowing him the access he wanted. Zane eased his body between her legs, watching her face as his shadow crossed over her and blocked out the light. He propped himself up on his elbows, and he kissed her again. She wrapped her arms around his waist, pulling him closer to her. With the very tip of his manhood he felt the warm, silky wetness that welcomed him. Finally he could take it no more. He plunged into her, the moment of connection so intense that they both had to gasp for air. He lay still for several moments, feeling her throb around him, savoring the sensation of being deep inside her. And then he began to move, slowly at first, deliberately, powerfully deep thrusts that pulled both of them closer to the precipice with each in-and-out movement. His pace grew faster and more urgent. He felt her urging him on. He felt her matching his momentum with powerful thrusts of her own. She pulled his face to her and kissed him, her tongue plunging into his mouth matching the rhythm of his body plunging into hers.

The sensation was almost too much for Zane. He struggled to hold on to the thin thread of control he had left. He felt her release as her cry filled the air around them. It was the signal he needed to totally lose himself in her body. With one last thrust, deeper and more powerful than any that had come before, Zane surrendered any last pretense of control and felt his release shudder through his body. A groan shot from his lips as his body stiffened for a hot, steamy moment and then relaxed. He collapsed against her, felt her arms cradling him close to her body as he gasped great gulps of air. He didn't trust himself to speak, had no idea what words would come out if he even tried. He just lay on top of her gathering his strength. Finally he collected his wits enough to attempt speech.

He dropped a gentle kiss against her cheek and murmured into her ear, "I don't think I've ever felt that good before." He felt more than saw the smile that was her response. As if suddenly aware he was crushing her into the mattress, Zane began to move off of her, but Jakarta held him fiercely, her arms still wrapped around his neck.

"No," she breathed, "don't go. Not yet." Perfectly content to do as he was ordered, Zane allowed himself to rest against her, feeling more at home than he ever had at any point in his life.

Chapter 5

The next day, Zane took Jakarta on another tour of his town. "This time," he said, "we'll try to stay a little off the beaten path."

"Whatever you say," she agreed amiably.

"Today we'll take a cemetery tour." Zane smiled. He eased his car away from the curb and started down the street.

"A what?"

"The cemeteries in New Orleans are fascinating. There's just so much history in them."

Jakarta looked skeptical. "History? In the cemeteries? Seems like the only thing you'd find in the cemeteries is dead people."

"Ah, that's because you don't look closely." Zane parked the car and led her through wrought-iron gates into a neglected cemetery. "This one hasn't had any new burials for years," he told her. "Some of the crypts here are from the Civil War."

"Why are there only aboveground crypts?" Jakarta asked. "Doesn't anybody get buried around here?"

"New Orleans is below sea level," he said. "If they

bury anybody, the coffin's likely to float up and drift down the street when there's a heavy rain."

"Oh," Jakarta said. "You know, we don't worry about that in Detroit. Our biggest problem is when somebody dies in the winter, it might be two or three days before the ground thaws out enough to bury him."

Zane laughed. "Guess every region's got its own problem. Ours is the water, and so to combat that they use the crypts. There's such history here. And it's so quiet."

"Well, it is a cemetery," Jakarta was quick to point out.

"Sometimes I just like to come here to think," Zane said.

"It doesn't seem a little bizarre to you? That you would just come here to think? Aren't you a little scared?" Jakarta asked as she eased around a crypt marker.

"Nah, the dead people aren't the ones you have to worry about," Zane said sagely. "Nobody here is going to hurt me."

"Okay." Jakarta shrugged. "I'll try to see what you get out of this place."

They walked along hand in hand for a while. Zane pointed out several crypts that were from the 1800s and some more recent.

"This is the final resting place for one of the town's biggest voodoo priestesses. See all the stones around the crypt?" Zane pointed at a modest crypt with small stones all over and around it. "People come here and ask her for help."

"She must really be powerful if people believe she can help them from beyond the grave," Jakarta observed.

"There's no accounting for superstitions," Zane said shortly.

"So you don't believe in voodoo?" she asked.

"I think it's a foolish superstition, but I was born and

raised in this part of the world, and I have a healthy respect for it because I've seen what people who do believe in it can do." Zane looked very serious. "I fear the practitioners of voodoo much more than I fear the power of voodoo itself."

"That seems like a fine line to draw, Zane," she said.

"Maybe. But it's a line nevertheless." Zane reached for her hand. "Come on. There's one more place I want to take you to before it gets too late."

They headed back to his car and drove to his apartment building where he parked in his reserved space.

"You wanted to take me back to your apartment before it got too late?" Jakarta looked amused.

"No, no." Zane shook his head. "There's a great restaurant here in the Quarter that I want to take you to. But parking can be kinda difficult, so I thought we'd walk. Is that okay?"

Jakarta nodded, and they headed into the center of the bustling French Quarter. It was early evening by then, and already the Quarter was filled with revelers.

"By later tonight, these people will all be drunk and throwing up in the streets," he said with great disdain in his voice.

"But it's not even Mardi Gras," she said.

"Yep. It's Saturday night in New Orleans. They don't need a Mardi Gras."

"It's such an alive town," she said.

"Alive is one way to put it." He smiled. "Here we are."

He stopped in front of a weathered brick building with a wrought-iron gate barring its entrance.

Jakarta read the sign out front. "Pat O'Brien's— Home of the World-Famous Hurricane. There's a line," she noted.

"Always at Pat O'Brien's. This is the place. But if you know somebody . . ." He walked over to a side door and knocked. Jakarta watched as the small light from the peephole disappeared and then reappeared as someone looked through the peephole and then moved away. Shortly the door was opened.

"Good to see you, Zane," the host greeted him. "It's been a while."

"Yeah, I've been pretty busy," Zane apologized. "But I have a friend visiting from out of town and I had to show her the world-famous Pat O'Brien's."

"Come on in, and we'll get you set up." The host stepped aside to allow them to pass. "Patio okay?"

"Perfect," Zane said.

After a moment, a hostess led them through the busy restaurant outdoors to the back to a beautiful courtyard filled with black iron tables. In the center of the courtyard there was a fountain that was an improbable mix of fire and water.

"That is amazing," Jakarta said. "It's so beautiful."

"Yeah, I love this courtyard," Zane agreed. "Even though the restaurant is always full and busy, somehow the courtyard manages to be private."

They were seated at a small table at the back. Their table was next to an iron privacy fence. Behind the fence was a brick wall, and spilling over the top of the wall onto the fence was lush greenery. A small candle in a glass globe would light the table once the early evening became late night.

"So, what's good here?" Jakarta asked.

"Well, if you don't get anything else, you have to get a hurricane."

"What's that?"

"It's a drink that has made this place famous. It's a frozen drink, very fruity, and it sneaks up on you," Zane informed her.

"Why, Assistant Prosecutor Reeves—are you trying to get me drunk?" Jakarta teased.

Zane cocked an eyebrow at her. "Do I have to?"

"I think we'd probably both have a better time if you didn't."

The pair shared a private laugh as the waitress approached. She handed them menus, first to Jakarta and then to Zane. She paused, studying Zane carefully as though she knew him. After a few moments of close scrutiny, she snapped her fingers.

"You're that prosecutor. R . . . Reeves, right?" she said as the name came back to her.

Zane nodded slowly. "Yes, I'm Zane Reeves."

"Yeah, I remember you." Her tone was accusatory. "You put my brother away."

Zane looked at the young waitress carefully. He figured her at probably twenty-four. Her dark brown skin was contrasted by her gold-streaked hair. As he studied her face, he tried to remember which case she was talking about.

"I'm sorry," he said finally, "I don't recall . . ."

"Sure, I imagine you wouldn't," she said. "Just another guilty kid in the parade, right? His name is Kelvin Davis, and you had him put away for ten to fifteen for armed robbery."

Zane sat quietly, unsure of what response she expected from him.

"You don't even remember him. Wow. . . ." She shook her head. "Okay, then, I'll be back in a few minutes to get your order." She spun on her heels and left.

Zane released a breath he didn't realize he was holding. "I'm sorry about that," he said to Jakarta.

"Does that kind of thing happen often?" she asked.

"No, almost never," he answered. "I brought you here to impress you, and look what happened."

"Oh, I'm impressed," she assured him. "That certainly left an impression on me." She scrutinized him carefully. "So how do you feel about that, Zane?"

"Feel about what? That waitress coming up to me with an attitude because I put her brother away?"

"Not that specifically, but how do you feel about having put her brother away—or any of the other brothers that you've put away?" Jakarta leaned back in the chair and crossed her legs. "I mean, what's it like for you? Knowing that you are putting so many of our people away for very long times?"

"I never think of it like that," Zane said. "I'm prosecuting criminals; I don't care what color they are. If they don't break the law, then they have nothing to fear from me."

"Yeah, I know, that's the company line that I would expect you to say." Jakarta waved dismissively. "But how do you feel? Does it make you sad to see the parade of young brothers going up the river to the penitentiary?"

Zane took a deep breath and considered her question. "It makes me sad to see the waste of such human potential," he said. "There are so many other things they could have done, so many other things they could have become."

"So do you ever cut them a break?" she asked. "Do you ever find that you prosecute those cases differently or more lightly because you want to help?"

"Absolutely not." Zane shook his head definitively. "That would compromise my integrity as a prosecutor, and that's all I have. If I get a reputation for being soft on the brothers, then I would be ineffective in my job."

"But you have a responsibility, don't you think?" Jakarta pressed. "When our people see you across the courtroom from them, don't you think they hope for a little, if not leniency, then certainly understanding?"

"I can't be held responsible for what they expect," Zane snapped. "I'm in that courtroom to do a job, and if doing my job requires that a young brother is going to be put away, then that's what's going to happen."

"I see," Jakarta said. "Justice is blind, right?"

"In my opinion, absolutely."

"But we both know that's not true, Zane. Look what you did for Savannah. When you didn't believe she was guilty, you helped find the evidence to free her. Are you telling me that the fact that Savannah is a black woman didn't influence your actions?"

"I hate to burst your bubble," Zane said, "but I would have done that for anybody. Anybody who I believed in as strongly as I believed in Savannah, I would have done anything to help. Because I believe in justice."

"Um-hm. Well, if you believe in justice, explain this to me: Why is it that the drug laws are so biased? How is that justice?"

Zane sighed. "You're talking about the crack versus powdered cocaine laws, aren't you?"

"Yes, I am," she said. "I've been reading quite a bit about that lately. It's clearly an issue of race. Crack cocaine, which is the drug of choice of black folks in the inner cities, carries two to three times the penalty of powdered cocaine, which tends to be the drug of choice of white folks in the suburbs. So, as a prosecutor, you must see a lot of people coming through charged with the possession or sale of crack and powdered cocaine. Is it justice to treat those offenders differently? How do you feel about that?"

Zane hesitated for a moment. "How I feel about that is until that law is changed, my job is to uphold it."

"But it's an inherently unfair law," Jakarta insisted, her voice starting to rise.

"I'm not disagreeing with that," he said, "but it's not my position as the prosecutor to change the law. Those decisions are made somewhere else."

"That sounds an awful lot like a cop-out to me," she said.

"I don't look at it like that. I think what I'm doing is protecting the good, law-abiding citizens of New Orleans. And if that means that some of the 'bruthas' have to go down for that to happen, that's a sacrifice I'm willing to make."

The waitress returned to take their orders. "Have you decided yet what you want?"

Zane looked up at her. "Actually, no, we haven't. We haven't even had a chance to look at the menus yet."

"Take your time, Mr. Reeves. There's no rush at all," the waitress said. "And one more thing I should have said to you when I mentioned my brother earlier."

Zane steeled himself for whatever was coming.

"You saved my brother's life by putting him away," she said sincerely. "He was running with a bad crowd and making some really bad decisions that probably would have gotten him killed within a year. Jail was the best thing that could have happened to him. It took him and me a while to realize it, but I have no doubts any-more—jail has saved his life. I guess I just wanted you to know that he's turned his life around in jail—going to classes, working on a degree—so that when he comes out he can do something productive. And I know for sure he would not have bothered to try and straighten his life up without this wake-up call. I just wanted you to know that."

"Thank you for telling me," Zane said. "I really appreciate that."

The waitress nodded and went to attend to another table.

Jakarta snorted. "Yeah, okay, point taken. But there's still some grave inequities in the justice system."

"I don't disagree with you," he said. "But I think there is a way to address them, and playing fast and loose with the law is not that way. Lawmakers make the laws, and prosecutors enforce the law. I think of myself as working the system from the inside."

She nodded. "You're talking about your political ambitions now, right? You've talked about them before in the e-mails you sent me."

"Maybe one day, I'll be able to help make a difference that way. But for now, I'm doing this, and I think it's important."

"Okay, I see your point," she conceded. She opened the menu. "So, what are we ordering?"

"You mean after the hurricane?" He laughed, tacitly agreeing to the change in subject.

Their week together flew past, and before Jakarta knew it she was back in Savannah's house, left with warm memories of her time in New Orleans. She had a hard time focusing on the mundane details of her life in Detroit. The city seemed so bland after New Orleans. She acknowledged to herself that a good part of the spice in New Orleans was Zane. She was surprised at how much she missed him.

They parted company without a definite plan for when they would see each other again. She expected that they would continue e-mailing and talking periodically, but they didn't have a plan for when again they would be in the same place at the same time. She was surprised to discover that she really wanted that.

The next time he calls, she decided, *I'll suggest that he come here and spend some time with me and the family.*

Jakarta even had fantasies about Zane moving to Detroit. *Surely there is a great career opportunity for someone with his skills in this town,* she thought. In her rational mind, she knew it was a pipe dream, but she considered bringing it up to him nevertheless.

If this relationship is going to move forward, she thought, *at some point we'll have to be in the same city for an extended period of time. And my whole family is here, so it would be great for Zane to come here too.* She rationalized her thought process. *I might just have to ask him about it,* she decided. *Wonder if he would ever consider leaving Louisiana.*

Chapter 6

It had been about a week since Jakarta's visit ended, and Zane was amazed at how lonely he was now that she was gone. It was as if she had taken the light with her when she left. He was more than a little stunned at his reaction to her, and his analytical mind could make no sense of it. But his Creole soul told him to accept the romance for the magic that it was.

He sat in his office only partially focused on the case files laid out in front of him.

"I've got some vacation time coming," he mumbled. "I wonder what Detroit is like this time of year." A sharp knock on the door interrupted his musing. He looked up and was surprised to see one of New Orleans's biggest political power brokers, Harland Thibedeaux. An energetic sixty, Harland had been a player in local politics longer than Zane had been alive. He was a big man, portly in a way that only a lifetime of fund-raising banquet dinners could create. Although he had never been elected to any office, Harland was easily one of the most powerful political mover/shaker in town. Zane stood to greet the parish's Democratic party chair.

"Harland, this is a surprise. What brings you down here to the courthouse?"

"It's good to see you, Zane," Harland said, shaking the hand that Zane extended to him. "It's been a long time."

"Yes, it has," Zane agreed. "Which makes me all the more curious. Are you here in the building for some sort of case?"

"No." Harland shook his head. "I have a proposition for you, one that I think you might be interested in." Harland pushed Zane's office door closed. "You don't mind, do you?" he asked, nodding toward the door. "I prefer a little privacy."

"No problem." Intrigued, Zane sat down and gestured for his guest to do the same. "What kind of proposition, Harland?"

"You probably know already that Senator Titus Reid is going to retire this year."

Zane nodded. "Yes, I had heard that."

"What you probably don't know is that Senator Reid is going to be retiring sooner than the end of his term."

"Oh?" Zane's curiosity was piqued.

"Reid is sick. He's fighting lung cancer, and he has decided that he does not want to spend whatever time he has left fighting political battles as well. So he's leaving midterm."

"I had no idea," Zane said. "I am so sorry to hear that. How is he?"

"He's dying," Harland said shortly. "But that's not really my concern here. Once Reid's seat is vacant, there will be a special election to fill it, and I want you to consider running for that spot."

"Me?" Zane's eyes widened with surprise. "Why me? I don't have that kind of experience."

"Of course you do." Harland waved dismissively.

"You are an assistant county prosecutor with a sterling record. You're young and energetic and idealistic and, let's face it, photogenic. All those things are important in politics today. Listen, Zane, the party has been watching you for a while now; plus we don't want to let this seat get away. I believe you to be the best candidate for it. What do you think?"

Zane hesitated, not sure what he did think about it. "Well, I made no secret of my political ambitions," Zane began. "But I figured I'd start out smaller, maybe a parish office, or maybe the state legislature. You're talking about going to Washington, running a statewide race. I don't know if I'm up for that."

"Scared of the challenge?" Harland asked.

"No," Zane said flatly. "But I am shocked, Harland. I don't know what to say to this."

"Well, don't say anything right now, Zane, just think it over."

"But I don't even understand why. Why me?"

"Why not you?"

"I've never run for anything. I've never campaigned. You know my position here is appointed."

"Yeah, but it's still a political appointment. You are involved in politics . . . whether you realize it or not."

"Yes, of course," Zane agreed. "But I didn't go before any voters. I've never done that before. You want me to go from having never been on a ballot or in an election to running statewide for the U.S. Senate?"

"Look, part of what we think makes you an attractive candidate is the fact that you are an unknown." Harland leaned back in his chair, causing the wood to creak in protest. "You don't have a long history to run from; you haven't made any huge public missteps that can be used against you. You know Louisiana politics— it'll chew you up and spit you out. Because you're an unknown right now, you get to start out fresh. The race will have to focus on the issues instead of the personalities."

"What makes you so sure about that? Seems like because I am unknown, the pundits and the public will be working overtime to find out what they can about me."

"Normally, you might be right about that, but this is going to be a special election, held specifically to fill the unexpired term. It's going to happen very quickly, not in the usual long cycle of campaigns. If we manage this campaign right, there won't be any time to do anything but focus on the agenda that you set—and the agenda that you set will be the issues."

Zane looked skeptical. "In my experience, there is always time for a little character assassination."

"Hey, politics can be ugly . . . but that's why we love it." Harland chuckled as he hefted himself out of the chair. "Now I know I've given you a lot to think about, but you're going to have to think fast and give me an answer. I believe you can do this. We can put the machinery in place that will ensure that this seat stays Democratic. You say the word and I will have a campaign infrastructure ready to roll in a matter of days."

Zane stood to shake his hand. "I will think it over carefully, Harland. Whatever happens, I'm really honored to be considered."

"We think you have what it takes, Reeves." Harland gripped Zane's hand firmly and held it. "But I'm going to need an answer right away—by the end of the week. If you don't want to grab for this golden ring, I've got to find somebody who will. It is essential to the balance of power in Washington that we hold on to this seat." After giving Zane an intense look, Harland let go of his hand.

Zane nodded. "I understand." He stood silently as Harland Thibedeaux left the office, leaving a curious energy in his wake. After the door was closed, Zane dropped heavily into his chair.

Thoughts swirled around in his mind as he tried to process what had just happened. *U.S. Senator? Me?* Zane reeled with the possibility of it. *Am I ready?* he wondered. He looked down at the file on his desk. *Is it really time for me to move on from this?*

He wanted some advice, and there were two people whose wisdom he had always trusted implicitly. He reached for the phone on the corner of his desk and began to dial. He paused. "Nah," he said aloud. "This is a good reason to head on up there." He cleared away the files on his desk and left his office.

"I'm going to be gone for the rest of the day," he told his secretary. "You can reach me on my cell phone if there's an emergency."

"Where are you off to?" she asked.

"Hammond," he said with a smile. "Gotta go visit Mama."

A little over an hour later, Zane parked in front of the stately home where he'd grown up. His mother and aunt had shared the home for over a quarter of a century. His aunt, having never married, stayed with her older sister even during Miss Naz's marriage. When Zane was seventeen and his father died, there was no question the two sisters would continue to share the home. It was a grand manor home, two stories, with a wraparound veranda circling the house. A porch swing and several groupings of wicker chairs and tables made it evident that Miss Naz and Miss Nita spent many hours on their elegant front porch. The lawn was carefully manicured, tended to by the yardman that Zane paid monthly. But the flowers were all Naz and Nita. They took great pride in the vibrantly colored beds of flowers that lined the walk and adorned the base of the veranda. It was early evening when Zane arrived, and to his surprise the sisters were not on the porch. He checked his watch.

Just in time for dinner, he thought, rubbing his hands together. He bounded up the porch stairs to the front door and entered the house after knocking once.

"Mama? Aunt Nita?" His voice rang through the house.

"Zane? Is that you?" His mother emerged from the kitchen in the back of the house.

"Yeah, it's me, Mama, but it could have been any-body. I swear, when are you and Aunt Nita going to start locking this front door?"

"We're fine, Zane." His aunt Nita came into the foyer, removing an apron from around her waist. "And I know you didn't come all the way up here to Hammond to fuss at us about our door." She wrapped him in a gi-gantic hug. "What are you doing here?"

Nazimoba Monroe Reeves and Juanita Monroe were unmistakably sisters. Their proud Creole heritage was displayed in their flawless café-au-lait-colored skin and silky black hair, which was just beginning to yield to strands of gray. Nita chose to wear her hair con-stantly in a bun, while Naz's chin-length bob style was a little more loose. The sisters shared similar patrician features: slender noses and naturally arched brows. Naz was the shorter of the two, but only by a few inches. The women had kept house together for over a quarter century and could almost think each other's thoughts. Their house was a collection of memories. Framed photographs filled almost every available inch of table and shelf space with mementos of the full life they were leading interspersed throughout. The house was spotless as always, and the rich smell of dinner cook-ing filled the front room.

Naz rushed over to her son and enveloped him in a hug. "Zane! I had no idea you were coming up. Why didn't you call?"

"I just decided to come up on the spur of the moment," Zane hedged. "I figured I'd surprise you."

"Well, you did." Naz punched him playfully in the arm. "Lucky for you we have enough dinner to share with you."

Zane chuckled. "Mama, I bet you have enough dinner to share with the entire block."

"Don't be sassin' me, boy," she ordered. "Just come on back and eat."

Zane followed his mother and aunt through the formal dining room, which was only used for special occasions, into the large, homey kitchen. Juanita moved immediately to the cabinet to fish out another place setting for Zane.

"Smells good," Zane said. "What are we having?"

"Just a little red beans and rice," Naz answered. "I didn't know you were coming," she said by way of apology. "I'd have fixed more."

"Mama, your red beans and rice will be plenty. I'm glad I'm here." He settled in at his childhood seat at the Formica-topped chrome table and began eating.

"Boy! Did you ask grace yet?" Nita demanded.

"Sorry, Aunt Nita," Zane said, contrite as a young boy. He put his spoon down and waited until his mother had blessed the food.

"Now," Naz said once the meal had begun, "I know my cooking is good, but I know you ain't smelled my red beans and rice all the way down there in New Orleans. So what are you doing here?"

"Well, I needed to get your opinions about something," Zane began.

"Go on, tell us," Nita encouraged.

"I have been asked to run for a U.S. Senate seat that is about to become available."

Both women set their utensils down and leaned back simultaneously, identical looks of pleased amazement on their faces.

"U.S. Senate?" Nita found her voice first. "Oh, Zane, that's amazing! What an honor. So what's the question?" she asked. "Of course you'll do it. You have to do it."

"Do I, Aunt Nita?" Zane said. "Do I really? I don't know if I think it's time yet."

"I don't know that you get to pick your time," Nita responded firmly. "If the party thinks this is your time, then this is your time. Very few men choose greatness, Zane. It is most often thrust upon them."

"It's going to take a lot of sacrifice," Zane said. "I'm probably going to have to quit my job and campaign full-time."

"It's a remarkable opportunity, Zane," Nita insisted. "You can't consider passing this up. You're a young man. You'll have many jobs—and if need be, I'm sure the prosecutor's office would be thrilled to have you back. But you have to go for this. You'll regret it forever if you don't."

Zane smiled, warmed by his aunt's encouragement. He turned in the chair to face his mother. "Mama? You've been awfully quiet. What do you think?"

"You're going to be so exposed to the public," Naz said finally, breaking her silence. "Are you sure you're ready for that? I watch the news, I see the kinds of things those people who are running for office have to do and say, and the kinds of lies they have to tell to get elected. Are you sure you're ready to be *that* person?"

"Mama, I don't have to be *that* person to get elected," Zane declared. "And if I have to be *that* person to get elected, then I won't get elected."

"That's what you say now," she said, "but there's something about political power that just corrupts seemingly good men. I don't want my boy going down that path."

Zane was silent for a moment, considering her words. "I see your point, Mama. Politics is a dirty business. But it's only as dirty as the people who are in it make it."

"I don't know if you're going to be able to change that system, Zane," Naz responded.

"Mama, that's what you said to me when I went to work in the prosecutor's office. 'I don't think you're going to be able to change that system, Zane.' But I feel that I've made a big difference."

"You have," she conceded.

"So why can't you trust my instincts this time too?"

There was a long pause as Naz studied him closely. "Zane," she said finally, "you know whatever you decide to do, your aunt Nita and I are always going to be behind you. But you came up here to ask my opinion and I'm going to give it to you. I think that politicians are crooks and politics is a business full of dishonesty and deceit. You're better than that. I've raised a better man than that. I don't want to see you falling into that sort of lifestyle."

"Oh, Naz, give the boy a break." Nita rolled her eyes impatiently. "He's a good man, and you're right—he has been raised better than that. He won't sacrifice his upbringing just for political gain. That's not who he is."

"Thank you, Aunt Nita," Zane said. "I hear you, Mama, I do. But—"

Naz cut him off. "But you've clearly made up your mind."

"I haven't made up my mind all the way, but I'm really leaning toward accepting. I wanted to hear what you two thought first." Zane lifted a spoonful of the red beans and rice.

"I think you have made up your mind." Naz's tone was dry. "And that's okay; it's your mind to make up. I suppose I should be grateful that you at least bothered to ask us about this decision."

"What does that mean?" Zane stopped in midchew.

"Don't think for one minute I've forgotten about that lady friend of yours that was coming to visit. You know, the one you didn't even introduce us to?" Naz pinned him under her piercing stare. "Why is that, exactly?"

"C'mon, Mama, there's nothing sinister about it. I just wanted to have a little time alone with her before I brought her up here so you all could rip her to shreds."

"Rip her to shreds?" Juanita looked indignant. "We do not do that."

"Oh, whatever." Zane laughed. "I just wanted to spend some time with her before I threw her to the wolves."

"Uh-huh. So can we expect to be meeting this young woman at some point?" Naz asked.

"I'm not sure," Zane said with a private smile tickling at the corners of his mouth. "Maybe."

His mother and aunt exchanged a look. "Uh-huh," they said in unison.

After dinner, Zane drove back to his apartment in New Orleans. All the way home, he thought about the advice he'd received from his mother and aunt. As he thought more about it, he realized there was one more opinion he absolutely had to hear before he could make any kind of decision. As soon as he entered the apartment, he reached for the phone and began dialing a number with a 313 area code.

"Jakarta! I'm so glad I caught you in. I have something I need to talk to you about." The words came out in a rush.

Jakarta was pleasantly surprised to hear his voice. "I didn't expect you to call until later on tonight," she said.

"Something's come up that I really need to talk to you about."

She was immediately concerned. "What? What's going on?"

He tried to calm her down. "No, it's a good thing. At least I think it's a good thing, and I want to know what you think. The chairman of the local Democratic party was just in my office and he told me that one of our U.S. senators is about to retire."

"Go on," Jakarta prompted.

"Jakarta, he asked me to run to fill the unexpired term."

"Wow," Jakarta breathed. "I don't know what to say. What are you thinking?"

"I think it's a phenomenal opportunity," Zane said, "but I'm so young, I didn't expect something like this to come to me so soon."

"Well, you have political ambitions. We've talked and e-mailed about that before."

"I know, but I thought that I would start with something a little smaller, like parish councilman or maybe state representative. But U.S. Senate? That's a huge leap."

"You don't think you're ready for it?" she asked.

"I don't know, it's a little intimidating."

"Zane, the chairman of the party would not have come to your office and approached you with this if they didn't think you were ready. I might not know a whole lot about politics, but I know there were probably any number of people he could have approached, but he asked you. That's got to count for something."

"So you think I should do it?" Zane said.

"I think only you can make that decision, but I think not doing it because you're not ready is not going to be a good enough answer. Because people are never really ready for new challenges," she said. "Sometimes, you just have to step up to it."

"That's what I was thinking," he responded. "I guess I just wanted to hear it from you."

"Honey, I think you will be wonderful at this. You have to do it because they came to you. You know how politics works—if you don't do it now, do you think they'll come to you ever again?"

Zane chuckled. "For somebody who claims not to be political, you certainly seem to know how these games work."

"That's just kinda common sense, Zane," she pointed out.

"Okay, well, here's the other part."

"Other part?"

"I know beyond a shadow of a doubt that I can't do this without you. I want you to come back to New Orleans and help me with the campaign."

The spoon that Jakarta had been using to stir her coffee clattered to the tabletop when she heard the words. "You're asking me to come back to New Orleans now?"

"We knew it was going to happen at some point. You didn't think we were never going to see each other again, did you?" Zane asked.

"No, certainly not," she was quick to say. "I just didn't think it was going to happen this soon."

"As you said to me, you can't always be ready for new challenges; sometimes you just have to step up to them. And I need you here. I need your guidance, your intelligence, your compassion." Zane paused for a moment. "I need you, Jakarta. I can't run this race without you."

"You're asking me to move to New Orleans. This is bigger than a week's vacation. You're asking me to pack up my things, leave my family for good, and come to Louisiana to help you run a campaign. Right?"

The line was quiet for a moment. "Um, yes. That's exactly what I'm asking you to do."

"And what happens after the campaign, Zane? Then what?"

"I have to be honest, baby, I don't know what. I guess it depends on whether we win or lose. I don't know what. I just know that for the next six months, until the special election is held, I'm going to need you here with me. Won't you please come down?"

"I'm going to have to think about this, Zane," Jakarta said. "I can't make a decision this big, this quickly."

"I understand," Zane said. "I will wait to hear from you and respect whatever you decide. But please, baby, I really want you to come."

"I'll get back with you in a few days," she said. "I promise."

When the call ended, Jakarta sat at the table, shell-shocked. *Can I do something like that?* she wondered to herself. *Well, why not?* she finally thought. *What am I doing here? It's eight o'clock in the evening, and I'm sitting in Savannah's kitchen, drinking my umpteenth cup of coffee today. Why wouldn't I go back to New Orleans?*

As she weighed the pros and cons of the choice before her, the answer seemed obvious to her. But she wanted a second, third, and fourth opinion. *I need to talk to my sisters,* she decided.

Once Zane gave Harland Thibedeaux his answer, the wheels of the campaign machinery kicked into high gear. True to his word, Harland had provided a campaign manager, a strategist, and workers ready to mold Zane into the perfect candidate for this election. Zane was amazed and a little overwhelmed by how quickly it had all come together.

Harland had arranged a meeting with Zane and people who would be running his campaign. The meeting, late one Thursday evening, was held in the conference room of the Orleans Parish Democratic Party Headquarters. When Zane arrived, he was ushered into the conference room where there was a long, oval-shaped table with four people already seated around it.

"I'm sorry," Zane said as he entered the room. "Am I late?"

"Absolutely not, my boy. Come on in." Harland stood and enthusiastically clapped Zane on the shoulder. "You are right on time. I asked these people to meet me a few minutes before you got here so we could talk behind your back." Harland led a chorus of laughter. Although Zane chuckled along, he was sure there was more than a grain of truth to that statement.

"Let me introduce everybody." Harland took charge of the meeting. "Zane, this is Elaina Winters, your campaign manager. She is the finest in the business; she will definitely steer this ship to victory." Zane reached out to shake the hand of a fifty-something white woman with intelligent eyes and graying hair pulled back into a neat bun at her neck.

"It's a pleasure to meet you, Zane," Elaina said. "I'm looking forward to working with you."

"Next to Elaina," Harland continued, "is Whitney Gramm. Whitney is a media strategist. She has been working campaigns for six or seven years now, and she knows lots of people in the media business. She's a good person to have on your team."

Zane nodded, acknowledging the young African-American woman wearing a tailored business suit. She looked every inch the professional, from her freshly styled hair to her highly shined shoes.

"You are going to look fabulous on TV," she said.

Zane laughed lightly. "Oh, I don't know about that."

"Next to Whitney, let me introduce Kennedy Bryant," Harland continued. "Kennedy will take care of coordinating all the volunteers that we'll need statewide to make sure that your interests are properly represented in every parish across this state."

Zane nodded at the slender young man whose most notable feature was a disheveled mop of brown hair that covered his head.

"That sounds like a pretty big job," Zane said to him.

Kennedy shrugged. "Sure, it's a big job, but it's always fun," he said.

"And last but certainly not least"—Harland gestured to the man at the end of the table—"is your campaign finance manager, Bradley Lockhart. I've never known anybody who could stretch a dollar or account for it as closely as Bradley."

"That's high praise coming from Harland," Zane said as he shook the hand of the forty-something bespectacled finance manager. "You must have a sterling reputation."

"Well, when you are dealing with public funds and donated money, you have to be aboveboard," Bradley said.

"I'm glad to hear you say that," Zane replied.

"Now, everybody," Harland's voice boomed in the conference room, "have a seat and let's get started. We have a lot to do to get our boy ready for prime time."

As Zane settled into his chair, he decided to bring up a subject that had been on his mind for a while.

"We have not talked about my platform. I would like to spend a few minutes giving you all an idea of what I'm all about and why I'm running."

The members of the campaign team looked curiously at Harland, then back at Zane. The silence in the room was deafening.

"Is there a problem?" Zane said, picking up on the undercurrent.

Again the others looked to Harland for an answer.

"No, certainly not a problem," Harland said finally, "and you're right, we do need to talk about your platform. But for this meeting right now, we wanted to focus on the strategy for how we will get you out there in front of the voters. The actual message is something we can craft later—"

Zane held up his hand to interrupt. "Wait a minute, let me make sure I have this right. You're concerned about communicating the message more than you're concerned about what the message is?"

"The media is the message," Whitney said.

"What exactly does that mean?" Zane asked.

"In a campaign like this one that's going to be abbreviated anyway, you don't have much time to communicate complicated messages to the voters. Typically in a longer campaign season, you have many different opportunities to reach the voters, and you can adjust your strategies as you go along." Whitney leaned forward, warming to her subject. "If you put out an ad that doesn't work, for example, you can change it or fix it or pull it off the air. With the special election, we don't have that sort of luxury. We have to hit it hard and hit it right the first time. So in many ways, the media is going to be the message. *How* you communicate to the voters is going to be just as important as *what* you communicate to the voters."

Zane sat quietly for a moment, processing the media strategist's words. "I'm not sure how I feel about that," he said finally. "That sounds like it's more style than substance. I thought we were trying to avoid that." He looked pointedly at Harland.

"You know politics, Zane," Harland chided. "It's almost always more style than substance. And let's be honest . . . one of the main reasons you were tapped to run for this office is that you bring a good deal of style to the table. Once we get you in there, then you can whip out your substance."

"I see," Zane said, unconvinced. "Well, go on then . . . let me hear what you have planned."

"The first thing we have to do is introduce you to the voting public," Elaina the campaign manager said.

"We'll do that with a series of commercials," Whitney interjected.

Kennedy spoke up. "And we'll have volunteers across the state stuffing envelopes to mail to all the registered Democrats."

"They'll stuff the envelopes with flyers," Elaina continued. "The flyers will have your biographical information, your political background, your picture, your slogan—"

"I have a slogan?" Zane interrupted.

"Not yet," Whitney said, "but we'll have one soon. Mmm . . . 'Zoom with Zane' or something like that."

Everybody around the table groaned.

"Okay, okay, it wasn't my finest moment," she admitted. "But you will have a slogan."

Zane turned his attention to Bradley Lockhart. "How are we paying for all this?"

"The party has started you off with some seed money, and all these mailings they're talking about will include fund-raising solicitations." Bradley paused briefly. "And there are, of course, some party faithful that we can always count on to come through for us in a big way."

Harland nodded his agreement. "Don't worry about the money. I wouldn't have started this train rolling if I didn't think we could afford to keep it on the tracks."

"Let's see, I don't get to worry about the money . . . I don't get to worry about the message. . . . What exactly am I doing?" Zane struggled to control his impatience.

Harland smiled. "You're going to be Zane Reeves, U.S. Senator—that's exactly what you're doing."

Zane sat back in his chair and listened as the people around the table continued their discussion about their plans for his campaign. Although the campaign team was brimming with enthusiasm, in many ways it felt more to Zane as if they were hired guns rather than committed political activists—paid to do a job rather than passionately working to effect change.

Zane Reeves, U.S. Senator . . . His mind echoed the words Harland had spoken earlier. *Yeah, but who is he? And* whose *is he?*

Chapter 7

Jakarta went to Savannah's office unannounced. She wanted to talk to her sisters about her decision separately this time. She didn't think she could take a big family powwow again. She wanted to start with Savannah, believing that her oldest sister with the new love in her life would be the easiest sell.

When Jakarta arrived at Dailey Plumbing, she found Savannah in her office with the phone cradled between her shoulder and her ear, scrawling furiously on a notepad. Jakarta knocked lightly, not wanting to interrupt. Savannah looked up and waved her in. She motioned to Jakarta to have a seat in one of the padded chairs facing her desk. Savannah held up her index finger to indicate that she'd be another minute or so on the phone. Nodding her understanding, Jakarta settled in the chair to wait.

"I have gotten a bid from your competitor for those same parts," Savannah was saying into the receiver, "and he has offered me a twenty percent discount." She was silent for a moment, listening to the response.

"Certainly I understand that we have been doing business together for a long time, but certainly you understand that I have to take my business where it is the most appreciated. So I will wait to hear from you as to whether or not you can meet this price . . . whether or not you want to keep Dailey Plumbing as a customer. I'll talk to you soon, Sal." Savannah hung up and turned to her sister.

"Sorry you had to wait, J. I didn't know you were coming in today. What brings you here?"

"Wow, listen to you—wheeling and dealing." Jakarta was impressed. "You really have taken to this running-the-business stuff, haven't you?"

"It was really much easier than I thought," Savannah said. "I'm just looking out for my family's interest. But you didn't come down here to talk about my business. What's up? What's on your mind?"

"Actually, something has come up and I'd like your opinion. Do you have a minute?"

"Sure," Savannah said as she cleared some papers off her desk. "Go ahead, shoot."

"It's about Zane—"

Savannah nodded. "Oh, what a surprise," she said dryly.

"Anyway," Jakarta continued, "he wants me to come back to New Orleans."

"Well, you had a good visit the last time. Why wouldn't you go back? I think it's great that your relationship seems to be going so well."

"Not for a visit," Jakarta said slowly. "He wants me to move there."

"Move to New Orleans?" Savannah hesitated. "Why?"

Jakarta was taken aback. "I don't know how to answer that. What do you mean 'why'?"

"Has he asked you to marry him?"

"No. . . ."

"Are you thinking about marrying him?"

"N-n-no," Jakarta stammered. "It hasn't even come up."

"So you're moving halfway across the country to be his live-in girlfriend?" Savannah's tone was incredulous.

"Um, well, yeah, I guess."

Savannah was quiet for a moment. "Jakarta, obviously you know the situation better than I do . . . but that seems like a huge life change and commitment for you to make, and based on what? To be his girlfriend?"

"But I don't think we can know what it's going to be until we give it a chance," Jakarta said defensively. "And I don't think we're giving the relationship a chance until we're both in the same place at the same time."

"And I suppose him moving to Detroit never even came up?"

Jakarta shook her head. "No. He's got a whole career and a whole life plan in New Orleans."

"Yeah," Savannah shot back, "and you've got a whole family here in Detroit."

"There's more."

"More?"

"He is going to be running in a special election to fill an expired term of a senator who is retiring. And it's going to be a lot of campaigning and he has asked me to help him with that."

"Oh."

"What does 'oh' mean?"

"That's a lot. I mean, you're talking about a major lifestyle change."

"I know."

"And my concern is that you are saying to me you want to move there to be with him and see how the relationship can develop, and that you're going to be in the middle of a campaign for the Senate. That's not real. It's not a real representation of what the relationship can be."

"What do you mean?"

"Come on, Jakarta, you're a bright woman. Campaigns are life in a fishbowl. How is that real?"

"But if he wins, it'll be life in a fishbowl anyway. I need to know if I can handle that."

"I see you've thought this through."

"I've tried. I've been thinking about nothing else since he asked me. You know, Savannah," Jakarta said as she folded her arms across her chest, "you were the one sister I thought would understand the most. I figured I'd get this argument, but I thought it was going to come from Paris. I'm a little surprised that you're saying this to me."

"You expected me to say, 'Follow your heart,' right?"

"Well, isn't that what you've done?"

"Yes, but for me, following my heart didn't take me away from my family and everything that's familiar to me and everything I value."

"It's not the same," Jakarta protested. "Savannah, you have ties here to Detroit that I never have had and I never will have."

Savannah sighed. "It sounds like you've made up your mind. So what is it that you wanted from me?"

"I don't know. I guess I wanted your approval; I guess I wanted you to be happy for me. I wanted you to tell me this is the right thing to do."

"I don't know if I can do that," Savannah said after a long pause. "What I can say to you is that I'll always have your back, I'll always be in your corner, and I'll always be here for you."

Jakarta stood to leave. "That sounds like you expect me to fall on my face."

"That's not how I meant it to sound, honest," Savannah said. "What I was trying to say is it's your life and whatever you decide to do, you know I'm here."

Savannah came out from behind her desk and hugged her sister. "You'll do the thing that's right for you—I'm sure of it. And I'm also sure that the thing that's right for you is not necessarily the thing that would have been right for me."

"I understand," Jakarta said, returning the embrace.

Savannah released her. "So, have you told Sydney and Paris?"

"Not yet, but I'm going to."

"Good," Savannah said firmly. "You can't just disappear into the night this time, J. Too much has happened and we've worked too hard to mend the fences."

Jakarta nodded. "I know, sis, I know."

In her car on the way to Paris's school, Jakarta reflected on the conversation with Savannah. *That did not go at all as I expected it,* she thought. *Maybe this is dumb.* When she arrived at Paris's school it was recess and she found her sister on the playground carefully eyeing a group of kids on the jungle gym.

"Jakarta!" Paris looked alarmed when she saw her sister approaching across the playground. "What are you doing here? Is everything all right?"

"Relax, Paris," Jakarta said. "Nothing is wrong. I just wanted to talk to you."

"Oh, well, what's up?"

"Is this a good time?" Jakarta asked

"Oh, sure, I'm just doing my playground duty for recess. I've got another twenty minutes before I have to get back to class. What's on your mind?"

"Well, something's come up and I really would like to get your opinion of it."

"Sure."

"It's about Zane."

"Go on."

"Uh, I, I'll just say it. He asked me to move to New Orleans."

"Move to New Orleans?" Paris repeated.

"Yeah, and I'm thinking about doing it."

"Well, then, what are you asking me?"

"That's almost exactly what Savannah said. I want to know what you think about it."

"You know what I thought when you came down here. I think that I love having us all here, I think that it's important for a family to stay close, and I think that you running off to be with this man is you once again running off from your family."

"It's not running off," Jakarta said defensively. "I just want to be with this man and see what can happen with this relationship."

"I hear you, I understand what you're saying. You're an adult and you have to do what you believe to be right for your life, but I would be dishonest if I acted as if I were happy about this."

"Paris, we're not the Ewings of Dallas living on a big ranch all together," Jakarta said. "We each have our own lives."

"Yeah, but we each live our own lives within fifty miles of each other, which I think is important. New Orleans is a long way away."

"But I'll still be a part of the family," Jakarta assured her. "It's not gonna be like before."

"Isn't it?" Paris said. "You know you have a history of just disappearing, and we go what seems like years without hearing from you."

"I promise not to do that. I'm through with that. I understand I need my family." Jakarta paused and took a deep breath. "There's more, P."

Paris sighed. "More?"

"Zane is going to be running for national office. There's a special election that's being held in a few months and he's asked me to campaign with him."

"Wow," Paris breathed. "That's really public."

"What do you mean?"

"Well, if you're going to be campaigning, you're going to be in the public eye. Are you ready for that?"

"You're talking about . . ." Jakarta's voice trailed off.

"You know what I'm talking about." Paris trained a stern look on her sister.

"I know," Jakarta said quietly, "and that was a long time ago. It's the past now."

"Yes, baby, it was a long time ago, but that doesn't mean it's going to stay in the past." Paris's voice was gentle. "Are you ready to possibly have to deal with it again?"

"I'm ready to be with Zane. And I'm ready to deal with whatever I have to." Jakarta's mouth was set in a determined line. "So what do you say, Paris? Can I count on your support?"

"You already know the answer to that," Paris said. "You know I have your back no matter where you are. I'm your sister."

"Thank you." Jakarta smiled. "I needed to hear that."

"So you've already told Savannah," Paris said. "How did she react?"

"Pretty much like you did actually. I was surprised."

"Well, Jakarta, we all love you and we want you to be happy. So when are you telling Syd?"

"I'm going to try to talk to her today."

"That ought to be an interesting conversation."

With trepidation, Jakarta approached the downtown Detroit skyscraper where Sydney's office was. She was certain that of all her sisters, Sydney's reaction would be the hardest for her, and surprisingly enough, Sydney's blessing was the one Jakarta wanted the most. She parked her car in the underground lot and emerged to the elevator. After punching the button for the seventeenth floor, she mentally rehearsed what she would say as she rode up the elevator. When she arrived at Sydney's firm, Jakarta waited while the receptionist announced her. After a moment she was escorted to Sydney's glass-walled office.

"Hey, Jakarta." Sydney came out from behind her desk to greet her. "What's going on? What on earth brought you all the way down here? Everything's okay, isn't it?"

"Yes, yes, everything's fine. So how are things going down here?" Jakarta asked.

"Well, you know, business is business. I have numbers to crunch and reports to read. I am positive, however," Sydney said, "that you did not come all the way down here to ask about my day."

Jakarta shrugged. "Well, so much for small talk."

"What's on your mind, J?" Sydney prompted.

"Have a seat. It's about Zane."

"Uh-huh," Sydney said as she leaned against the edge of her desk.

"Why is no one surprised when I say that?"

"I take it you've already talked to Savannah and Paris about whatever this is."

"Yeah, I have, and nobody seems surprised when I say it's about Zane."

"Come on, Jakarta," Sydney said. "Your whole life has been about Zane these last few weeks. Of course it's about Zane."

Jakarta blushed slightly. "My whole life hasn't been about—"

"Never mind, J," Sydney said. "Just tell me what's going on."

"I suspect I already know what you're going to think about this, but Zane has asked me to move to New Orleans."

"Why? Does he have a job for you?"

Jakarta grinned. "Well, sorta."

"I hope 'mistress' isn't the position you're thinking of accepting."

"Sydney!" Jakarta was dismayed. "Why do you always go *there?*"

"And why do you always try to act like that's not where I should be?"

"Yeah, well, this time you're wrong. Zane is going to be running for office and he's asked me to help him campaign."

The statement seemed to have caught Sydney's attention. "Is that so? What's he running for?"

"U.S. senator."

"U.S. senator?" Sydney rubbed her fingers across her chin, impressed. "Wow . . . that's a big deal. There are only a hundred senators in the entire country. And he's running to join that club? That's huge!"

"Well, if you say so—and thanks for the civics lesson." Jakarta's tone was sarcastic. "But whatever size deal it is, Zane's going to run, and he's asked me to come help."

Sydney contemplated her sister for a few moments silently. Jakarta began to feel uneasy under the scrutiny.

"What?" Jakarta said finally, breaking the long silence between them.

"Are you sure this is a good idea?" Sydney said.

"Moving to New Orleans, or campaigning with Zane?"

"Both—either." Sydney leaned forward. "Look, if you've already talked to Paris and Savannah, I know they have already given you the argument about family and commitment."

Jakarta nodded.

"So maybe I can give you a different perspective. Campaigning for a national office like that is a huge commitment of time and money and energy. Not to mention how very public it is. Zane will be pulled in a thousand different directions. He's going to have to smile when he doesn't feel like it, shake hands when he's exhausted, and kiss up to people he would normally ignore. In other words, he's going to have to live his life in a fishbowl."

"I already know all that, Syd," Jakarta said impatiently.

"I don't think you do," Sydney countered. "I don't think anybody can really know until they've lived that experience. And here's my concern: These days everything is fair game. Candidates routinely have their personal lives picked apart. And, Jakarta, if you are a part of his personal life, if you are standing next to him on the campaign trail, you become fair game too."

"No, it wouldn't happen like that." Jakarta shook her head vigorously. "I wouldn't be next to him while he's giving speeches or anything. I'll just be with him. I don't have to be in the limelight. I'll stay in the shadows."

"Uh-huh," Sydney said noncommittally. "J, I think

you really need to give this some serious thought. Because whether or not you want to admit it, whether or not you want to deal with it, if Zane is running for office and you're with him, then you're running for office too. And I'm not sure if you're ready for what could happen. Have you really thought this through?"

Jakarta sighed heavily. "I know what's on your mind, Sydney. Paris said the same thing. But that was a long time ago. It's behind me."

"Of course it's behind you," Sydney said. "The point I'm trying to make is, if you get up front, it won't be behind you anymore."

"I think you're wrong," Jakarta said flatly.

"I think you want to believe I'm wrong," Sydney said. "Because you don't want to deal with it. Clearly you've already made up your mind to go to New Orleans and do this with him."

"Well, before I started talking to my sisters today, I was on the fence," Jakarta said. "But now I'm sure. I need to do this, Syd. I need the excitement that this will bring. And more than anything, I think I might actually love Zane."

Sydney rolled her eyes. "More romantic nonsense."

"Maybe," Jakarta said. "Just tell me you'll support me, Syd."

Sydney rose from her perch on the corner of the desk. "You knew that when you came in here," she said as she hugged the younger woman. "Whatever else happens, you know we Raven sisters always have each other's back."

"That's what I was counting on," Jakarta said cheerfully as she returned the embrace. "I've got to go, Syd. I've got some packing to do."

"Well, that shouldn't take very long. You can pack everything you own in a duffel bag," Sydney teased.

"Let's hear it for traveling light." Jakarta laughed.

Serious again, Sydney said, "I hope you aren't making a mistake, Jakarta."

"I'm not, I'm sure of it." Jakarta felt a confidence she hadn't experienced before. "I'm sure of it."

Chapter 8

This time when Zane met her at the airport, he didn't hesitate to wrap her in his arms. "I'm so happy you decided to come," he whispered into her ear. "I don't know what I would have done if you hadn't agreed to help me do this."

Jakarta returned his squeeze with a fierceness that surprised and pleased him. "I'm glad I came too," she said. "Are you sure you want me with you?" She pulled back to meet his eyes.

Zane correctly saw the fear and concern in her eyes. "Yes, I need you with me," he said without hesitation. "I don't know what these next few months are going to bring, but I know I need you by my side, whatever happens."

She nodded. "I'm just worried—"

"Shhh." He put his finger against her lips. Slowly he slid the finger away and replaced it with his own lips. He kissed her long and slow and deep, oblivious of the looks of the airport patrons.

"What was that for?" she asked breathlessly when the kiss had ended.

"That was for now and for the future . . . come what may."

Jakarta nodded.

"Come on, baby, let's get your suitcase," he said.

"You don't think I checked my bag again, do you?" Jakarta grinned.

"Well, so what did you do with your stuff?"

"I had my suitcase overnighted to your address," she said. "It should be here before ten A.M. tomorrow."

Zane threw his head back and laughed. "That had to be expensive."

"Yeah, but this way I'll know for sure that it will get here, and if it doesn't, then the shipping company will be able to track it a whole lot better than this airline." Jakarta had a smug expression on her face.

Zane laughed again.

"Hey, once bitten, twice shy," she said.

"Okay then. If we're not waiting on any luggage, let's go." He paused for a moment, looking deeply into her eyes.

The ride from the airport was quiet this time. Zane's and Jakarta's hands were clasped over the gearshift, their fingers entwined, gently caressing. Once in his apartment, Jakarta went to the refrigerator and pulled out a bottle of water. "So what do we do first? I've never campaigned before."

"Me either," Zane answered. "Not really. I've worked on other people's campaigns, but certainly I've never been the candidate before. But the first thing we're going to do is have a meeting with my campaign staff."

Jakarta giggled. "I love the way that sounds . . . 'my campaign staff.' So official."

"Don't tease me," Zane said. "It's all so new to me."

"When's the meeting?" Jakarta asked.

"Tomorrow at noon. We'll go to the party head-quarters, and I'll introduce you all around."

"Now you're sure this is the right thing?" Jakarta asked him again. "What will your campaign staff think about you bringing me along?"

"I want you to be with me." Zane was firm. "I want you to be a part of this campaign. So it's important that they know who you are; and it's important that they know how much you mean to me. I don't care what they think."

"Okay." Jakarta didn't sound convinced. "If you say so. But that's tomorrow at noon. What are we doing until then?" Jakarta put her hands on her hips and tapped her foot.

Zane said, "I thought we'd stay in for dinner tonight."

Jakarta smiled slightly. "Excellent suggestion."

"And then after that, I just bet we could find something to fill the time." His smile was sexy and inviting. He pulled her into his arms and kissed her deeply, passionately. "I really missed you," he said softly.

She laced her fingers behind his neck and pulled him closer. "I really missed you, too."

The next evening, Zane had called a meeting of his campaign team at their borrowed space in the Democratic party headquarters building.

"I want you to meet them all," he said as they prepared to go to the meeting. "We're going to be working very closely with these people for the next six months, and I want them to know who you are, and know how important you are to me."

"Oh, I don't know if you need to go there," Jakarta said. "Let's just do the introductions."

"Let me handle this," Zane said.

When they arrived at the headquarters, the team was already assembled.

"Thanks, everybody," Zane said when he entered the room. "This meeting won't last but a quick minute. There's someone I wanted you all to meet. She's going to be around, helping during this campaign, and I thought you should know her." Zane reached for Jakarta's hand. "Everybody, this is a very special friend of mine from Detroit, Jakarta Raven. Jakarta, these people are determined to get me elected to the Senate." Still holding Jakarta's hand, Zane walked her around the room to each person.

"This is Harland Thibedeaux. Harland is the parish party chair. I've told you about Harland."

"Yes, you have." Jakarta smiled broadly. "He tells me you're the one who talked him into this."

"I'm the one that put the offer in front of him," Harland corrected. "He dove at it on his own." Both men laughed.

Zane moved Jakarta to the next person. "This is Elaina Winters. Elaina will be campaign manager."

"Nice to meet you," Jakarta said.

"The pleasure is mine, Ms. Raven," Elaina responded.

"Please, call me Jakarta. I want to help out however I can. Whatever you assign me to do, I'm happy to do it."

"Good." Elaina nodded. "There's going to be plenty to do in the next six months."

Zane moved on. "This is Kennedy Bryant. Kennedy is our volunteer coordinator."

"So maybe I should be asking you what I need to do, since you're in charge of the volunteers," Jakarta said with a smile.

"Oh, we'll find something for you to do, don't you worry one minute about that," Kennedy said. "By the way, I have some family in Detroit. We'll have to sit down and compare notes one day. Maybe we know some of the same people."

Jakarta looked at the thin, young white man and thought, *Umm, probably not.*

"This is Bradley Lockhart. He's our campaign treasurer."

"Pleasure to meet you," Jakarta said. "You'll have to tell me how somebody would go about donating to Zane's campaign." Jakarta was thinking of her sister Sydney's deep pockets.

"That's information I'll be happy to give you," Bradley said.

"And this is Whitney Gramm. Whitney is our media specialist. They tell me she is one of the savviest media people in the state," Zane said.

"I absolutely am." Whitney grinned. "It's not just hype."

Zane smiled at her. "We're counting on that."

"It's a pleasure to meet you, Whitney," Jakarta said.

Whitney nodded. "Likewise, I'm sure. Zane is a wonderful man and he's going to make a great candidate. I hope you're ready for quite a ride."

"I think I am," Jakarta said. "But I've never been through this, so I don't really know what to expect. I'll look to you professionals to help me and make sure I don't do anything dumb."

"Yes, we'll take care of that," Whitney said. "We will definitely stop you from doing anything dumb."

If Jakarta noticed the tone in the other woman's voice, she decided to let to slide.

The next day while Zane was at work at the prosecutor's office, Jakarta decided to go to the headquarters to see how she could help. She knew that the campaign had not begun in earnest, since Titus Reid had not yet retired. But she figured she could start laying some groundwork to help out when the campaign did begin.

She caught a cab to the headquarters office, and when she entered, Kennedy Bryant was already there.

"Kennedy! You're just the man I was hoping to find," Jakarta said cheerfully.

"Hi, Jakarta. What's up?" The young man smiled at her.

"I know you're in charge of volunteers, and I've come to volunteer. What can I do to help?"

"There's not really a whole lot to do just yet, since the campaign hasn't really started yet."

"Yeah, I figured that." She nodded. "But there must be something that I can do. Come on, put me to work. I'm putting myself in your hands."

"Actually," Kennedy said, "I was just folding these letters that will be going out asking people for donations as soon as Titus announces. So if we can get all of these stuffed and ready to go, that would be a big help. How are you at envelope stuffing?"

"One of my many talents," Jakarta said brightly.

Kennedy laughed. "Well, come on then." He led her to a long table that was covered with stacks of letters and envelopes. "We're sending one of these letters to every registered Democrat in the state of Louisiana," he said. "So there are quite a few envelopes that need to be stuffed. Each envelope will get a letter, a reply envelope, and a brochure—which hasn't come back from the printer yet. We were going to wait and stuff them all at once, but Elaina thought it would be more efficient to stuff the letters and reply envelopes and get them organized for bulk mailing. That way when the brochures come in, those can be added and the mailing will be ready to go."

"I don't know anything about bulk mailing," Jakarta warned.

"That's okay. We have labels coming from the state party headquarters, but they aren't here yet, so we're going to do the labels and the brochures at the same time." Kennedy pointed to the two stacks nearest them. "Right now, all we need is the letters and the reply envelopes stuffed."

"So I don't have to worry about keeping them in any kind of order?" Jakarta asked.

"Nope, just stuff them and set the finished ones off to the end of the table."

"Oh, you're singing my song, Kennedy. That sounds like a job I can handle."

Kennedy smiled. "Thanks a lot, Jakarta, this is going to be a big help."

Jakarta settled down at the table and began stuffing envelopes. Kennedy left her side to take care of other business in the office. Jakarta scanned through the letter as she folded. It was from Senator Titus Reid asking the registered Democrats of the state to give the same support to Zane that they had always given him. Jakarta wondered if Titus Reid had even seen these letters, but then decided that he must have.

She had been folding and stuffing envelopes for about a half hour when Whitney arrived. The media specialist was wearing a stylish purple pantsuit with a long duster-style jacket. Her hair was done up in a French roll.

"Jakarta," Whitney said, a note of surprise in her voice, "I didn't expect to see you here."

"I just came down to help out," Jakarta said. "Kennedy thought it would be helpful if I stuffed these envelopes, so envelope stuffing is what I'm doing."

Whitney took in Jakarta's walking shorts and T-shirt

with a look that spoke volumes. "Yes, well, I'm sure we all appreciate your support."

"That's what I'm here for, Whitney," Jakarta said. "Zane asked me to come here specifically to support him in this campaign, so I'm looking for ways to do that. If you have any thoughts about how I might be able to help Zane, I'd love to hear them."

"I'll keep that in mind." Whitney nodded. "Now if you'll excuse me, I have a couple of calls I need to make to reporter friends of mine. Just like you, I too am going to use all my skills to help Zane get elected." Without any further conversation, Whitney turned and left the table where Jakarta was working.

"Well, all righty then," Jakarta said when Whitney left. "Somebody's a little full of herself." Jakarta shrugged it off and continued stuffing the envelopes.

A couple of hours later Zane showed up at the headquarters. He walked over to the table where Jakarta was finishing her stuffing job and kissed her on the cheek. "I hoped I'd find you here. When I called the apartment and you didn't answer, this was the only other place I could think to look."

"Well, congratulations, Mr. Prosecutor," she teased. "You've found me. So now what?"

Zane reached for her hand and gently pulled her up from the chair. "We're going to take a little road trip," he said.

"Where? Someplace exotic, I hope?"

"Maybe not so exotic." He smiled. "We're going up the road a bit, to Hammond. It's time for you to meet the grande dames."

"Oh." Immediately, Jakarta felt anxious. "Are you sure it's time?"

Zane laughed easily. "It's going to be fine . . . they're going to eat you up."

"That's what I'm afraid of," Jakarta mumbled.

They left the headquarters and went to his car. During the ride to Hammond, Jakarta peppered Zane with questions about his mother and aunt. She wanted as much information as possible so she could make a good impression on them.

"What difference does it make what their favorite colors are?" Zane asked. "Just relax and be yourself. They'll think as much of you as I do, I'm sure of it."

"Zane, you're an only child, raised primarily by your mother and your aunt. I guarantee you, they will not see me the same way you do," Jakarta predicted.

A throaty chuckle escaped from Zane. "I should hope not," he said.

Jakarta made a face at him and sighed.

When they arrived at the sisters' home, Naz and Nita were working in the yard. Naz saw his car pull up first. She stood and pulled off her gardening gloves. "You're making quite a habit of surprising us, Zane," she said when he emerged from the car. "And right around dinnertime again. Your timing is amazing." She smiled at him.

"Mama, it's like radar . . . I always know when you're about to put dinner on the table." He walked around to the passenger side and opened the door for Jakarta. "I've got someone I want you two to meet." He helped Jakarta out of the car.

Nita had joined Naz by then, and the two of them stood in front of their veranda waiting for their first glimpse of Zane's mystery woman.

Jakarta felt self-conscious as she stood to meet them. She noted their gardening clothes: Naz in capri pants and a smock, Nita in long Bermuda shorts and a button-down shirt. She marveled at how much they looked alike. She never saw the resemblance people said existed between her and her sisters, but the similarity between these sisters was unmistakable.

Zane made the introductions. "Mama, Aunt Nita, this is Jakarta. Jakarta, the grande dames of Hammond, Miss Naz and Miss Nita."

"It's a pleasure to finally meet you," Jakarta said, walking toward them with her hand extended.

"Yes, finally," Naz said tersely. "I was beginning to think Zane was hiding you from us. Maybe he was afraid I'd say something rude about your hair. He knows how I feel about dreadlocks." She shook Jakarta's hand briefly, completely ignoring Zane's disapproving look. "I understand you're from Detroit?"

"Yes, ma'am," Jakarta answered, Naz's comment about her locks still stinging. "My sisters are still there."

"Sisters?" Nita asked as she shook Jakarta's hand. "How many do you have?"

"There are four of us," Jakarta answered. "And my oldest sister has two teenagers."

"That's quite a family," Nita observed.

"Did they have any problem with you leaving them to come down here?" Naz asked.

Jakarta paused a moment. "Um, no, ma'am. They were very supportive of my decision. They think the world of Zane."

"Well, who wouldn't?" Naz replied. "I assume you two can stay for dinner?" She addressed Zane.

"Sure, sounds great," Zane was quick to agree.

"Come on in then, it's almost ready." Naz turned to head into the house. "Zane, please show your friend where she can wash up for dinner." Nita followed Naz into the house, leaving Jakarta and Zane alone outside.

"Yeah, they're gonna eat me up all right," Jakarta said ruefully.

Zane was apologetic. "Just give them a chance. It takes them a while to warm up to new people."

"New people, or new girlfriends?"

"It's going to be okay." He kissed her forehead. "I promise."

"Ooo, Zane," Jakarta teased. "Your first campaign promise. Hope this one is more reliable than the typical campaign promise."

Anxious but determined to see it through, she followed Zane into the house.

Dinner was strained, with Naz and Nita probing and picking, and Jakarta on the defensive the whole night. It was all Jakarta could do not to scream in relief when she and Zane finally got in the car and headed back to New Orleans.

"They are much better at that dinner-table grilling than my sisters," Jakarta said wearily. "And I thought my sisters were the champions of the world. I'll have to call and let them know they've been outclassed."

"I'm sorry, Jakarta." Zane squeezed her hand. "It's just their way. They're very protective."

"I understand. I just hope they come to see you don't have to be protected from me."

"I already know. Does that count for anything?" Zane asked.

Jakarta smiled weakly at him. "More than you can imagine."

Chapter 9

By the time the weekend came, Zane was champing at the bit, ready to start campaigning. He and Jakarta met Elaina and Whitney at the campaign office.

"So, where do we start?" Zane asked, clapping his hands together eagerly.

Elaina checked a clipboard. "There's a grocery store opening where we're going to present you, and then you've got an appearance at a music festival in the park."

"All this today?" Zane said, amazed.

"This is going to be a short campaign," Elaina reminded him. "We've got a lot of ground to cover and a lot of name recognition to build and not a whole lot of time."

"Okay," Zane said, "bring it on." He reached for Jakarta's hand and squeezed it. "You ready?"

She nodded. "Absolutely."

When they reached the grocery store there were several dignitaries and wanna-be dignitaries on the platform. "Who knew grocery store openings would generate this much attention?" Zane said to Whitney.

"In the political season, everything generates this

much attention," Whitney said. "Wherever two or more are gathered," she said, grinning, "there'll be a politician nearby."

Zane grinned and took a place on the platform next to a fire marshal, a councilwoman, and an alderman. He was introduced as the assistant prosecutor of the parish, not the candidate for the Senate. He said a few words, congratulated the representative of the Piggy Wiggly, and stepped aside to make room for the alderman to speak.

After the event was over and he had shaken a few hands, he immediately sought out Elaina. "Why prosecutor and not candidate?" he said.

"Because you're not officially a candidate until there is officially a race. We know that Senator Reid is about to retire, because he told Harland. Reid hasn't made it public yet though. So we're just jumping out of the box early. Trying to get you some exposure before the other side knows and the race begins in earnest."

"Okay. So, I guess I should have been briefed about this more carefully. Am I not supposed to say anything about what my vision is for the state?"

"Not yet," Elaina told him. "So far we just need you to smile and look handsome. When the time comes for you to start talking about substantive issues, we'll let you know."

"Okay, then," Zane said, unconvinced.

"That didn't feel much like campaigning," Jakarta observed when the team had gotten back into the van.

"Think of it as the precampaign," Elaina said. "We need to position Zane first, so people will know who he is, before we start running for office."

"Oh," Jakarta said. "You know, this is all new to me."

"Yeah, we know," Whitney said shortly.

Jakarta again felt animosity from the media strategist. *I wonder if this is going to be a problem,* she thought. She held her tongue for Zane's sake, not wanting to cause any friction among his inner circle. When they arrived at the venue for the music festival, Elaina briefed him on this stop. The festival covered many acres and had numerous stages set throughout the venue. Each stage featured a different type of music. There were vendors scattered all around the festival grounds, hawking everything from food to clothes, music to souvenirs.

"Now remember, you're not running for anything. You're just greeting the crowds and welcoming people to New Orleans," she reminded him.

"How is it that I've even managed to get onstage if that's all I'm doing?" Zane looked a little confused.

"Harland's got some very powerful friends." Elaina smiled. "Just smile and wave and come on down from there."

"Gotcha," Zane said.

Jakarta couldn't help thinking he was being treated very much like some sort of windup campaign doll. *Wind him up, point him in the right direction, and watch him do what we say.* Zane held his hand out to her. Jakarta slipped her hand into his and walked with him backstage where he would wait to be introduced. There was a zydeco band playing. The infectious beat had Jakarta tapping her toes and swiveling her hips to the rhythm.

"You like zydeco, huh?" Zane noticed the movement.

"I didn't know I did until now. Is that what I'm listening to?"

"Yeah. It's swamp music."

"Huh?"

"Well, that's where it comes from, the swamp. But it's everywhere now."

"Well, yeah, I love it. What is that . . . Is that a washboard that guy is playing?"

"Yeah. One of the hallmarks of zydeco," Zane said. "Tell you what. Why don't we go out tonight and I'll take you somewhere where we can listen to some more?"

"I would love to do that," Jakarta said. "Are you sure you're going to have time?"

"Sure I'm gonna have enough time. I'm not running yet. Remember?" They laughed together.

Jakarta looked out in front of the stage and saw the crowd. To a person, they seemed to be dancing to the zydeco beat. "How have I never heard this music before?" she said. "I think of myself as a woman of the world."

"If you don't get to Louisiana much, you wouldn't have heard it," Zane reasoned. "Although it is spreading throughout the country now."

The band finished their set, and the audience erupted into gales of applause. "That was so cool!" Jakarta said.

"I promise, we'll find another zydeco band tonight."

They watched as a local D.J., who was serving as master of ceremony for this particular stage, stepped out and led the audience in another round of applause for the band that had just finished.

"While they break down the stage and get ready for the next act, there's a local celebrity who'd like to bring you greetings." The D.J. looked over in Zane's direction and waved him out. "Ladies and gentlemen, please join me in welcoming Orleans parish assistant prosecutor Mr. Zane Reeves."

A polite smattering of applause greeted Zane as he walked out onto the stage.

"Good afternoon, everybody." His voice unexpectedly cracked a little. He cleared his throat and tried again. "Oops," he said into the mike. "Good afternoon again, everybody." The crowd applauded the second effort. "I am Zane Reeves, assistant prosecutor for Orleans Parish, and I bring you greetings from the parish courthouse. I hope you all have a wonderful day here in our parish. If you're visiting just for the day, please take advantage of all the wonder that New Orleans has to offer. And remember, stay out of trouble, 'cause you don't want to see me across from you in the courtroom." He spoke with an almost parental severity. "Have a good afternoon, everybody." He waved and left the stage. The crowd applauded a little more enthusiastically as he was leaving.

"Whew!" he said to Jakarta. "That was much harder than the grocery store opening."

She gave him a brief, encouraging hug. "How come?"

"There were a lot more people here, I think."

"Well, you'd better get used to talking to big crowds," Whitney said as she joined them backstage.

Zane shrugged. "I guess it's something that will just come easier the more I do it."

Elaina walked over to them. "Yeah, we're going to give you plenty of opportunities to do it, too. By the way, there's a party fund-raiser that Harland wants you to go to tonight."

"Tonight?"

"Yes," Elaina said. "He's gathered up some of the party's deepest pockets and they want to meet you and talk with you before they decide whether or not to give you a donation."

"And it has to be tonight?" Zane said.

"Well, this is the night that Harland set it up for," Elaina answered with a question in her voice. "Is there a problem?"

Zane looked at Jakarta. "Well, we kinda had plans," he said.

"No, that's okay, Zane," she chimed in immediately. "This is more important. You go on and go to this dinner. You and I can reschedule our plans with no problem."

"Are you sure?" he said to her.

"Of course I'm sure. This is important. You do this."

Zane kissed her briefly on the cheek. "You are the best. I knew having you here with me would be a good thing."

Jakarta just smiled and pretended not to see the look of mild disgust on Whitney's face.

"Tell you what," Zane said. "Why don't you come with me, and after it's over you and I can go on and find some music?"

Jakarta was just about to accept when Elaina chimed in. "No, I don't think that's such a good idea this time, Zane. The people are just going to want to meet you and get to know you. We don't want there to be any distractions."

"Distractions?" Jakarta said.

"I don't mean that in a bad way," Elaina was quick to assure her. "You are a new face around here and a beautiful young woman at that. These donors are almost exclusively older men and we don't want their attention to wander from Zane."

"I see," Jakarta said. "It's okay, honey. I'll just wait for you at the apartment."

"I don't know if I like this," Zane started to protest.

"It's just for a few hours, Zane. Go on and do what you have to do."

Reluctantly he nodded. "But I will make it up to you, I promise."

"I know." Jakarta smiled.

"We should be heading out," Whitney said.

"Already?" Zane asked. "We just got here. I wanted to show Jakarta more of the festival."

"Actually, you should get back and get cleaned up for tonight. This is a pretty big night for you. You really have to wow these donors."

"I understand that," Zane said. "But it is only three o'clock. I have plenty of time to get prepared."

"Well, we'd like a few minutes with you to discuss what you're going to say to them," Elaina said.

"I can't even talk to these people about my platform?" Zane said. "These people have to know I'm running for office."

"Yes, of course you're going to be talking about your platform tonight," Elaina was quick to assure him. "That's what we want to talk about. We want to go over that with you."

"Are you suggesting that you're going to tell me what I believe in and am running for?"

"Absolutely not," Whitney said. "We want to hear from you what that is and then help you craft the best way to convey that message."

"And you don't think I can do that on my own?" Zane said, growing impatient.

"We don't think you have the same sort of political experience that we have, and we understand that there are certain ways to say things that are better than others. That's all. We're just trying to hone the message, not change the message."

"Uh-huh," Zane said. "Okay. Well, look. You all go on back to the van and Jakarta and I will be along shortly. Before we leave here, I want to get something to eat."

Whitney opened her mouth to protest but Elaina put her arm on the younger woman's arm. "That's fine, Zane. You know where the car is. Don't take too long, though." The two women disappeared into the crowd.

"What was that about?" Jakarta said.

"I guess that was about me finding out that this campaigning thing is going to be more challenging than I expected."

"I don't understand, Zane. It's like they want to run you and mold you."

"Yeah, but isn't that the way this sort of thing is done?"

"But shouldn't you be true to who you are?"

"I have been. I've not been asked or instructed to do anything that would compromise who I am. And if they do, I'll just refuse."

"I'm sure you know what's best," Jakarta said.

"What does that mean?"

"It means that I don't know anything about this and that I'm just here to be with you. And I trust that you know what you're doing."

"I do," Zane assured her. "I do."

She changed the subject. "Okay. So what are we going to eat?"

"You ever had a shrimp po' boy before?"

"A shrimp what?" she said.

"Po' boy. It's a sandwich. You'll love it. Come on." He led the way to one of the vendors in the park.

Chapter 10

In the car, on the way back to Zane's apartment, Elaina and Zane sat in the front, Elaina driving, and Jakarta and Whitney sat in the back. Jakarta tried to make herself as inconspicuous as possible as she listened to Zane's campaign team prep him for the night ahead.

"Wear a dark suit," Whitney was saying. She had leaned forward behind Zane, her arms resting on the back of the seat near his head. "Wear a dark suit and a conservative tie. It'll make you seem very authoritative. That's going to be important because you're so young and these money men are going to have questions about sending someone of your age up for statewide office." Zane nodded.

"It won't be a dais kind of thing. It's going to be a small group, probably fifteen to twenty people. I suspect it'll be all men, not their wives, which means it's going to be very 'clubby,'" Elaina said. "Braggin' and lyin'." They chuckled a little. "You will be served dinner and Harland will most likely have you at tables of eight. And Harland will have picked who will be at your table. He'll brief you on that when you get there.

But you'll have to make sure you work both tables. When dinner is over, Harland will formally introduce you and it will be your time to speak. So, now you tell us, what is the message you want to communicate? Why are you running for Senate?"

Jakarta sat up a little straighter in the car, anxious to hear that answer herself.

"Well, beyond the power and prestige of the position, which, let's be honest, that's certainly a big part of it, I want to run for Senate because I want to help my people to work on bringing about more equity between men and women. I want to have an impact on the amount of money that is spent on education in some of the poorer areas of Louisiana. There is not enough federal money coming into the school districts, and those children are in danger of being left behind. I am concerned about the environment. I would like to see tougher penalties for environmental polluters. Overall I want to improve the quality of life. Not just for the people of New Orleans, but all the people in Louisiana."

Jakarta smiled, proud of his answer and impressed by his passion. Neither Whitney nor Elaina spoke for a few moments.

"Well . . . ?" Zane said.

"Okay. Couple of things," Whitney began. "You could actually say that power thing, because those men will understand that. The power and prestige appeals to them."

"That was kinda just for us," Zane said.

"No, but it shouldn't be, is the point I'm making," Whitney replied. "That's one thing. Second, you're not gonna want to say I want to help 'my people.' You're going to want to say you want to help 'all people,' because in a statewide election you can't just be a candidate for people of color."

"Okay." Zane nodded. "That makes sense."

"Also," Elaina inserted, "that environmental polluters

line might not fly with this crowd. There are probably oil men in the room and they are not gonna want to hear that you want to crack down on their businesses."

"But I do!" Zane said. "Some of the things they're getting away with down in the gulf are criminal."

"I'm not disagreeing with you," Elaina said. "I'm saying this might not be the right crowd to say that to."

"I thought the message was mine," Zane said.

"The message is yours. But you don't have to tell everybody everything every time."

"Okay," Zane said. "I see your point. Anything else?"

"The parity in pay is not going to be as important to these people."

"So I can't talk about that either, you're saying?"

"It's a question of audience, Zane. Parity in pay is gonna work real well when you talk to women voters or NOW. For this group, that particular issue can stay on the shelf."

"Well, so far I get to tell them I want to be a senator because I want to be powerful and because I want to help all people. Is that basically it?"

"That's what I heard," Jakarta chimed in, able to hold her tongue no longer. "You're not letting Zane be who he is."

"Of course we're going to let him be who he is," Whitney snapped. "Who he is will have to be defined for this crowd."

By then they had reached Zane's apartment building. Elaina parked the car in front. "Well, if you'll excuse me, I'm going to go on up to the apartment. It's been a very interesting day," Jakarta said. "I imagine I will see you ladies later."

"Count on it," Whitney said.

Zane handed her his keys. "I'll be up in a few minutes, baby."

"Take your time," Jakarta assured him. "I just feel a

need for a long hot bath." She exited the car and walked across the courtyard to his apartment.

"I don't think much of how this is going so far," she muttered to herself. "And I'm not sure what I'm doing here."

By the time Zane entered the apartment Jakarta had finished her bath and was sitting on the sofa wrapped in a thick cotton robe, reading a magazine. She looked up when she heard him enter. "Wow, that must have been some strategy session," she commented.

Zane shrugged. "Well, we went through several issues and I feel pretty well prepared for tonight."

"So what did Whitney and Elaina decide you could talk about?"

Zane gave her a look. "They felt that tax cuts, especially the cut in the capital gains tax, and incentives to companies to move their business into Louisiana would be issues that would resonate with this crowd."

"I see," Jakarta said. "And how do those issues resonate with you?"

"That's cool. I'm okay with those," Zane said.

"You're sure about that?"

"Why are you questioning me?" he asked, his brow furrowed.

"You know, Zane, I've been sitting here thinking a lot about why I'm here and what I'm supposed to be doing for you. And I'm not prepared to just be your campaign groupie. You asked me to come here, I assumed, because you value my input and my opinion."

"You know I do," he said.

"Then I have to tell you that I feel like you are in danger of compromising who and what you are. These women are telling you what to say."

Zane was quick to disagree. "That's not true. These

women are telling me how best to communicate what it is I want to say."

"That seems like a fine line to me."

"But it is a line," Zane said. "These are issues that I agree with. I don't have any qualms with anything I'm going to be talking about tonight. And I'm not a political veteran and neither are you. But the political veterans tell us that some messages are better with some audiences. That just makes sense to me on a logical level. It has nothing to do with politics."

"So, you're okay with everything?"

"I am," he assured her.

"Then I'm gonna be okay, too. But, Zane, I am going to point out to you when I think you're straying away."

"So you're not going to be my campaign groupie, you're going to be my campaign conscience." Zane smiled and leaned over the couch to kiss her.

Jakarta felt the familiar stirrings of desire that were awakened in her every time Zane's soft lips and insistent tongue touched hers. "Well, I could be a campaign groupie some of the time," she answered when he pulled away. He smiled at her. "I need to go on and get cleaned up now before I'm late."

Jakarta nodded. "Okay, I'll be here when you come back."

"I love the way that sounds," Zane said. He kissed her on her forehead and disappeared into the bedroom. A short time later, he emerged freshly showered and shaved, wearing a navy blue suit with a crisp white shirt and navy tie with a yellow paisley pattern on it. A pocket square made out of the same paisley material completed the ensemble. Jakarta gave a low whistle when she saw him, fully appreciating the fine cut of his suit and the fine way the man inside wore the suit.

"You look like new money," she said, smiling.

"Thanks," Zane answered. "Conservative enough, you think?"

Jakarta, in her mind's eye picturing the muscles that rippled across his back and the firm solidness of his chest and the strength of his thighs, nodded. "Yeah, you're pretty conservative enough," she said, smiling.

"What?" Zane insisted. "What are you smiling about?"

"I'm sorry, Zane. I just was imagining you without that suit on, and conservative is not the word that comes to my mind."

Zane blushed slightly. "You're going to make it hard for me to focus on this dinner tonight," he teased.

"Just focus on getting through it and coming on back here."

"I can do that," he said.

She rose from the couch and as she crossed the room toward him, unfastened the belt tie on her terry cloth robe. The robe fell open and revealed her nakedness underneath. She was pleased by the sharp intake of breath she heard Zane make. When she reached him, she wrapped her arms around and pulled him into a hug, pressing her body hard against him. She felt his body immediately respond to her.

"Hurry home," she said in a low, thick voice. "I'll be your campaign groupie tonight."

Zane dipped his head to kiss her and they kissed, a disappointingly brief kiss.

"If I don't get out of here right now," he said hastily, "I'll never make it."

Jakarta nodded as she stepped back from him, retying her robe. "Hurry back," she said.

He sighed and shook his head as if trying to clear his thoughts, and after grabbing his keys from a hook near the door, he headed out.

"See you soon," he called as he closed the door behind him.

Jakarta, tingling from his kiss and his nearness, plopped down on the sofa. "Not soon enough," she muttered.

Chapter 11

They fell into an easy pattern. Zane was still doing his prosecutor job during the day, but at nights and on the weekends he was becoming a new and more visible presence around the parish. Elaina, Harland, and Whitney carefully crafted a strategy that had him in the public's eye, but not in the public's face. The time was approaching, according to Harland, that Senator Reid would announce his early retirement.

"Once that happens," Harland had warned, "it'll be a free-for-all. People scrambling to get candidates together for a special election to fill that seat."

Zane had asked on several occasions who his opposition might be.

"You don't have any opposition within the party," Harland assured him. "You are our choice."

"That's good to know," Zane acknowledged, "but I meant from the Republicans. Who are they sending?"

"I'm not sure yet, because they don't know yet that they need to put somebody up. But when they find out and start looking through their ranks for somebody to get behind, I suspect their gaze is going to land on John

Primus," Harland said. "He's a state legislator from Baton Rouge, and he's pretty well connected within the Republican power structure. It would be a logical jump for him to make. He'll be tough to beat," Harland conceded. "But you've got the best chance to do it, I believe."

"When will we know?" Zane asked.

"I imagine once Reid announces his retirement, we'll know within a matter of hours."

Zane let out a low whistle. "That quickly?"

"Louisiana politics moves very fast," Harland assured him. "But don't worry about who they're going to put against you. We're just going to run the best race you can run . . . and that will be good enough."

"Thanks for your confidence, Harland. Really, you don't know what it means to me."

"I'm sure it's not misplaced."

Thinking back on that conversation now as he sat at his desk at work, Zane reflected on Harland's words: *"Louisiana politics moves very fast."* Looking at the crush of paperwork on his desk, he had a realization. *Once this campaign begins in earnest, I'm probably going to have to ask for a leave of absence from my job. I'll be up and down the road constantly, all over this state. Elaina tells me to expect eighteen-hour days.* He felt curiously energized just thinking about it. *It's going to be a wild ride,* he thought and smiled.

Later that evening, Zane and Jakarta were in his apartment sharing one of the rare quiet evenings they had these days. Over a meal of red beans and rice that Jakarta had prepared while Zane was at work, they chatted about the minutiae of the day.

"This is nice," Jakarta said. "It's nice to just be alone and spend some time with you."

"I agree," Zane replied, "and you're going to turn into a New Orleans cook yet."

"I've been going through those cookbooks in your kitchen. They're easier to follow than I expected. I'm going to try my hand at gumbo before the week is out."

"Gumbo?" Zane shook his head. "That's a big undertaking. You think you're ready?"

"The question is, do you think you're ready?" Jakarta laughed.

A sharp rap on the door interrupted their laughter.

"Who is it?" Zane called as he rose to answer.

"Whitney. I have some wonderful news!"

Jakarta caught the sneer she felt building before it slipped out. *I don't like that woman,* she thought yet again. *And I don't trust her.* But she decided, as she always did when Whitney was around, to keep her own counsel.

Zane opened the door to admit the media strategist. Whitney was more casually dressed than Jakarta ever remembered seeing her in a pair of tight jeans—*you can see her pulse in those,* Jakarta thought caustically—and a white cotton poet's blouse with soft ruffles at the neck and cuffs. Her hair was loose this evening, not pulled back into the ponytail she usually favored, but loose around her head in a page boy, a section of hair tucked behind her ear.

"I have amazing news." Whitney bounded into the room enthusiastically. "You are going to want to hug me when you hear this." She spoke to Zane.

"Good evening, Whitney," Jakarta called from across the room.

"Oh, hi, Jakarta. I didn't see you there."

Jakarta nodded but said nothing.

"So what's this fabulous news?" Zane asked.

"I was able to pull a few strings and get you featured in *Ebony* magazine."

"You are kidding," Zane said. *"Ebony?* How? Why?"

"They do a yearly article on the top bachelors of the year. And you're going to be featured in that." Whitney's smile was smug.

"Top bachelors?" Jakarta asked. "How does that help politically?"

"Any exposure is good exposure," Whitney said tersely. "And this is going to be excellent exposure." She turned her attention to Zane. "There are pictures of all the bachelors included with the article, but some of them get more prominent positions than others, and you'll be one of the first ones mentioned in the article—probably with a bigger picture too. I'm going to get our photographer on that so we can get several shots of you right away to send off to *Ebony."*

"Wait, hold up." Zane shook his head. "I agree with Jakarta—how does this help politically?"

"Any exposure, particularly national exposure, is good. Name recognition is what we're trying to build here. So the people who read *Ebony* will see your name, see your face, know who you are, and then later, when they go to the polls, maybe they'll remember you." Whitney placed her hand on his arm. "It's all good, Zane, this is all good. And believe me, it was hard to manage. They select those bachelors months ahead of time. But—"

"You know a friend of a friend, right?" Jakarta said sarcastically.

"Well, it pays to have friends in high places." Whitney's answer was disdainful.

"And you're sure this is a good thing?" Zane asked, either missing or choosing to ignore the undercurrent between the two women.

"Oh, this is one of the best things possible," Whitney

assured him. "Wait till you see how much attention you get because of this."

I don't think he needs that kind of attention, Jakarta thought, but again kept her own counsel.

"I'm also working on getting you in *People,*" Whitney added.

"Why *People?*" Zane asked.

"They do an annual roundup of the sexiest man alive—"

Jakarta could no longer hold her tongue. "Aw, c'mon. The sexiest man alive is usually a celebrity. It's been Brad Pitt, and Mel Gibson, and Denzel Washington. How are you going to get Zane in there?"

"No, no. He won't be the sexiest man alive," Whitney conceded. "But as a part of that issue they always do features on other men in categories, sexiest fireman, sexiest pediatrician, and this year, sexiest politician. And I'm working hard to make that be you."

"And you feel that portraying him as sexy and eligible is a good way to have the voters take him seriously as a Senate candidate?"

"We're reaching out to all kinds of voters here, Jakarta," Whitney said as if speaking to a dull-witted child. "The voters who read *People* are not necessarily going to respond to the same thing as the voters who read the *Wall Street Journal.* We are reaching out to all demographics; and women, whether we like it or not, are going to be Zane's strongest constituency."

"Seems like pandering to me," Jakarta said.

"We are just trying to do whatever we can to get our guy elected." Whitney smiled at Zane.

"Are you okay with this, Zane? You haven't really said anything."

"You know, I never really thought of myself as sexy."

"The sexiest men never do," Whitney said. "But take it from me and Jakarta, you are sexy. Right, Jakarta?"

Jakarta felt a certain need to stake her claim. She rose from across the room to stand between Whitney and Zane. She placed her hand on his chest and rubbed the fabric of his T-shirt, enjoying the contrast of the soft fabric against the texture of his chest hair underneath. "You are most definitely the sexiest politician ever," she said as she leaned up on her tiptoes to kiss him. Zane gave himself over to the kiss. After a moment Jakarta stepped back and turned toward Whitney. "I'm sure you'll do what's best for him," Jakarta said to her, noting with smug pleasure the look of angered indignation on her face.

"Just let me know what you need me to do, Whitney," Zane said. "Was there anything else?"

"No," Whitney answered.

"Okay then, so we'll see you tomorrow sometime?"

"Yes, I'll try and set that photo shoot as soon as possible, so I'll let you know when."

"Great, I'll look forward to it." Zane put a hand on her shoulder and walked her in the direction of the door. "We'll see you later. Thanks for everything."

"You're welcome, Zane," Whitney said as she smiled up at him. Clearly reluctant to leave, she had obviously run out of reasons to stay, so with a nod to Jakarta, a nod that Jakarta accepted as at least a momentary concession, Whitney proceeded through the door.

As soon as Zane closed the door behind Whitney, he turned to Jakarta. "Okay, now what was that all about?"

Jakarta rolled her eyes. "I don't know what you're talking about."

"Yes, you do. Tell me," Zane insisted.

"The woman is a barracuda," Jakarta said. "She's clearly got her eyes on you and I'm not havin' it."

Surprisingly, Zane laughed. "I think you're misreading the situation."

"Oh, come on, Zane, you're a smart man. You're a

prosecutor, for God's sake. You're used to divining people's motives. Top eligible bachelor, sexiest politician alive, and you think that's about the election?"

"Yes, I do."

"Okay, well, how come she didn't come in here and say that she's going to get you on *Black Enterprise*'s list of up-and-comers or the *Wall Street Journal*'s roundup of the most influential? That's not what she had for you. What she had for you was sexy and eligible, and you don't think there's a message in there somewhere for me?"

"I can't speak on Whitney's motives," Zane said finally. "I can only tell you where my heart is. So it doesn't matter what she's up to, if in fact she is up to something, because my heart belongs with you."

Ruffled feathers smoothed, Jakarta surrendered to the kiss he planted on her. *Yeah, well, that witch better remember her place.* The thought passed through her head right before she surrendered to the sensual cloud Zane was creating around them.

Whitney was infuriated. She sat in her car outside Zane's apartment, stewing. *That bitch,* she thought. *Who is she anyway? Where did she come from? How has she gotten such a hold on him?* She sat for a moment longer, considering her options. *I need to know more about this Jakarta Raven,* she decided. She started her car and eased away from the curb.

Whitney returned to her office and began her search. Detroit was all she knew about Jakarta Raven. So it was the only place she knew to start. She started with an Internet search. The Raven name came up, but not associated with Jakarta. Instead it was Savannah Raven. Whitney settled back in her chair, grabbed a bottle of beer, and continued to search.

* * *

Much later, as Jakarta and Zane lay side by side in his massive bed, Jakarta asked, "You feel okay about this?"

"What?" Zane asked sleepily.

"This plan that Whitney has."

"Oh, are we back to that again?" he asked, not opening his eyes.

"You know, Zane, I'm supposed to be your campaign conscience too. I just want to make sure you're okay with this."

"I think it'll be fun," he said.

"Okay."

"You don't sound like you believe me."

"If you think it'll be fun, then I believe in you. I just had to ask. So what are you going to wear?"

"Wear?" Zane finally opened his eyes.

"Well, yeah, she said that she was going to be arranging a photo shoot in the next day or so. What are you going to wear?"

"I hadn't given it a second thought."

"Well, then, let's decide." She pushed him playfully and he rolled over to the end of the bed.

"Now?" he asked.

"No time like the present," she prodded. She climbed out of bed too and went to his closet. "Do you think a suit or do you think something more casual?"

"Oh, I don't know." Zane sighed.

"Well, maybe for the *People* thing, it should be something more casual." She began her search through his closet.

Back in her office, Whitney was conducting a few searches of her own. Her search for Raven in Detroit had brought up a story about a tragic car accident involving a Daniel and a Jewel Raven some eleven years ago. Daniel and Jewel had been killed in an accident with a drunk driver. The article said that the husband and wife were survived by their four daughters: Savannah, Sydney, Paris, and—Whitney's eyes narrowed—Jakarta. "How intriguing," Whitney said as she took another sip from her beer bottle. She continued her search, determined to understand everything about Jakarta Raven.

Two days later, Harland called all of the principals involved in Zane's campaign to a meeting. "The announcement is going to happen on Thursday, the day after tomorrow," Harland told them. "I've spoken to Senator Reid and he's going to be making his announcement on Thursday. He's going to give us 120 days to have a special election and fill his seat. This is it, boys and girls. This is the moment that we've been waiting for. The campaign starts, in earnest, on Friday."

Everyone around the table nodded. A curious energy fairly crackled in the room around them. They were ready, biting at the bit, anxious to move beyond the precampaign maneuvering and into the actual campaign.

"I want to thank you all for everything you've done so far," Zane said. "And if this is any indication, I am clearly running with the best team available behind me."

Elaina stood and passed a manila folder to everyone at the table except Jakarta. "I'm sorry, Jakarta, I didn't know to expect you."

"That's okay. I'll just look on with Zane," she said as she scooted her chair closer to Zane, so she could look over his shoulder at the materials.

"This is our statewide rollout strategy," Elaina said.

"The top sheet has the itinerary for the first week. Zane, you realize that you're gonna have to—"

"I know, take a leave of absence from my job. I already talked to my boss about it. He's very supportive."

"The steps are outlined there on the top pages. The next few pages are our speaking points and target points. Kennedy"—Elaina turned to the man in charge of volunteers—"how are we fixed on volunteers?"

"Well, I've primed our volunteer captains of the major cities. They know that as soon as the announcement is made, we are going to be ready to roll, and they assure me that we are going to have the support we need."

"Excellent," Elaina said. "And, Bradley?"

"Zane's been very convincing so far." Bradley nodded his approval. "Our coffers are full. We can afford a bus to carry the team and the press core around the state."

"Wonderful," Whitney said. "I have several reporters lined up and ready to hit the road with us. A bus will make that much easier."

"Well, then, it sounds like everything's under control," Harland said. "In a few months, we'll be electing our state's next senator. I have every confidence that that's going to be Zane Reeves." Applause from the assembled group met Harland's words.

As promised, Senator Reid made his announcement that Thursday, and also as promised, the intensity of their campaign efforts kicked up a notch. Jakarta felt very much like one of those cows in a movie she'd seen, swept up in a tornado and hurled around without its permission, with no ability to control what was happening. She could only cling to Zane and hold on for the ride.

* * *

The bus Bradley had secured for them was a large, Greyhound-style passenger bus with plush, comfortable seats and a bathroom on board. The bus had been slightly modified, some of the back rows on either side having been moved to make way for a small workspace for Zane, and a curtain installed around the back bench so he could have a private sleeping area. In addition to the campaign team, the passengers on the bus consisted of representatives from the major newspapers around Louisiana, a couple of Kennedy's volunteers, and two men who would share the driving duties.

In a very short time, Jakarta fell into the rhythm of their days. In the morning they would roll into a town for a day where Zane would meet with the local authorities and appear at some public event, usually something like a park dedication or a department store opening. After the public event, Zane would often meet for hours in private with strategists and donors. At night, there was inevitably some fund-raising event that he had to attend. Jakarta went to as many of those events as she could, but the schedule was too jam-packed to do everything. She wondered how Zane managed it, but then she realized that the campaigning itself energized Zane and fed him in a way that sleep and rest would never be able to.

The tension between Jakarta and Whitney was still there but they had, through tacit agreement, come to an uneasy truce. The focus had to be on Zane and what was going to be best for Zane's candidacy. Each woman seemed to inherently understand and accept that fact.

Despite being with Zane, Jakarta felt lonely and alone. Very often she actually was alone while Zane tended to a campaign duty that she either couldn't or didn't want to attend. And now on top of everything else, she was feeling a little homesick. *I wonder how everybody's doing back home,* she thought. She talked to them often, and to varying degrees her sisters remained supportive, but except when she was with Zane, she was feeling very isolated.

Chapter 12

"Have you seen this month's *Ebony?*" Sydney's voice boomed through the receiver when Jakarta answered the phone at Zane's apartment.

"Hello to you too, Syd," Jakarta said dryly. "I'm fine, and you?"

"Yeah, yeah . . . how you doing? How's the weather? Blah, blah, blah." Sydney sounded agitated. "Never mind all that. Have you seen this month's *Ebony?* I couldn't believe it."

Jakarta sighed. "Oh, you must be talking about the eligible bachelor thing, right?"

"My God, yes! Why would you let him do something like that?"

"His campaign people felt it would be good exposure for him. You know, it's all politics." Jakarta barely hid her annoyance.

"Uh-huh," Sydney said skeptically. "Have you read this article? Or seen this picture?"

"No, I haven't seen it at all. We talked about it several weeks ago, but then I didn't think anything else about it."

"Well," Sydney drawled, "if I were you, I would head on out to the nearest newsstand and get a copy of this month's *Ebony*. You really should see this for yourself."

"Why, Syd? What does it say?"

"It's just . . ." Sydney paused. "You know what? You should see it for yourself. I will say this—that is one good-looking piece of man you've got there. That picture in the magazine makes him look good enough to eat."

Jakarta chuckled. "Well, that was kinda the point, I think."

"I don't know, sis. I'm not sure if you want that sort of point out there. But get the magazine and judge for yourself. You're closer to the situation than I am, and I've never participated in a senatorial campaign, so I'll defer to your judgment." Sydney sucked in a deep breath of air. "But Lord, have mercy, I was just stunned when I saw it."

"Now you've got me curious," Jakarta said. "I'm going to have to go and get one."

"Yeah, you do that." Sydney giggled. "Talk to you later." Sydney disconnected.

Wonder why he didn't mention it, she thought. *He must have a copy of it.*

Curiosity piqued even further, Jakarta decided to set aside the laundry she had been folding and head out to get a copy of the magazine. She found one at a nearby newsstand in the Quarter. Unable to wait another moment, she quickly opened the magazine and flipped to the page where the article began.

She was initially impressed by the array of bachelors *Ebony* had assembled. They were all really handsome men. She was even more impressed by the diversity in their ages. Zane's profile was in the first five the magazine presented. The picture featured him standing in front of the parish courthouse, his leg propped on a park bench, his elbow resting casually on his knee, his suit jacket slung over his shoulder, his tie slightly loosened at the knot. He was smiling into the camera, that sexy smile she had come to look forward to seeing.

"Zane Reeves, thirty-two, assistant prosecutor, New Orleans, Louisiana." She smiled as she read aloud the caption under his picture. *That's my man,* she thought. *It's all just politics,* she repeated to herself, *it's all just politics.*

"Zane Reeves is an active member of his community, serving on several boards and participating in various victim advocacy programs. Zane has political aspirations because he believes being a lawmaker is the best way to help the community. Zane's active lifestyle and busy schedule have not left him much time for a social life, but he wants to change all that. Zane is looking for a woman who is politically minded and committed to improving our society. 'The woman I would be interested in,' Zane says, 'is not afraid to get her hands dirty in the process.' "

Jakarta felt her temper begin to rise as she read the profile under his picture. Suddenly, she could no longer convince herself that it was just politics. *This looks like woman-shopping to me,* she thought. *Damn that Whitney. What is she trying to prove?*

Jakarta grew angrier and angrier as she stewed over the feature. *How could he allow this to happen? I don't see how this has any political benefit at all.* She started walking back to the apartment, hoping the exercise would help her work off some of her anger.

When she arrived at the apartment, she saw Zane's car parked out front. Any anger she had managed to walk off on the way back flared up again with a vengeance. She stormed up the stairs to the apartment and flung open the door.

"Oh, so is this what you are now, an eligible bachelor?" Jakarta slapped him in the chest with the copy of *Ebony* magazine she'd opened to his picture. "So what exactly am I doing here, Mr. 'eligible bachelor'?"

Zane was dumbfounded by her attack. "Wait, wait, wait. Hold up!" he said, holding his hands out in front of him. "It's not like that and you know it. This was just a campaign thing. We thought it would be good exposure."

"This is the kind of exposure you want?" Jakarta demanded. " 'Zane is looking for a woman who is politically minded and committed to improving our society.' " She sneered the words. "Did you notice in here"—she pulled the magazine back and pointed to blurb copy toward the end—"the magazine has instructions on how women can contact the bachelor of their choice? So is that what you're after?"

"It's just politics, baby. You know that."

"Uh-huh. That's what it is today. Who knows what it'll be six weeks from now when the letters start pouring in?"

"I swear to you, Jakarta, it's not like that. I'm not looking for anybody else. I want to be with you."

"Uh-huh."

"It's true. I am your eligible bachelor and that's it."

Jakarta tossed the magazine on the bedroom dresser and turned to him. "My eligible bachelor?"

"All yours," he said.

With both hands she grabbed the short-sleeved oxford shirt he was wearing and ripped it open, causing most of the buttons to fly off in the process. Zane flinched but said nothing.

"My eligible bachelor," she repeated. He nodded his agreement. She pulled him toward her and led his head down to meet hers. Holding his face between his hands, she kissed him deeply, pushing her tongue into his mouth, staking her claim. As she kissed him she eased her hands away from his face and onto his shoulders, forcing the opened shirt onto the floor. Her hands moved between them, unfastened the belt, and released him from the khaki walking shorts he had campaigned in earlier. With both hands she held him, cupping him in one hand, caressing his shaft with the other.

"My eligible bachelor," she purred the words. "Mine." She watched as his eyes rolled back in his head slightly, and he nodded in the affirmative.

"All yours," he breathed.

She gently directed him to the bed. He lay on his back waiting while she quickly pulled off her dress, stepped out of her panties, climbed onto the bed. She deftly applied a condom to his straining erection. Straddling him, she eased herself down onto his erection.

"Mine, right?" she said breathlessly.

"All yours," he assured her again. He started to move but she stayed him with a hand on his chest.

"Be still," she demanded. He did as he was bid. She moved instead, riding up and down on his shaft, feeling him filling her and reveling in the sensation of him sliding in and then out of her.

"I don't know how much more of this I can take, Jakarta," Zane breathed heavily. He looked at her, gave her a pleading look. Jakarta bent at the waist and kissed him deeply.

"All mine?"

"All yours," he breathed. She moved her hand from his chest, giving him permission to move with her. Together they thrust and parried, feinted, and drove each other to the brink of ecstasy. Zane propped himself into a sitting position and pulled her legs around his waist. That slight movement pushed their bodies even closer together. She could feel the tight button of her ultimate pleasure pressed against his pubic bone, tantalized by the coarse hair at the base of his shaft. They rocked together with more intensity and more urgency. Jakarta felt the waves of her fulfillment begin to spread throughout her body. She pressed her breast against his face. He willingly took a nipple into his mouth and teased it with his teeth. That was the final straw. Jakarta exploded against him, yelling his name over and over again. Her release sent him over the edge shortly after. With his hands wrapped around her bottom, he pulled her in closer as he thrust harder into her and held her there for one earth-shattering moment until he groaned his release. Spent, she collapsed against him. Still in a sitting position, he supported her for a while, running his fingers through her locks and cooing sweet words of endearment against her ear.

"All yours," he promised. She felt tears welling in her eyes because of the sincerity she heard in his voice.

"All yours, too," she promised.

Chapter 13

Zane sat in his campaign office the next morning reviewing the week's schedule. He noticed that the following day's activities would have him campaigning in Hammond. He was feeling a little guilty because he had not talked with his mother and aunt very much since the campaign began in earnest. *I can fix that tomorrow,* he decided, reaching for the phone on his desk.

"Hi, Mama," he said cheerfully.

"Who's calling?" Naz said sarcastically.

"Aw, c'mon, Mama. Don't be that way," Zane coaxed. "I'm sorry I haven't called much lately. But the bus is going to be in Hammond tomorrow for a campaign stop. I'm giving a speech."

"Really?" Naz sounded excited. "Where are you going to be? I want to be sure to come."

Zane gave her the address of the auditorium where he'd be giving his speech. "And afterward, I was hoping you'd let me take you and Aunt Nita out to dinner."

"Out to dinner? Don't be ridiculous," Naz said dismissively. "I insist that after the speech, you all come over here for dinner."

"All?" Zane sounded incredulous.

"Yes. I want to meet this campaign team I keep hearing so much about. Just bring the whole campaign over here to the house. Nita and I will fix a big dinner and we'll all sit around and get to know one another."

"Mama, that's probably twenty-five people," Zane warned. "You know, the bus travels with press and volunteers as well as staff."

"Well, invite whoever you think should come, but the more the merrier," Naz insisted.

"Are you sure about this?" Zane questioned again.

"Absolutely! You know how much Nita and I love to cook."

"Okay," Zane said, "I'll put you on the schedule."

"Put me on the schedule?" Naz harrumphed. "I shouldn't have to schedule time with my son. And can we expect your little friend, um, Jezebel to join you?"

"Mama, you know that is not her name."

"I can't keep it straight. What is it again?"

"Her name is Jakarta." Zane enunciated the name slowly.

"That's some kind of name—Jakarta. What does it mean anyway?"

"It doesn't mean anything, Mama. It's the name of a city in Singapore." Zane sighed. "But it seems to me it takes a whole lot of nerve for a woman named Nazimoba to talk about somebody's name."

"Don't get sassy with me, boy," Naz snapped.

"Yes, ma'am." Zane's voice was singsongy. "But yes, Jakarta will be joining us. She's been traveling with the campaign."

"So you've got your own little campaign groupie, huh?"

"It's not like that, Mama, and I don't really have time to go into it with you."

"I'll see what it's like for myself," Naz drawled.

Not willing to get further into that argument, Zane chose not to rise to the bait. "We'll see you tomorrow night around eight, Mama."

"That'll be fine, sweetheart." Naz's tone was syrupy sweet. "See you then."

As Zane hung up, he drummed his fingers thoughtfully on the desktop. *What is it about Jakarta that Mama is having such a hard time with?* Shrugging it off, he decided that was a problem for another day. His immediate concern was preparing for the speech the next day in Hammond.

Dinner the next day at Naz and Nita's house was a raucous affair. When Zane announced that dinner was at his mom's, the entire bus wanted to come—press, volunteers, staff, and all. At about 8:30, thirty-four road-weary souls descended on the stately antebellum home. True to Naz's word, she and Nita had cooked up enough food to feed the entire crowd and then some. The hardened political press relaxed and enjoyed a meal of red beans and rice, crawfish étouffée, jambalaya, shrimp Creole, pecan pie, and gallons of sweet tea. Naz and Nita had set out the good dishes.

"Nothing's too good for my boy," Naz had said, and between the two of them, they had more than enough dishes for everyone who came to eat that night. In short order, it seemed every square inch of the house and the veranda was filled with people eating, laughing, talking, and enjoying the feast Naz and Nita had prepared.

"Mama, you've outdone yourself." Zane pulled her

into his arms and smothered her with a bear hug. "I can't believe you went to all this trouble."

"It's no trouble." She beamed up at him. "I'd do anything for you."

Jakarta stood quietly off to the side of them. "Everything really is delicious, Miss Naz. Zane told me you were an excellent cook. . . . Now I see he wasn't exaggerating."

Naz regarded the younger woman carefully. "Well, he might be a little biased."

"No, really, everything is delicious," Jakarta insisted.

"Well, thank you. Please help yourself to some more." Naz turned her back to Jakarta, making it clear that for her the conversation was over. "Zane, finish introducing me to the rest of your staff." She pulled Zane in the opposite direction away from Jakarta.

Zane threw an apologetic shrug over his shoulder at Jakarta and then linked arms with his mother and led her to a small pocket of campaign staffers.

"Well, I can see I've got a fan in Miss Naz," Jakarta mumbled.

"Don't pay her no mind." Nita came up to stand behind Jakarta. "She doesn't think anybody is good enough for Zane, so she tends to be very protective."

"I suppose I understand that," Jakarta said slowly.

"It's okay," Nita assured her. "You seem to be a fine young woman, and Zane clearly thinks very highly of you, so that's good enough for me."

Jakarta nodded gratefully. "Thank you, Miss Nita."

"Just give Naz some time, she'll come around."

"Hope you're right about that," Jakarta said as she watched Zane and his mother across the room, Naz clearly holding court in her house. "I really hope you're right about that."

*   *   *

Naz was deep in conversation with Whitney. "Zane tells me you're a media specialist. What pray tell is that?"

Whitney smiled indulgently. "I am in charge of Zane's commercial image. I work with the media, both print and broadcast, to make sure we're getting Zane's message out clearly."

"I see. And how does one prepare to become a media specialist?"

Whitney took a sip from the glass of tea she was holding. "Well, I was a communications major at Xavier in New Orleans."

"That's a fine school." Naz nodded her approval.

Whitney smiled. "And political science was my minor. Media specialist is a great job that allows me to combine both of those skills."

"Weren't you lucky to find something that you enjoy doing and that you're good at?" Naz looked impressed. "So what do you think our boy's chances are?" Naz nodded toward Zane, who had struck up a conversation with a volunteer across the room.

Whitney's eyes narrowed as she looked over at Zane thoughtfully. "With that charm and that style, I think Zane is a shoo-in."

"Exactly the right thing to say." Naz laughed. She reached for Whitney's hand. "Come out on the veranda and sit with me awhile, young lady. I'd really like you to tell me what I can do to help Zane get elected." Naz steered Whitney outside to a quiet corner of the verandah.

What are you up to, Nazimoba? Jakarta thought as she caught a glimpse of the pair before they disappeared through the door.

Chapter 14

"Finally!" Whitney said triumphantly. "I found it. I knew there had to be something." She leaned back in her chair and gloated. Whitney had been almost single-minded in her determination to find some dirt on Jakarta. Her persistence had finally paid off.

"Wait till they find out about this. That ought to send little Miss Raven on her way." She reached for the phone and placed a call. "Michael, I need a copy of a file, please. Yeah. It's a little dicey but I bet you can get it for me. It's a police file. Jakarta Raven. From ten years ago." She gave him a phone number. "Fax it to me as soon as you get it, and then send me the hard copy. I need it right away. Thanks, Michael, you're the best." She hung up the phone, a grin spreading across her face. "Yep, this ought to do it."

She made one more phone call. "Mr. Grey, this is Whitney Gramm. How are you today, sir? Listen, some information has come up about Zane Reeves's campaign that I think you ought to know. Can I come by later this evening? Thank you so much, sir."

She hung up the phone and went to go stand by the

fax machine. The fax machine hummed and sprang to life. Whitney watched the pages as they emerged, her glee growing with each passing moment. "Oh, this is perfect." She chuckled.

Her ecstasy was complete when the final page emerged. Instead of text, this page consisted only of pictures, one front view and one side view: Jakarta Raven holding a plaque with a nine-digit number across the bottom and the words COOK COUNTY DEPARTMENT OF CORRECTIONS across the top.

"Oh, this is rich." Whitney began to laugh hysterically.

In her car on the way to her meeting Whitney considered whether she should let Elaina or Harland know what she had found.

"Not yet," she decided finally. "Mr. Grey is the right place to start. As the biggest contributor to this campaign, he'll be the one they all listen to. He understands what the stakes are, anything else will be a piece of cake."

She parked her car outside the restaurant where he had agreed to meet her. Patting her bag, she felt the reassuring weight of the fax pages that she was carrying in a folder.

Just a matter of time now, she thought.

It was about six o'clock and Jakarta was awaiting the room service meal she had ordered from the hotel kitchen. Zane was off in another part of town at a meeting, but she couldn't remember with whom. "It's probably the Kiwanis tonight," she decided. Not up to another rubber chicken dinner and roomful of strangers' faces, Jakarta had decided to stay back at the hotel. She was just about to change into her lounging pajamas when the phone in the suite rang.

"Hello," she answered on the second ring, thinking maybe it was Zane.

"Jakarta Raven please."

"This is Jakarta," she answered, curiosity in her voice.

"Ms. Raven, we haven't met, but my name is Gerard Grey, and I am one of Zane's campaign contributors. Actually, I'm the biggest of Zane's campaign contributors."

"Yes, Mr. Grey," Jakarta said, worry replacing curiosity, "how can I help you?"

"I was hoping you could meet me for a drink this evening."

"Why is that?"

"There are a few things I'd like to discuss with you if you don't mind." Mr. Grey's voice had a tone Jakarta couldn't quite identify.

Jakarta cocked an eyebrow. "And we can't talk about these things on the phone?"

Mr. Grey was insistent. "Actually, I think it would be better if we met face-to-face. I won't take much of your time, Ms. Raven, I promise, and it will be very important to Zane's campaign."

"Okay," Jakarta agreed. "Where would you like to meet?"

"There is a bar called Stumpy's two blocks down from your hotel. Could you meet me there in thirty minutes?"

"Give me forty-five," Jakarta said, "and I'll be there. How will I know you?"

"Oh, I'll know you, Ms. Raven. I'll be looking for you." The phone clicked and the dial tone filled her ear.

What the hell is that all about? Jakarta wondered. She considered not going, but her curiosity got the better of her and she realized she was going to have to find out. She headed to the bathroom of the suite to freshen up.

When she arrived at Stumpy's, she looked around the bar expectantly. She was immediately approached by an older white man, whose ruddy complexion indicated he probably spent more time than he should in the sun.

"Hello, Ms. Raven. Thank you so much for coming."

"Mr. Grey, I presume." Jakarta's tone was dry.

"Yes." He extended his arm in the direction of the room. "I have a table waiting for us; won't you join me?" He led the way to a small round table in the far corner of the bar.

"Something has come to my attention, Ms. Raven, and I'd like to talk to you about it. I need your help."

"I'm not sure how I can help you, Mr. Grey, but I'm certainly willing to listen."

He had a really bad toupee—comical almost. Jakarta was having difficulty focusing on what he was saying, his "hair" was so distracting.

Why doesn't someone tell him? she kept wondering. *Doesn't he have a wife or girlfriend or somebody in his life who could stop him from coming out looking like a fool?* She struggled not to laugh and point.

"So surely you can see my concern," Toupee Man was saying.

"Huh?" Jakarta forced herself to focus on his face and avoid looking at his hair. "I'm sorry, Mr. Grey, my mind wandered for a moment. "What were you saying?"

Mr. Grey's sigh barely masked his impatience. "I was saying, Miss Raven, that Zane has a real chance in this special election . . . and a real chance to go all the way."

Jakarta cocked her head and favored him with an impatient look of her own. "That's a good thing—right?"

"Yes, Miss Raven. It's a very good thing. Zane is young and talented, focused and dedicated."

"I already know that," Jakarta fairly snapped at the man. "What is your point, Mr. Grey? There's obviously something on your mind." She leaned across the table closer to him. "Why don't you just tell me what it is?"

Mr. Grey moved back slightly, as if trying to stay out of arm's reach. "I had hoped it would be obvious, Miss Raven. Zane cannot afford any—um—liabilities. He has an uphill battle as it is, and it's important for him to avoid any unnecessary baggage."

Suddenly, Jakarta did not find Mr. Grey nearly as funny anymore. Suddenly, he seemed sinister and menacing. Suddenly, Jakarta no longer felt the urge to laugh.

"Mr. Grey," she said in carefully controlled tones, "unless I have totally misunderstood, you just called me a liability and unnecessary baggage all in one breath."

"I am sorry if I have offended you, Ms. Raven." Mr. Grey did not seem sorry at all. "But there's too much at stake for the party not to cover all its bases. We've got a lot invested in Zane and I'm just suggesting that until the campaign is over that you—"

"You want me to leave."

"I want what's best for the candidate and the campaign and the party," Mr. Grey said. "I trust you want the same."

"I want what's best for Zane. I don't quite understand why you think that would be me leaving."

Mr. Grey reached into a briefcase Jakarta had not noticed before and retrieved a folder. He slid the folder across the small table to her. The air was wrenched out of Jakarta's chest as she recognized the pictures stapled to the front of the folder.

"You know what, Mr. Grey? This meeting is over."

Jakarta jumped up from her chair with such force that it toppled backward.

She practically ran out of the bar, away from Mr. Grey, and away from that horrible folder. Outside, she hailed a cab, desperate to put as much distance as possible between her and her past. She struggled to fight back the tears. *What if he's right?* she thought. *What if I am holding him back? Once those horrible stories start again, how can they not hold him back?*

"Where to, lady?" The cabdriver half turned in the seat to face her. She sat for a moment, not sure where to go. This wasn't her town. Zane and his campaign people were the only people she knew. She realized with a sinking feeling that she really didn't have anywhere else to go.

"Never mind," she said finally. "I guess I'm going back to the hotel." She exited the cab.

The driver shrugged and pulled away from the curb in search of his next fare.

When she completed the short walk back to the hotel, she could not face being in that lonely room by herself. Not tonight. Tonight she felt the need to be around people. *Preferably people who love me,* she thought, *but none of them seem to be available.* She was suddenly feeling more homesick than ever before.

She chose to go to the hotel's bar and selected one of the cocktail tables off to the side of the small dance floor. She wasn't consciously looking to get picked up, but maybe subconsciously she needed to feel that she had some value to somebody.

When the waitress came over, she ordered her favorite drink—"Absolut Mandrin and cranberry juice with a twist of lime, please"—and then settled back in the chair to watch the couples on the dance floor. When her drink arrived, she sipped it slowly but did not derive the pleasure she usually found in the beverage.

She tried to keep her mind blank and not think about the conversation she'd just had, but the music wasn't loud enough and the drink wasn't strong enough to drown out his voice, his offensive words, and the insecurities they raised.

In her mind's eye, she saw Zane in the *People* magazine pictorial, looking relaxed and confident and— dare she think it?—sexy. And then her mind produced the image of him from *Ebony* magazine—one of the most eligible bachelors—suit coat slung over his shoulder, tie loosened at his neck, beaming into the camera.

The waitress reappeared with a second drink, interrupting Jakarta's thoughts.

"I didn't order another drink," Jakarta said.

"No, you didn't. The drink is from the gentleman at the bar." The waitress pointed across the room.

Jakarta looked, and found herself pinned under the gaze of a tall, thin, light-skinned man who was wearing a navy blazer with a gold T-shirt underneath. He smiled and tipped his head to her. Jakarta lifted the drink and nodded by way of thanks. He motioned with his fingers, clearly asking if it would be okay to join her. Before she even realized what she was doing, Jakarta had nodded her assent.

"Hi," the man said as he approached her table. "I'm Charlie." He pulled out the chair across from her and dropped down into it.

"Hi, Charlie." Jakarta nodded. "Thanks for the drink."

"You are more than welcome," he said. "I couldn't help noticing you sitting all alone. I can't believe you're not waiting for someone."

"How do you know I'm not?" Jakarta said.

"I . . . I just assumed . . ."

"That's always a dangerous thing to do, Charlie." Jakarta gave him a flirtatious smile. "Assume."

"If you'd like me to leave . . ." Charlie made a move to stand.

"No, no. You are welcome to stay."

Smiling again, Charlie leaned forward in his chair. "I didn't catch your name."

"Um . . . my name is—ah—Ann," she said finally, not sure if this Charlie followed the state news and might recognize her from the campaign.

"Hi, Ann," Charlie said. "So . . ."

"What's a nice girl like me doing in a place like this?" Jakarta cocked her head to the side.

"I probably would have been smoother than that, but yeah, basically."

Jakarta shrugged. "Just killing some time, Charlie, just killing some time. What brings you here?"

"Well, it's a nice bar, nice people to meet. I'm just trying to unwind after a long day at work."

"And what is it you do, Charlie?"

"I'm a systems engineer."

Jakarta looked at him blankly.

"What that means is . . ." He proceeded to launch into an explanation of the duties and responsibilities of a computer systems engineer.

Jakarta could feel her eyes glazing over. *What are you doing?* she thought to herself. *Send this guy on his way. Why are you even letting him stay here?* Some small part of her rational mind shouted, *This is not what you want . . . this is not what you need. Send him away! Go to your hotel room!* The voice was getting more and more panicked.

"Hush!" Jakarta said aloud.

"I'm sorry?" Charlie looked hurt.

"Oh, oh," Jakarta started as if suddenly realizing she was not alone. "I . . . I . . ." she stammered for a moment, "didn't . . . I didn't mean it to sound like that,

Charlie. It's just that, um, I, ah, I wanted to dance," she said quickly. "We can talk some more about your job later, but I love this song. Would you dance with me?"

The look of surprised hurt on Charlie's face melted away and was replaced with an ear-to-ear smile. "Sure, I'd love to dance."

He took her hand and led her to the dance floor. Jakarta found herself held far too closely in the arms of a stranger while the sultry voice of R. Kelly sang, "I don't see nothin' wrong with a little bump and grind."

Good Lord, she thought, *this is what I said was my favorite song?* As the dance continued, Charlie began to get aggressive. Jakarta pulled back from him, trying to maintain a safe space between their bodies.

What on earth are you doing? the voice in her head was screaming now. *Get away from this man!*

She was just about to take her own advice when Whitney Gramm, Zane's media specialist, stepped up to them.

"What is going on?" Whitney demanded.

Jakarta jumped back from Charlie as if she were a guilty teenager who just got caught by her mother making out.

"What are you trying to do?" Whitney said. "Completely torpedo this campaign?"

"What does this have to do with the campaign?" Jakarta demanded. "I'm just having an innocent dance with a new friend."

Charlie smiled stupidly at Whitney, not understanding the tension between the women.

"Look," Whitney snapped, "you have to know there's no such thing as an innocent dance with a new friend, especially not now, and especially not with you."

Jakarta said, "I'm not running for anything."

"Don't be a fool, girl," Whitney hissed, "of course you are running. As long as you stand next to that man

you are running with him. And if you're not running
for him, then you are running *against* him." Whitney
grabbed Jakarta's upper arm tightly. "Let's get out of
here before one of the press who are covering this campaign sees you in here."

"H-hey!" Charlie said as Jakarta was led off by Whitney.

"Thanks for the drink, Charlie," Jakarta called over
her shoulder, "it was nice meeting you."

"Nice meeting you too, Ann," he called to her retreating back.

"Ann, huh?" Whitney said as she pulled Jakarta
through the hotel lobby toward the elevators. "At least
you had sense enough not to use your real name."

"You know, I didn't want to be Jakarta for a while,"
she said. "I wanted to get away from it all for a minute."

"Looks to me like what you wanted to do was sabotage this campaign," Whitney answered. "But you've
got to know how important this is to Zane. What the hell
were you thinking?"

Jakarta looked away from the media strategist's angry
stare.

"No . . . I guess you weren't *thinking* anything," Whitney huffed.

The elevator arrived, and the women entered. Whitney
pressed the button for their floor, and Jakarta stood in
the back of the small box, as far as she could get from
the disapproval that was radiating from Whitney in almost visible waves.

When they reached the floor, Whitney walked with
Jakarta to the room that Jakarta shared with Zane and
stopped Jakarta before she put her key card in the door.

"I won't mention this to Zane," Whitney said. "This
time. But don't you ever let anything like this happen
again."

Jakarta didn't answer, but instead swiped her card

through the reader and pushed the door open as quickly as she could. As she suspected, the room was empty. Zane was most likely still out with either the Elks or the Moose or the Optimists, eating chicken or jambalaya or banana splits, and shaking hands or kissing babies or schmoozing financiers. Exhausted, emotionally and physically, Jakarta kicked off her shoes and lay on the top of the comforter, curled up into the smallest ball she could manage. She lay there on the top of the bed, too keyed up to sleep.

It was several hours later when she heard Zane come into the room. And even though sleep would not come to her this night, she closed her eyes and feigned sleep because she didn't feel up to talking. She heard him come across the suite to the bedroom, felt him wrap her in the comforter, and felt the shift in the bed as he climbed in. She was grateful that he had been thoughtful enough to cover her, but irrationally a little miffed that he didn't even attempt to awaken her.

She was tortured by her thoughts, and unlike Zane, who she could tell from his steady, even breathing had fallen immediately to sleep, Jakarta was wide awake, replaying the conversations and events of the night in her head.

She could hear Mr. Grey and his thinly veiled criticism. She could still feel the unwelcome touch of the stranger named Charlie on the dance floor. And she relived the shame she had felt when Whitney pulled her from the bar.

It's like I'm trying to self-destruct, she thought. *Why do I do these things? I know better. What am I trying to prove here? Maybe I don't want Zane to win.* The thought startled her. *Maybe I'm trying to make sure he loses so I won't have to live this political life.*

That possibility had never occurred to her before, so

she focused on it and turned it over in her mind, trying to see if there was any truth to it. By the time the pink light of sunrise slipped in through the hotel window, Jakarta had made her decision. Although she knew she could never tell Zane the whole truth, she knew she had to leave.

I have to let this election go on without me, she decided. *Zane will be better off running his campaign without me hanging around his neck like some kind of albatross.*

She eased out of bed, showered, and changed. By the time Zane's wake-up call came, rousing him for his pancake breakfast with the Daughters of the American Revolution, Jakarta was dressed and ready to go.

"Good morning, baby," Zane said sleepily as he stretched the night's kinks out of his back. "You're up bright and early. Are you going to the breakfast with me this morning?"

"Um, no," Jakarta said. "Actually, baby, I'm heading back to Detroit for a while."

"What? Why?" Zane sat up in bed and the sheet fell away, revealing the solid wall of his chest. Jakarta had to look away so she could hold on to the will to say what she had to say.

"I talked to Savannah yesterday," Jakarta lied, "and she's having some kind of problem with my niece, Stephanie. I want to go and help her out."

"But why?" Zane insisted. "Paris and Sydney are there; they can help. Why do you have to go?"

"Stephanie and I have always been very close and she trusts me more than she trusts her other aunts. I just feel like I can do more good there than I can here."

"What are you saying?" Zane shoulders slumped from the weight of his disappointment.

"It's going to be okay, honey. It's just for a little

while." Jakarta tried to soothe him. "You go and run the best campaign the state of Louisiana has ever seen, and I'll see you later."

"When?" Zane persisted. "When will you be back?"

"I don't know how long the situation will take to resolve itself," she said, thinking not at all about her sisters and her family in Detroit. "I'll be gone as long as it takes. But you'll be fine, I promise. You're in good hands. Elaina, Whitney, and the others will take really good care of you."

"But I'm going to miss you." Zane's voice was plaintive.

"I'll miss you too, baby, but this is best for now." Jakarta crossed the room to stand by his side of the bed. She reached out and gently stroked her hand across his cheek. His morning preshave stubble felt like a caress in her palm.

"Okay," Zane said finally. "I won't try to keep you from your family if they need you. But please come back as soon as you can. I'm going to be miserable without you."

Jakarta bent slightly and kissed him on the cheek. "Baby, you'll be too busy to even know I'm gone," she said sadly. "Now go on and get cleaned up. The Daughters of the American Revolution are waiting for you."

"When are you leaving?"

"My flight is at ten oh five this morning." Jakarta managed a weak smile.

"So soon?"

"The sooner I go, the sooner things will be taken care of." She saw questions begin to cloud his face. "And there's no time for a cross-examination, Mr. Assistant Prosecutor . . . you have pancakes to eat, and I've got a plane to catch."

Clearly reluctant to let that be the last word, Zane eased out of bed. He stood next to her, clad only in pale blue boxer-briefs. He pulled her into his arms and held her close. From neck to knees, their bodies connected, generating heat, filling Jakarta with longing. Then after a soft kiss, he released her.

"Hurry back," his voice rumbled in his throat.

Not trusting her voice to maintain her facade, Jakarta could only nod.

PASSION'S DESTINY

Chapter 15

Despite what she had told Zane, Jakarta wasn't at all convinced that Detroit was where she needed to go. She felt the all too familiar panic in her throat that surfaced whenever this situation threatened her.

I need to just disappear, she thought. *It was fun while it lasted but I knew it was too good to be true. I need to just go and let them all be at peace without me. I did just fine before I came home and I'll do just fine when I'm gone.* It was a familiar argument that she had waged with herself in the past but this time it didn't ring quite as true. This time she realized that even though her family would be just fine without her, she would never again be okay without them. So almost instinctively when the cabdriver showed up to take her to the airport, she made arrangements to catch a flight to Detroit.

She went home to Savannah's house on automatic pilot. Not thinking, not feeling, much like the way lemmings go to the sea, or the swallows return to Capistrano, or buzzards return to Hinckley, Ohio, she knew instinctively that when she got to Savannah's house she would be safe.

When she arrived at her sister's house, it was early evening. Savannah and the children were having dinner. Using her key, Jakarta opened the door and entered. Savannah came into the hallway to see who was entering her house.

"Jakarta," she said with a surprised look on her face, "what on earth are you doing here?" She stopped in midsentence, apparently reacting to something she saw in Jakarta's face. "What is it, Jakarta? What happened?"

Wordlessly Jakarta crossed the foyer to her sister and collapsed in her arms.

"What is it, Jakarta? What happened?" Savannah's voice was frightened now.

"They know." Jakarta's voice was muffled. "Zane's campaign people, they know. They know about me. They know what happened." The words were disjointed, but Savannah was able to figure it out.

"How?" she asked.

"I don't know how but they know, and they say that if Zane's opponent finds out, he'll use it against him and that'll be the end of it. I couldn't let that happen to him, Savannah, I just couldn't. It means too much to him, and he means too much to me."

"I don't understand, you just left?"

"I had to, what was my alternative?"

"You are upset," Savannah said. "Go on upstairs to bed and get some rest. We can talk about this once you've had some rest."

"There's nothing to talk about. I did the only thing I could do."

Savannah nodded. "I understand, J, but what you need to do right now is go upstairs to bed."

Jakarta allowed herself to be led to the stairs. "I really am tired, drained is more like it."

"Go on upstairs, we can talk about it tomorrow." Gratefully Jakarta hugged her sister one last time before mounting the stairs to the guest room.

When Jakarta emerged the next morning for coffee, she was not at all surprised to see an assemblage of sisters in Savannah's sunny kitchen.

"What took so long?" Jakarta said dryly. "I expected you all here last night."

"Savannah told us you needed to rest, so we decided this morning would be soon enough," Paris said, holding a cup out to her sister.

"So what happened, baby?" Sydney said gently.

"You were right, Syd, the past never really does stay buried, does it?"

"But what happened?"

"It's pretty typical, I would imagine, for these sorts of political maneuvers. One of the biggest donors to Zane's campaign took me out for coffee one evening to let me know that they knew. He showed me the mug shot." Jakarta's eyes welled up. "I don't know how he got it, or even how he knew to look for it, but he had it . . . he showed it to me. He told me if they were able to find it, Zane's opponents would be able to find it too. He told me as long as I stayed next to Zane, I put myself in the line of fire. And he told me even if I could take the heat, it wasn't fair to make Zane suffer too." Jakarta's tenuous thread of control snapped then, and she started to cry. "And I knew he was right. I could put his whole candidacy at risk. I couldn't make Zane go through that."

"Did you even tell Zane?" Savannah asked. "Did you let him decide if he wanted to go through it?"

"It's not for him to decide," Jakarta said sternly. "Because I know what he would say, and he'd be wrong."

"J, you can't keep running from this for the rest of

your life," Paris said gently. "Sooner or later you have to face it."

"I have to face *it*." Jakarta emphasized the pronoun. "Not Zane, and not now. Did you all come here to convince me to go back to Louisiana? Because that would be a completely different song than the one you were singing a couple of months ago."

"No," Sydney said. "You're right about one thing. The media and his opponent would absolutely eat Zane alive with the information. But I think that Savannah has a point. He deserves to have the opportunity to make that decision for himself. You can't unilaterally make this choice for him."

"There is no choice." Jakarta stood and pushed away from the table. "I can't let him make that choice. This election is too important."

"So have you come home to stay?" Paris asked.

"I don't know about 'to stay,' Paris," Jakarta said, wearily rubbing her eyes. "I know I've come back home for now."

"That's good enough for us." Savannah stood and gathered their coffee cups from the table. "Now, I bet we all have some work to get to this morning—right, girls?" She looked at Sydney and Paris.

They nodded and stood to leave, hugging Jakarta on their way out of the kitchen. Warmed by her family's love as she knew she would be, Jakarta congratulated herself for having the good sense to come home this time.

"Wonder if it's too early to call." Zane checked his watch. "Six-thirty A.M., I don't want to disturb them but I do want to check on Jakarta." Having accepted Jakarta's answer for leaving, Zane was anxious to touch base with her and see if the crisis had been resolved. He was still debating with himself on whether or not to call when he heard a knock on the hotel room door. Elaina Winters, his campaign manager, burst into the room, clipboard in hand.

"Good morning, Zane," she said cheerfully. "Glad to see you up and about."

"The day starts early on the campaign trail." He repeated the phrase she had said to him many times.

"Well, at least one of you is listening," Elaina said impatiently. "Where is Jakarta? Is she ready to go?" Elaina looked around the suite.

"Jakarta left last night," Zane said as he stuffed papers in his briefcase.

"Jakarta left?" Elaina's brows drew together in question. "Why? What's going on?"

"Relax," Zane said. "It's only for a little while. She had a family emergency she needed to tend to back in Detroit."

"Is that right?" Elaina said. "Well, how long will she be gone?"

"I don't really know," said Zane. "But I expect her back as soon as possible."

"I see. So you're flying solo?"

"Just for a while," Zane said.

"I understand. Well, in today's itinerary we head to Shreveport."

"Shreveport is up at the other end of the state," Zane said.

"I know. We're going to start at Shreveport and work our way back across."

"Okay, whatever you say."

"Come on, we have to go."

Zane hesitated and checked his watch again. "Okay, I can call from the bus," he decided.

"Whatever, let's hit it." Elaina held the hotel room

door open for him and Zane headed out, on his way to Shreveport.

News of Jakarta's departure spread quickly through Zane's campaign bus. Elaina spent most of the morning stamping out the rumor that something went wrong in their relationship and that Jakarta's departure meant that they were breaking up.

"Everything's fine," she assured staff and the press that traveled with them. "There was just a family emergency she had to go tend to. Everything's fine."

Zane in his customary seat toward the back of the bus used his cell phone to try to reach Jakarta in Detroit. When the answering machine at Savannah's house picked up, he disconnected without leaving a message, disappointed not to have talked to her. Whitney Gramm came and stood in the aisle in front of him.

"Can't reach her?" she asked.

"No, I guess whatever's going on has them out of the house. I'm sure I'll hear from her soon," Zane replied as he closed the flip on his cell phone.

"Well, just let her get in touch with you. Just give her some time to sort out whatever's going on," Whitney said, "and I'm sure she'll get in touch with you as soon as she can."

"Uh-huh." Zane nodded slowly. "What's going on?" he asked

"Well, when we get to Shreveport, you're going to have to—"

He cut her off. "No, not with the campaign, not with Shreveport, what's going on?"

"I don't know what you mean," Whitney said.

"Somehow, I think you do."

"Well, but I don't. All I know is that this is going to

be a big day for you and this is where your attention needs to be focused."

"We're not finished with this, Whitney."

"Whatever you say, Zane," she said as she returned to her seat. Something about her demeanor triggered the prosecutor in Zane.

She's hiding something, he thought. *I know it beyond the shadow of a doubt.* Before he had a chance to think more about it, a reporter from the *New Orleans Times-Picayune* came back to talk to him.

"Whitney put me on your schedule for a one-on-one during this bus ride. Is now a good time?" he asked.

Zane immediately clicked into campaign mode. "Sure," he said, "have a seat. Let's talk." For the moment, he put his concerns for Jakarta on the back burner.

Back in Detroit, Jakarta sat alone in Savannah's house, curled up in an overstuffed armchair, cradling a mug of tea in her hand. She tried to clear her thoughts but the images kept running through her mind. She could almost hear the metal clang of the cell door as it closed, she could smell the stench of humanity that lived in the concrete walls of the cell. But more than anything, the image that kept torturing her was that smile. That sick snake-oil-salesman smile. The rest of the features had faded away, but like the Cheshire Cat, that smile remained. It made her sick to her stomach, but she couldn't erase the image from her mind. Anxious to escape it, she climbed out of the chair, reached for the remote on the nearby table, and turned on the television. She turned it up as loud as it would go, hoping the sound of a game show blaring through the house would somehow deafen her to the sound of the judge banging his gavel, the sounds of the handcuffs slapping around her wrists, the sounds of her own weeping that filled her ears. "It's been almost ten years," she berated herself. "Why can't I let it go? Why does it still haunt me like this?"

Somehow she knew that *The Price Is Right* would not be enough to protect her from the rush of memories that assaulted her. Instinctively she knew that the only way to stop the noise in her head this time was going to be to face it directly and deal with it. But she wasn't ready. "Not yet," she muttered to herself, "not yet." She wiped a tear that threatened to run down her face. "Not yet."

Much later, she was in that same spot when she heard the front door open. She thought it was the kids coming home from school, so she didn't rise from her chair. She was sitting there morose when Paris entered the room.

"Hey, sis," Paris said.

"What are you doing here?" Jakarta asked. "Why are you here in the middle of the day like this?"

"It's not really the middle of the day," Paris corrected her. "Actually, it's four o'clock. Aren't the kids home from school yet?"

Jakarta shrugged. "I didn't hear them come in, but that doesn't mean they're not here. I just don't know. But what are you doing here?"

"It's Wednesday," Paris said, holding aloft two plastic grocery bags. "We have dinner tonight. Remember?"

"Oh, yeah," Jakarta said. "Family dinner. I had forgotten." She sat silent for a moment, and then glared at Paris. "But dinner is not until six-thirty. Why are you here already?"

"I told Savannah I'd help cook this week, but that's only part of the reason I'm here already. I want to talk to you, before the night gets too hectic."

"Talk to me about what, Paris?" Jakarta's voice was flat.

"I want to talk to you about this decision you've made not to tell Zane what's going on," Paris said gently.

"He doesn't need to know," Jakarta said firmly. "He never needed to know. He was never supposed to find out."

"That's not real, Jakarta," Paris said. "If this man means to you what he seems to mean to you, then eventually he would have found out."

"I can't argue that point with you," Jakarta said. "But he doesn't have to find out now. Not this way. Not because somebody's using it against him in this campaign."

Paris looked concerned. "But you run the risk of him being blindsided by it. If you don't tell him, somebody else will. You told me that they know. They may have told him already. He deserves to hear it from you."

Jakarta shook her head sadly. "I just can't, Paris. I can't face it right now. I can't bring it into his world right now. He's working so hard to become a senator . . . and he'd be a wonderful senator." Jakarta studied her sister, unshed tears in her eyes. "I can't bear the responsibility of being the reason that he doesn't get that opportunity."

"You are making decisions for him that you have no right to make," Paris said firmly. "If he is half the man that you think he is, he'll understand. And if he isn't that man, if he doesn't understand, then that's something you need to find out right now."

"What are you saying to me, Paris? I thought you would be the one, of all my sisters, who would be happy that I'm back here with my tail between my legs."

"Baby, I never want to see you hurting," Paris said. "I don't know why you would say something like that to me."

"Not the hurting part, maybe," Jakarta conceded, "but I'm home, back in the fold of the family. Here for Wednesday dinner. Doesn't that make you happy?"

"Not if it had to be like this." Paris shook her head. "You love that man, Jakarta. Obviously. You can't ignore that. Love is way too hard to find. Trust me, I know."

Something in her sister's tone roused Jakarta from her own troubles.

"What do you mean, Paris? What's going on?"

"It's nothing." Paris turned away.

"Obviously it's something, P. Tell me what's wrong."

"We were talking about your problems right now, Jakarta," Paris said tersely.

"I'm tired of talking about my problems. That's all anybody's been talking about since I got back into town. Humor me—I need a diversion. What's going on?"

"It's nothing new," Paris said with a sigh. "I met a guy who I thought had some potential, I thought he liked me, but it didn't pan out."

"There's apparently more to this story than that," Jakarta insisted. "Tell me."

"Yes, but it's so sad and pathetic that I don't like to admit to it," Paris said.

"I won't tell anybody," Jakarta promised. "It'll be our little secret. Come on, tell me."

"Okay, if you must know, I met him on-line on one of those on-line matchmaker services. We had been exchanging e-mails for a couple of weeks. I really thought we were connecting on several levels. We had a lot of the same interests and hobbies; he was intelligent and not intimidated by my intelligence. I really thought we were off to a good start."

"It all sounds very promising," Jakarta said, "so what happened?"

"What happened was we met in person and he got a look at me," Paris spat.

"What are you talking about?" Jakarta was confused.

"The Web site encourages everybody to post a picture. I did, but it was just a head shot. You know the one that they did at the school last year for the yearbook? It was just head and shoulders."

"Oh, I remember that picture. It was a good picture, you looked pretty in it."

"Yeah, I thought so too," Paris agreed. "So he'd seen my picture and I'd seen his. He was pretty good looking—balding and wearing glasses but still a good-looking man. But more than his looks, I thought our mental connection was strong. So we agreed to meet—at a public place, because that's how you're supposed to do it when you meet on the Internet—at a restaurant. He was there when I got there. As I approached the table and he stood to greet me, his face fell. I could see it in his eyes—I've seen it before. He was disgusted by my size."

"Oh, Paris," Jakarta said, "I know you're exaggerating. You're just hypersensitive—you act like you're the fat lady in the side show. You're just a little overweight."

"Yeah, says you, the skinny one in the family," Paris said bitterly. "But I've seen that look before. I see it on men when I'm in the grocery store, I see it on men when I go to the movies or the mall—they look at me, and then they look away. If they even bother to look at me to begin with. Sometimes they just look through me. But I really thought that this guy was going to be different. I thought he knew me well enough as a person that he would be able to look beyond me as a body. But I guess all men have an image in their mind of what they want, and if that woman doesn't walk through the door, then they're outta there."

"He just left?" Jakarta asked.

"No, he was gracious enough to tough it out through

the meal, but I could tell that he was no longer interested. I have some experience with this kind of rejection, I know what it looks like." Paris sighed. "I never sent him another e-mail, waiting to see if he would send me one. But he didn't. We haven't had any contact with each other since." Paris affected a nonchalant shrug. "Another one bites the dust."

"You're being too hard on yourself, P," Jakarta said. "If that man, to quote what you just said to me, was half the man you thought he was . . . half the man you deserve . . . he would not have cared about your weight. He was obviously not the one for you."

Paris rolled her eyes. "I don't know that the one for me exists, Jakarta. Maybe fat chicks don't get love."

"Oh, honey . . ." Jakarta got up from the chair and hugged her sister.

Paris returned the hug as she surreptitiously wiped her eyes. "I don't want to talk about it anymore. I want to talk about this situation with Zane."

"Yeah? Well, I don't want to talk about that anymore," Jakarta said. "Why don't we go into the kitchen and start dinner together?"

Paris nodded. "Yeah." She chuckled. "That's probably a good idea."

Shreveport went very well for Zane. The crowds were large and supportive and receptive to his promise of equity in school funding and stricter environmental controls. As usual the day was full, a rally to begin the day with and a fund-raising dinner to end it with. By the time he got to his hotel room in Shreveport, he was exhausted. "I'll call Jakarta in the morning," he decided, right before he dropped off to sleep.

Three rooms down the hall from him, the campaign team was still awake.

"So she left," Elaina said.

"Zane bought the story that she gave him as to why?" Kennedy asked.

"Yes. If we can just keep him busy, he won't have time to look for her. So we're all agreed—it would be best for the candidate if we keep her away until after the election?" Whitney asked.

Elaina, Kennedy, and Bradley all nodded in approval. "Agreed." They turned to look at a figure that stood away from the group near the window. He had a manila folder with a mug shot stapled to the front of it in his hand.

"Agreed, Harland?" Elaina called to him.

Harland looked up from the document he had been studying and nodded his head slowly. "Agreed," he said, "absolutely agreed."

The next stop on the "Zane Train," as the team had taken to calling their bus, was Natchitoches. There he was interviewed by a local television anchor and judged a crawfish pie contest. The day went well but Zane often found himself missing and thinking about Jakarta. *She would've loved that crawfish pie,* he thought as the bus rolled down the highway to the next stop. *And that woman who made the winning recipe, Jakarta would've gotten a kick out of that crazy apron she was wearing.* Zane smiled thinking about Jakarta. He reached for his cell phone to call her, but then caught a glimpse of his watch. *It's well past midnight. I don't want to call this late,* he decided. *I'll call in the morning for sure.* He put his phone back in his pocket and laid his head back, hoping to catch at least a few hours of sleep before his next stop.

*   *   *

The next few days passed in a flurry of campaign stops and strategy meetings. It seemed that constantly he had either a meeting or a fund-raiser, or an appearance to make. The schedule was starting to tire him out. Whenever Zane had a moment to himself, all he wanted to do with it was sleep.

This night, Zane was temporarily back in New Orleans, a brief pit stop before he had to board the Zane Train to weave their way through the countryside to the next stop. He was in the campaign office reading through some briefing notes, when he suddenly realized it had been a week since Jakarta left for Detroit.

Damn, he thought, *I hope everything is okay with her and her family. Why hasn't she called me?*

As he thought about it he realized that maybe she had called. *I never take my cell phone with me on campaign appearances, she might have tried to call and missed me.* Zane considered that possibility. *But she could have left a message. What's going on?*

He checked his watch and saw that it was 1:00 in the morning. *I don't care,* he decided. *It's been a week and I need to talk to Jakarta. Somebody in that house will just have to wake up. I need to talk to her tonight.*

He reached for the phone on his desk and was about to dial when Whitney approached him.

"Zane, what are you still doing here? I figured you'd be at home crashed out by now."

Zane shrugged. "What are you still doing here? I thought I was the only night owl."

"I was finishing up the plan for our media buy. I needed the scheduling software I've got on the computer here," Whitney explained. "But I'm not the candidate; nobody cares if I've got bags under my eyes. You really should go home and get some rest."

"Yeah, I'm on my way, but I have to make a call first."

"This time of night?" Whitney's brows drew together in a question.

"I know it's late, but I need to talk to Jakarta." Zane began to punch the numbers on the phone.

Whitney placed a finger on the switch hook and disconnected the line. "You shouldn't call her," she said.

"What are you doing, Whit?"

"I don't think it's a good idea for you to call her, Zane. Obviously she needs her space."

"What are you talking about? She left to be with her family because of some kind of family emergency. What do you mean 'her space'?"

"And how long ago was that?" Whitney said. "And she hasn't contacted you, not even once? Maybe this campaign stuff was just too stressful for her and she wanted to take a rest."

Zane was quiet, considering Whitney's words.

"Nah, that's not it," he said finally. "She wouldn't do that, or she wouldn't do that without telling me. But whatever, I just need to talk to her and figure out what's going on. And tomorrow is going to be another full day, so I'm calling tonight. So if you'll excuse me . . ." Zane said expectantly.

"Really, Zane, I don't think it's that great an idea. Seems like she's made her feelings about this situation very clear in that she hasn't bothered to call you, not on your cell phone, not at your apartment, and not here at the campaign headquarters in over a week. Just let her be. Your focus needs to be on the campaign."

Slowly, Zane replaced the phone handset on the base. "What's going on, Whitney?" he said. "This is the second time we've had a conversation like this about Jakarta. You know something that you aren't telling me. What is it?"

"What makes you think I know anything?" Whitney hedged.

"Whitney," he said, "I make my living figuring out what's on people's minds and figuring out when they are lying. I know for certain that you're lying to me about something. Tell me what's going on." He pinned her under his penetrating gaze. "Tell me now."

Whitney looked away and fidgeted for a minute. "Would you trust me if I said there are some things that are just better left unsaid?"

"No, I wouldn't," Zane said emphatically. "Now tell me what's going on and tell me now."

There was a long, tense silence between them. "How much do you know about Jakarta?" Whitney said, finally.

"I know she's from Detroit, I know she's got four sisters—" Zane stopped in midsentence. "Why?"

"Did you know she had been arrested?"

"What!" Zane looked at her with disbelieving shock.

"See, Zane? There are some things you are better off not knowing."

"You're lying," he said angrily. "She was never arrested. Why would you say a thing like that? Damn, Whitney, I knew you were a little jealous of her, but this?"

Whitney grew angry. "It's the truth, Zane. I'm not jealous of her, and I wouldn't make something like this up."

Zane stood from his chair; his face was a mask of skepticism.

"Okay, you don't believe me. . . ." Whitney left his office and stalked across the headquarters to her desk. She snatched open a drawer and pulled out a file. Stomping back to him, she slapped the folder on the desk. "See for yourself."

Zane looked down at the cover of the manila folder and stapled on the front were two mug shots—a front view and a side view of Jakarta.

"No, this can't be," he breathed.

"There is information in there about Jakarta that could potentially compromise your campaign. So she generously agreed to leave, so you wouldn't be tarred by your association with her."

"Information like what?"

"It's all in there. Look for yourself if you want." Whitney's voice turned pleading. "But I think you should let it go and focus on the campaign. It is all that matters now. If you want to go to Jakarta when this is all over and sort things out, then fine. But for now, your mind, body, and soul need to be here focused on getting elected."

"No," he said, pushing the folder away from him. "I'm not reading this file. I'll find out everything I need to know from Jakarta."

"What?" Whitney said. "Jakarta is in Detroit."

Zane put some papers in a briefcase and moved toward the door. "I know that. But I have to see her, and I have to see her now."

He stormed out of the office and slammed the door behind him.

Chapter 16

Zane showed up at Savannah's house in Detroit, in the middle of the afternoon, unannounced. He wasn't sure where he would go if Jakarta wasn't there, so he was prepared to sit on Savannah's stoop all day, if necessary. *I have to see Jakarta, and I have to see her today,* he thought. *She's going to explain this to me, face-to-face.*

He paid the cabdriver who had brought him from the airport, and squared his shoulders as he approached Savannah's door. He pressed the button for the doorbell, and listened to the chimes ring throughout the house. He had his finger on the button to press again, when the door slowly opened.

Jakarta's eyes widened, and her mouth dropped into an O shape. "What are you doing here?" she whispered.

"Tell me the truth."

Jakarta shook her head. "There's nothing to say."

"Don't!" The word burst from Zane's lips. "Don't do this, Jakarta. You owe me an explanation, and I want to hear it from you, not them."

"You're talking about the campaign people."

"This isn't something I need to hear from anybody other than you. Let me in, and let's talk."

Jakarta stood behind the closed screen door, using the mesh as a protective barrier. "You shouldn't have come," she said.

"How could I not come?" Zane asked. "I love you, Jakarta." He felt his eyes fill with tears.

"You've never said that to me before," she said.

"But that doesn't mean I never felt it before," he said. "And maybe I never really realized it until this moment. Please. Let me in. We need to talk."

Jakarta nodded. "Yes. I guess we do." She held the screen door open and stepped aside as he passed her into Savannah's house. "Come on in to the kitchen." She closed the door and led him into the back of the house. "Let me get some coffee."

"I don't want any coffee," he said. "I just want to know what's going on."

"Well, I want some coffee, even if you don't," she said. "And I'm going to tell you. I'm going to tell you everything."

Once they were seated at the dinette table, coffee mugs in front of each of them, Jakarta leaned forward and rested her elbows on the table. "So. What do you know already?" she asked.

"All I know is that somebody on my campaign team has a folder that's got a mug shot of you stapled on the front of it."

"Did you read the folder?" Jakarta asked.

"No," Zane answered. "I didn't want to learn whatever this is from a folder. I didn't want to read 'Just the facts, ma'am.' I want you to tell me."

"So you came all the way here so that I could tell you this? You should have just read the folder." Jakarta was suddenly impatient.

"Or you should have just told me whatever it was to begin with!" Zane's impatience matched her own.

"I couldn't tell you," Jakarta said. "It never even occurred to me that you would have to know."

"How could I not have to know, Jakarta? There's a mug shot of you! You're going to have to tell me, and right now. We can dance around this all day in this kitchen, you saying I didn't need to know, me saying you have to tell me, but the reality is now I do know something is going on, and you're going to have to fill in those blanks for me."

Jakarta took a deep breath. "Okay. Here goes. That mug shot was taken ten years ago. I had been arrested for assault. Those charges were eventually dropped." She fell silent.

"Clearly there's more," Zane said. "Am I going to have to pull this story out of you bit by bit?"

"No. I'll tell you, but you're not going to like it."

"I don't like it already," Zane pointed out.

Jakarta began again. "Our parents died when I was twenty. They were killed in a car accident caused by a drunk driver. Did I ever tell you that?"

Zane nodded.

"When that happened, it was the hardest thing I'd had to deal with up to that point in my life."

Zane's cellular phone erupted just at that moment, the shrill ring causing both of them to jump. "Damn," he said. "I thought I turned that thing off." He snapped it off the clip on his belt, and checked the caller ID. "Damn," he repeated softly, "it's Elaina." Shrugging, he set the phone on the table in front of him, unanswered. The ringing continued.

"Aren't you going to get that?" Jakarta said.

"No. Nothing is as important right now as you, and hearing this story." The ringing finally stopped, and Zane reached for the phone again, this time to turn it off. After he turned it off, he pushed it to the side. "Go on. What happened when your parents died?"

Jakarta took a deep breath and closed her eyes, allowing herself to go back to that black time when her whole world turned upside down. "When Mom and Dad were killed, I was a sophomore in college. I had really only gone to college because Mom and Dad expected me to. I wasn't enjoying it at all, and I was being a little rebellious. I wasn't studying very hard. I was much more the party girl than the student. When Paris called me to tell me what had happened, I just fell apart. I broke down. I couldn't take it. I was wracked with guilt. I felt that somehow it was my fault that Mom and Dad had been killed. And killed by a drunk driver. That was just too profound. It seemed to me at the time that God was punishing me for squandering the opportunity I had been given. I had actually been out at a party drinking that night Mom and Dad got killed. It didn't matter, in my mind, that they were killed in Detroit, and I was partying in Virginia. All that mattered was that somebody had left a party drinking and killed my parents at about the same time I had left a party drinking. It was all just too much for me."

Jakarta stopped, swallowing hard, determined not to cry. Zane said nothing, just sat patiently waiting for her to continue.

"After the funeral, I was just lost. I dropped out of school and came back to Detroit. I needed to be here among familiar things and people who loved me. I was the only one still living at home with Mom and Dad by then. All my sisters had started their own households, so when the insurance settlement came and it was time to sell Mom and Dad's house, I was the one with the primary responsibility of packing everything up, deciding what we were keeping and what we were getting rid of. To me, that was like losing them all over again. I just couldn't take it."

She paused, trying to find the right words. "I had a breakdown," she said finally. "I had to be hospitalized. I went into a severe depression. I tried to close myself up away from the world, and nobody—none of my sisters and none of my friends—could reach me."

She stopped talking to study Zane closely, looking for any sign of revulsion or pity in his face. She saw none. "I was in the hospital for almost a month, undergoing therapy and taking antidepressants until the doctors felt I was ready to come out and try to face the world again." She fell silent once more.

"Go on," Zane prompted gently, as the silence stretched between them.

"There was one doctor, when I was in the hospital, who I really responded to. His name was Dr. Stuart Sullivan, and he was"—she shrugged for a moment— "and I suppose still is, one of Detroit's most prominent psychiatrists. Everyone kept telling me how lucky I was that Dr. Sullivan had taken an interest in my case. 'One of the best!' " Jakarta mimicked one of the many nurses who had sung Dr. Sullivan's praises to her. "He started treating me while I was still in the hospital and offered to continue working with me on an outpatient basis after I went home. I thought that was such a wonderful, generous thing for him to do, because his practice was so full, and he was not accepting new patients. So I sort of latched on to Dr. Sullivan. I know now that he encouraged that dependence. He said it was 'therapy.' " She spat the word bitterly. "He said that the transference of emotion from my missing parents to him was completely normal, and to be encouraged, because it meant that I was healing."

Jakarta's tone was filled with contempt. "The first

time he touched me, it freaked me out. Oh, but he was quick to soothe me. 'It's all a part of the therapy, Jakarta,' he'd said. 'It's all about helping you to relax and let your feelings come to the surface.' He started out massaging my shoulders, working the tension out of my neck, he said. And then his hands were on my arms. At first, it seemed innocent enough. I was very tense, and very stressed. After a few sessions of just those innocent shoulder massages, one day he . . ." She paused, and her voice broke for a moment as she tried to find the words. "He put his hands on my breasts."

The words were soft, and Zane leaned in to hear.

"He said that was therapy too. He said that pent-up frustration in any form—including sexual—was bad for my recovery. So he fondled me." She was silent for several long moments. "I thought it was wrong, but I trusted Dr. Sullivan so completely, I figured he was the expert, not me. He was the doctor and I was the patient. If he said this was what I needed to help me get back to feeling normal again, then I was willing to accept that." She shook her head, disbelievingly. "I should have known better."

Zane interrupted at that point. "You were ill and young, and he took advantage of you. That wasn't your fault."

Jakarta shrugged. "Maybe. But a few visits later, fondling my breasts and placing my hand on his erection was no longer enough for him. This particular visit, he decided we needed to have sex. Oh, he didn't call it that—he called it intensive touching therapy. He wanted me to undress and lie on his couch . . . as a sign of trust, he called it. And he was going to undress and just lie there with me." She mimicked the words, "to prove that he could be as vulnerable as I was. I have no doubt that had I done that, we would have had sex before that session was over. By then, I had lost my trust in Dr. Sullivan. The things that he was doing and the things that he was suggesting didn't feel like therapy anymore. They felt like abuse. And I was in my right mind enough to know that these things were wrong. I refused and told him that I would not be seeing him anymore. He grew very angry and said that I couldn't just walk away from my therapy like that. He said I wasn't ready to be out of treatment. I remember laughing when he said that. I said, 'You call this treatment? I'm paying you a hundred bucks an hour to try to have sex with me? That's your idea of treatment? I don't think so, Dr. Sullivan.' It was the healthiest I had felt since before Mom and Dad died. I turned around and left his office right then, determined to be done with therapy in general and Dr. Sullivan in particular."

"Well, that was the right thing to do," Zane said. "But, Jakarta, I still don't understand. . . ."

"Oh, there's more." She sighed. She got up from the table and warmed up his coffee from the pot she still had on the stove. "Sorry I don't have any beignets." She smiled weakly. "Best we can do around here is jelly donuts."

Zane waved dismissively. "Tell me what happened," he said, refusing to allow her to change the subject.

"My sisters wanted to know why I had stopped seeing Dr. Sullivan so abruptly. They knew how much I respected him, and how much I felt he had helped me. They didn't understand why I had stopped. I didn't want to tell them at first, I was so embarrassed and ashamed about what he'd done, but finally I told them." Jakarta smiled, remembering the rush of support she'd received from her sisters. "They were outraged, horrified. Savannah wanted his head on a platter, but Sydney decided that rather than his head, we should go for his license on a platter. So with their encouragement and against my better judgment, I filed ethics charges against him with the medical board, and criminal charges with the city. I was scared; I knew it was going to be his word against mine. I knew he was a prominent psychiatrist and I was a former mental patient, but I also knew I was telling the truth and the truth had to be told. Paris convinced me to see the charges through when she said that if he'd done it to me, he'd probably done it to other women too. I knew she was right, and I knew I had to do whatever I could to stop him from abusing his position."

Zane nodded. "I'd have taken a case like that in a heartbeat," he said. "Medical professionals like that need to be put in jail."

Jakarta sighed. "That's the reaction I'd hoped I would get from the prosecutors and the ethics board when I approached them."

"But that's not what you got," Zane said matter-of-factly.

"No." Jakarta's voice was hard. "That wasn't what I got at all. The ethics board conducted an *investigation.*" Using her fingers, she mimed quotation marks in the air as she spoke the word. "But it was little more than a love fest for Dr. Sullivan. The panel reminded me of his sterling reputation in the community and how many people he has helped. They even suggested that I was lucky that he had agreed to take my case and help me through my grieving process. One of the members of the ethics board was a woman, and she disappointed me most of all. She wouldn't even entertain the idea that maybe what I was saying was true. She even suggested that perhaps what I was experiencing was an unhealthy transference of emotion. That perhaps he had rejected my advances and maybe this was my way to pay him back. I have always wondered if she was sleeping with him, because that was exactly what he'd said in his testimony before the board."

Jakarta's eyes looked not at Zane, but at the past. "Oh, Dr. Sullivan was smooth that day. I was terrified and nervous, and there he sat at the ethics board hearing with this slimy grin convincing the other doctors that this was just a case of a poor disturbed young woman who had obviously fallen in love with him, trying to wreak some havoc on his career because he had rejected me. It was a humiliating experience, but in all honesty I didn't have any faith going in that the ethics board was going to do anything to him. I figured it was a good ol' boys' club, and they'd all protect one another. I had my real hopes pinned on the criminal charges that I'd filed with the city." She took a deep breath. "But once the ethics committee dismissed my charges without comment, it really weakened my credibility with the criminal proceeding. We both had to take the stand in open court. I told my story, I told them everything he had done to me." Her voice grew hard and bitter as she told the story. "He didn't even bother to have a lawyer at the proceeding. When the prosecutor finished with me, Dr. Sullivan questioned me, acting as his own counsel. By the time he got finished, he'd made me look like some lovesick puppy bent on revenge. Or worse, some recent escapee from the loony bin. It was even more humiliating than what had happened with the ethics panel, because at least that hearing was closed. This was in open court. And he took that opportunity to be onstage in front of the judge and gallery. The charges had generated a little publicity because of who Dr. Sullivan is. The suggestion that he may have been involved in the sexual abuse of a patient had brought the newspapers out in full force. They were all there that day, that horrible day in court when he picked me apart."

Zane ached to reach out to her, but he didn't want to interrupt the cathartic stream of words that flowed from her.

"Since it was only a probable-cause hearing, there was no jury. So the judge went back in his chambers—seems like he was only gone for ten or twelve minutes—and came back and declared that I had not presented enough evidence to warrant a full trial. The case was dismissed." Jakarta rubbed her face with her hands. "A few people in the court applauded once Dr. Sullivan got off. He stood up, thanked the judge, and then turned to me." Jakarta's face had taken on an angry look, her teeth clenched and her eyes hard and flinty as black onyx. "He said to me, 'I hope one day you'll be feeling better, and whenever you're ready, we can resume your therapy.' " Jakarta spat the words. "He actually came over and said that to me. It was too much, Zane, it was just too much. I leaped up from the chair and lunged for him. I was determined to claw his eyes out, rip that lying tongue out of his head. If the system wouldn't punish him, then by God I would."

Her face became animated as the words tumbled from her in a rush. "I had reached him and had jumped on his back when the court bailiffs rushed over and pulled me off of him. It took two of them to control me, I was so angry and so filled with indignation. They pulled me off of him, handcuffed me, and took me away. I was later charged with assault—that's where the mug shots came from. After I'd spent the night in jail, Dr. Sullivan came down and had all the charges dropped. It made him look even more magnanimous with the press, that he was willing to forgive me because obviously I was so distraught. Made it seem like he was much more concerned about my mental health than he was about any sort of punishment for my actions. But before he dropped all the charges, before he made a public display of his generosity, he came to my cell. He said to me, 'Wouldn't it have just been so much easier to go on and let me make love to you, Jakarta? You would have enjoyed it.'

"After that whole experience, I was convinced that you can't really fight the system, and I pretty much lost my faith in mankind. And so that was when I started running. When I was released from jail, I left Detroit and headed west. I didn't know where I was going and I didn't care. I just knew I needed to get away and put some distance between me and that situation. I started doing self-destructive things, trying to medicate myself to ease my pain and humiliation. I fell into a series of really bad relationships with really stupid men, and I made some bad choices. Nothing illegal, but really stupid things. I had a little money from the insurance and the sale of the house when Mom and Dad died. So I didn't need to work, I just kinda drifted around. And probably would have kept drifting if Dwayne hadn't disappeared and Savannah hadn't needed me. That was the first time in a long time anybody really needed me. And when I came home, I discovered how much I really needed my family."

"And that's what brought you to me," Zane said. "So let me make sure I understand this. The arrest and mug shots were because you attacked this Sullivan in court because he got away with abusing you."

"Yeah, guess that's it." Jakarta nodded.

"Well, baby, how is that your fault?" Zane asked gently. "That is a completely understandable situation. Why wouldn't you have told me that?"

"I couldn't think of any reason why you would need to know," Jakarta said. "It happened ten years ago. And it happened to me. It didn't have anything to do with you, and it certainly didn't have anything to do with your campaign. Why would you have needed to know about it?"

Zane shook his head. "Maybe I didn't, initially. But, Jakarta, once it came out, you should have told me. You shouldn't have let Whitney try and tell me what was going on."

Jakarta hung her head. "I know. But I didn't want to cost you this election. I needed to get away from you so that nobody else would find out. So far, only your team knows, and they wouldn't use it against you. But what happens when the other side finds out?"

"I know that they will," Zane said, "but we'll cross that bridge when we come to it. I need you to be with me, Jakarta. Please, please, come back to Louisiana with me."

Jakarta gave him a look of stunned disbelief. "After everything I've told you and everything you know about me now, you still want me to come back to Louisiana with you? You still want me to be on the campaign trail with you?"

Zane looked at her as if she'd lost her mind. "Of course I want you to be with me. I need you there with me." He laid his hand on the table palm up, beckoning her to place her hand in his. When she did, he squeezed it gently, and rubbed his thumb across her knuckles. "Baby, nothing you've said here today changes the way I feel about you. It helps me to understand you more, and I'm so sorry that you had to endure that experience—I would do anything if I could take that away from you—but, Jakarta, I love you. And that's all that matters to me. I need to have you with me. I cannot do this without you. Remember, you're my campaign conscience."

Jakarta smiled. "I don't know what to say. I had no idea . . ."

"You had no idea what?" Zane demanded. "That I loved you?"

"Zane, you've never said that to me before," Jakarta pointed out. "Why now?"

"Baby, I guess I always thought you knew. I know that you love me."

Jakarta looked away from his penetrating eyes.

"You do, I know you do," Zane insisted. "I can feel it when you hold me; I can see it when you look at me; I can hear it when you call my name; I can taste it when you kiss me. I didn't need you to say it."

Jakarta looked up and met his eyes with an intensely intimate stare. "I do love you, Zane," she admitted, "and that's why I left Louisiana . . . and that's why I can't go back to Louisiana with you. If I'm there, somebody will pull this whole sordid incident out and use it against you."

"We'll deal with that if we have to. But I'm not going back without you. I'm not."

He rose from his chair and came around the table to kneel next to her chair. She wrapped her arms around his neck and hugged him close to her heart.

"Zane, if you want me to be with you, then I'll come."

"Thank you." His voice was muffled against her skin. "Thank you. I know I couldn't do this without you."

At that moment, Savannah, who had come home for lunch to check on Jakarta, walked into the kitchen. "Oh!" she said.

Zane stood. "Hi, Mrs. Dailey . . . I mean Ms. Raven. Good to see you again."

Savannah's look of astonishment traveled between Zane and Jakarta. "Um . . . nice to see you again, too, Mr. Reeves," she stammered. "What on earth are you doing in my kitchen?"

"I came to get my woman," he said simply.

Jakarta smiled up at him. "I'll be heading out later on today, sis," she said to Savannah. "Zane needs me."

Savannah's face broke into a broad smile. "Good," she said. "It's about time."

Chapter 17

As Jakarta packed her things and prepared for the trip back to Louisiana, Zane turned on his cell phone and checked his messages. There were four, all urgent, all frantic, all from Elaina. He erased each message, and then placed a call.

"Zane!" Elaina's voice blasted his ear. "Where on earth are you? Why haven't you called me back? We need you here! You've missed two scheduled events already. I'm having a hard time coming up with excuses to explain where you are."

"Calm down, Elaina," Zane said, "before you bust a blood vessel or something. I'll be back tonight. I'll be there to handle whatever's on the schedule for tomorrow."

"Where are you?" Elaina demanded.

"That doesn't matter," Zane replied. "All you need to know is I'll be back tonight. You don't have to keep tabs on me every second of every day."

"Yeah, Zane, I do," Elaina snapped. "That's what I do. I manage your campaign. And I can't manage your campaign if I don't even know where my candidate is."

"All you need to know is I'll be back tonight," Zane repeated stubbornly. "I'll call you when I get to town."

"So you're out of town? That's great, Zane, real responsible." The phone clicked in his ear.

Zane chuckled. *Wait till she sees what I'm bringing back with me.*

Jakarta appeared, carrying a duffel bag.

"Is that all your stuff?" Zane asked.

Jakarta laughed. "Sydney once said to me that I could pack my entire life in a duffel bag, and I guess she's not far from wrong." She dropped the duffel and went over and hugged him. "Actually, this is all I need." Standing on her toes, she reached to kiss him. He bent to meet her lips and an explosion of sensation rocked through them both.

"I missed you," he murmured against her mouth. "Don't ever leave me again."

"I'll be by your side as long as you want me there," Jakarta promised.

"That means you'll be by my side forever."

They kissed again; their tongues mingling, tasting, promising. After a few moments, Zane pulled away. "We've got a plane to catch," he said.

"Let's go then." Jakarta nodded, ready to face whatever came.

"What exactly did he say?" Whitney demanded of Elaina. "Where is he?"

"He wouldn't tell me where he was," Elaina answered. "All he would say is that he'll be back in town tonight."

"In town?" Whitney keyed in on the words. "So that means he's not in New Orleans?"

"Well, yeah," Elaina said impatiently. "And I bet you can guess where he's gone as easily as I can."

"He didn't go after her," Whitney hissed. "He couldn't have . . . not with what we know about her."

"There's no accounting for taste." Elaina shrugged. "Clearly, he loves her."

"You're wrong about that," Whitney said flatly. "Infatuated maybe, addicted to the sex maybe—but in love with her? I don't think so. She is so wrong for him."

Elaina cocked an eyebrow at the younger woman. "Wrong for him politically or personally?"

Whitney sneered, "Is there a difference?"

On the plane ride back to New Orleans, Jakarta tried to steel herself for what was coming.

"They're going to be pissed that I'm back, you know," she said to a dozing Zane.

"Who?" he mumbled groggily.

"Your campaign staff, your funders—hell, everybody who's seen that cursed file." Jakarta struggled to keep her voice low.

"Oh, well." Zane shrugged. "They'll either like it or they won't. In any case, I couldn't possibly care less. They are with me to do a job, and their job is to help me get elected. That doesn't have anything to do with running my personal life."

Jakarta shook her head. "I'll bet they would disagree with that."

Zane stretched in the seat, apparently unconcerned. "So? That'll be their problem."

"No, Zane, that'll be our problem. You can't forget that your biggest contributor is the one who chased me out of Louisiana in the first place." Jakarta looked worried.

Zane leaned over to kiss her lightly. "You can't forget that I love you. That's the only issue that matters here. This campaign is supposed to be focused on the issues, not the past of my girlfriend. I won't let it disintegrate into a personality contest." His face grew hard, and his eyes darkened. "And Mr. Grey, Harland, and whoever else will have to understand that backing me doesn't mean they own me. Grey was way out of line, and I'm going to tell him so."

"Don't alienate him, Zane," Jakarta advised. "You may need him in the future."

Zane snorted at that and rolled his eyes. "What I need," he said as he stretched languorously, "is a nap. Let's not worry about anything else, at least right now. We have each other, and nothing is ever going to be stronger than the two of us together."

Jakarta's fear began to melt away under the warmth of his words. She lifted her arm and placed it around his shoulders, gently guiding his head to rest against her chest. "I do love you," she said softly.

"I know," Zane mumbled as he got comfortable and drifted back to sleep.

"Elaina thinks he's bringing her back." Whitney barely controlled her fury as she stood in Harland's office at the party headquarters. "She thinks that despite the risks, he's bringing that woman back here."

Harland shook his head sadly. "That wouldn't be a good choice—"

"It absolutely would not," Whitney interrupted. "She'll ruin everything."

Harland studied her carefully. "As I was saying, that wouldn't be a good choice, but it's Zane's choice to make. We're just going to have to control the story the best way we can."

"Control the story?" Whitney struggled not to come unglued. "Harland, you've got to be kidding. That woman was hospitalized in a mental ward and arrested for assault. A story like that is too big to control."

"It shouldn't be that difficult to do, especially for someone with your talent," Harland said firmly. "The election is a few weeks away. All we have to do is keep Jakarta out of the limelight until then. Who cares if it comes out after Zane gets elected? By then, it would only be a mild scandal, over and done with before we know it." Harland gave Whitney a stern look. "All you have to do is control it until after the election."

Whatever! The word screamed in Whitney's head, but she chose to say nothing. She stomped back to her office and spun quickly through her Rolodex looking for a number. Once she found what she was searching for, she snatched the card out of the file and shoved it in her purse. She headed out to her car, started the engine, and drove around the corner—out of sight of the headquarters office. She parked on the side of the road and pulled out her cell phone and the number she'd pulled out of the Rolodex. Dialing quickly, she punched in the Hammond number.

"Miss Naz, this is Whitney Gramm from Zane's campaign."

"Oh, of course, Whitney! How nice to hear from you." Naz's tone changed. "How are things? Is everything okay?"

"Actually, there's a problem, Miss Naz," Whitney said, "and I'm hoping you can help me with it."

"A problem with Zane?" Naz immediately jumped, on the alert. "What is it? What's going on, Whitney?"

"I hope I'm not being an alarmist," Whitney began, "but actually, it's about Zane and Jakarta."

"Oh." Naz drawled the word. "So the problem is Jakarta."

"After a fashion," Whitney said. "Miss Naz, I've only

called you because you asked me to let you know what you could do to help Zane get elected."

"Tell me, Whitney. What's going on?"

Quickly, Whitney briefed Naz on Jakarta's troubles. "It's not that I have anything against Jakarta personally," Whitney lied, "I'm just concerned that once people find out about that, they'll judge Zane based on her. And he doesn't deserve that. He's a better man than that."

"Clearly," Naz agreed. "How can I help?"

"He is away right now . . . he's gone to Detroit," Whitney said.

"Oh, is he?" Naz's tone was sharp. "He didn't tell me he was going out of town."

"It was a spur-of-the-moment thing. I'm afraid he's gone up there to bring her back here."

"What?" Naz said. "Does he know what you just told me about Jakarta?"

"He knows some of it. He went to Detroit to get the whole story from Jakarta. I can only guess how she's going to spin the truth to make herself sound good." Whitney struggled to control the snarl she felt building in her throat. "I'm sure by the time she's finished, he'll have forgiven her for everything."

"Fool boy," Naz snapped. "He always has been a sucker for romance."

"Well, Miss Naz, maybe you can talk some sense into him," Whitney suggested. "Maybe you can make him see what's at stake here. I have a feeling that you and Zane have always been close and he's always listened to you."

"You're very perceptive," Naz said. "I'll talk to him. And failing that, I'll talk to her."

"I hope you don't think I was out of line to call you," Whitney said.

"I'm glad you did, child. I'm glad you did." Naz was firm. "Somebody has to be looking out for Zane."

Whitney nodded vigorously. "I have been saying that all along."

The next morning, when Zane and Jakarta arrived at the Reeves-for-Senate campaign headquarters office, Elaina, Whitney, Harland, and Kennedy Bryant the volunteer coordinator were already gathered, along with several campaign volunteers.

"How good of you to join us," Harland said sarcastically as Zane entered the conference room.

"Not now, Harland." Zane pulled Jakarta into the room. Varying reactions met her reappearance. Kennedy seemed surprised to see her; Elaina and Harland did not, wearing looks of "I told you so" on their faces. Whitney was obviously struggling to appear emotionless. Jakarta keyed in on the media strategist's face.

"Hi, everybody," Jakarta said cheerfully. "I'm glad to be back. Everything worked out fine in Detroit. The crisis was averted."

Whitney apparently gave up her struggle to control her emotions and glared at Jakarta.

"Look," Zane said, "Jakarta is back, and Jakarta is here to stay."

Harland opened his mouth and began to protest.

"Stop!" Zane held up his hand. "I know what you're going to say, and I don't care. Jakarta's past is Jakarta's past. It has nothing to do with me, it has nothing to do with this campaign, and it has nothing to do with Louisiana's future. So we are going to get over this, put it behind us, and focus on the issue at hand. This campaign is what matters."

"Of course this campaign is what matters," Whitney

snapped. "And don't kid yourself into thinking Jakarta's past is not going to effect Louisiana's future."

"Not if we don't let it," Zane said confidently. "We're the ones who are going to control this story. And we're going to control it by not letting it be a story at all. Now"—he turned to Elaina—"what's on our agenda for today?"

After the meeting, Jakarta decided it would be best if she left the headquarters for the day, to give the staff a chance to adjust to her return, or a chance to tear into Zane privately. When she returned to their apartment, she felt a need to relax and unwind.

A good long soak will suit me just fine, she decided. She picked a book from the shelves and headed to the bathroom to run her water.

Jakarta was in the bathroom finishing her bath when she heard the key in the lock and heard the door swing open. She glanced at a nearby clock. *It's a little early for Zane to be home,* she thought.

She wrapped herself in a fluffy cotton robe and headed toward the living room to greet him. She was stopped in her tracks at the sight of Nazimoba Reeves, her hands placed firmly on her hips.

"Somehow I knew I'd find you here," Naz said disdainfully. "Is what I've been hearing true?"

Startled, Jakarta could not fully process either Naz's presence or her words.

"Well, answer me," Naz demanded. "Is it true that you're about to ruin my son's career?"

Jakarta shook her head vigorously. "What are you doing here?" she asked.

"I think that's the question I've come to ask you,"

Naz countered. "If your real question is how I got in, I've always had a key to Zane's apartment. Ever since it was just a dorm room in college, I've had a key. That's the kind of relationship we have. Now it's your turn. What are you doing here?"

Jakarta pulled the robe closer to her body. "I'm here because Zane wants me to be," she said. "He came to Detroit to get me. I didn't want to come back . . . he insisted."

"Sometimes men don't know what's best for them," Naz said. "Sometimes, the women who *love them,*" she said the words with great sarcasm, "have to make the hard choices for them. That's why I'm here."

"Is that right?" Jakarta said. "And what do you think is the hard choice that has to be made here?"

"From what I'm hearing, you are a liability to his career. You're going to be the reason he doesn't get elected to the Senate."

Jakarta hung her head, unable to fully defend herself, because Naz was voicing some of the same thoughts that had run through Jakarta's mind.

"Miss Naz, I hear you, I know your concerns. I have said some of those exact same words to Zane. But he insisted." Jakarta met the older woman's eyes. "Maybe you should be having this conversation with him. And what is it that you've heard, and how did you come to hear it?"

"What I heard was that you are a criminal with a record and that you went to jail for assault."

"Miss Naz, then you've only heard half the story." Jakarta shook her head wearily. "Yes, ma'am, I did have some trouble, but it's so much more complicated than that. And it seems to me that even if you don't like me, you ought to trust Zane's judgment enough to know that I wouldn't be here if he didn't believe it to be the right thing."

Naz rolled her eyes dramatically. "Men are not always the most objective judges when it comes to matters of . . ." Naz paused, apparently trying to pick the most delicate phrasing. "Matters of the libido."

Anger and outrage fully consumed Jakarta at that point. "Miss Naz, I'm trying very hard to give you the respect that you've earned for your position as Zane's mother, but I am not going to stand here, in this place that I now consider my home, and listen to you disrespect me and my relationship with your son. It's not just about sex, and I would think you would know him better than that. I am not leaving. He asked me to come back to be with him, and that's what I'm going to do. I hope you are able to come to terms with this, but if you aren't I hope that you're going to be respectful enough to keep your concerns to yourself. Now if you'll excuse me, I have to get dressed." Jakarta turned without waiting for a response and strode back to the bedroom. In the room, she resisted the urge to slam the door, closing it with a quiet click instead.

Jakarta listened closely trying to hear when Naz left the apartment. A few minutes longer than Jakarta expected her to stay, the door finally opened and closed. Jakarta heaved a sigh of relief.

She heard? Jakarta thought. *Wonder how she heard anything.* Suddenly, she knew. *Damn that Whitney.*

Chapter 18

Later that evening, Zane was in his office when the phone rang.

"I need to speak to you right away." The voice on the phone belonged to Harland. "I need to talk to you and I need you to come down to my office."

"What's up, Harland?" Zane said impatiently. "I'm kinda in the middle of something."

"What you're in the middle of is a campaign. And that's what I need to talk to you about. I need you to get here, and I need you to get here within the next forty minutes." Harland was insistent. "It's important that we speak."

"I'm working on the proofs of a new campaign brochure that's going out," Zane said.

"That can wait, this cannot. I'll see you in forty minutes." Harland disconnected the call, not allowing any further discussion.

Zane looked at the receiver in his hand angrily, as if his anger could reach Harland through the buzzing dial tone. It was on his mind not to go, but he suspected he knew what Harland wanted. "The sooner I get this over with, the sooner it will be over with," he decided.

He read through a few more paragraphs of the ad proofs, and then he packed up his briefcase and left the office on his way to meet with Harland. He deliberately took his time, and arrived in Harland's office ten minutes later than the appointed time. He knew it was a small, passive-aggressive thing to have done, but somehow it made him feel better anyway. When he entered Harland's office, he was surprised to see that the two of them would not be meeting alone.

In Harland's big office, there was a massive wood desk. It always reminded Zane of the desks elementary school principals use to try to intimidate the kids. Harland sat behind the desk in an oversize leather chair. Sitting across the desk in one of the three visitors' chairs was Gerard Grey. Zane's eyes narrowed at the sight of Grey. He knew from Jakarta that Grey had been the one who approached her and encouraged her to leave.

"Harland, Gerard," Zane said tersely. "You should know that I don't appreciate being summoned down here like some kind of lackey." Zane jumped onto the offensive. "The work I was doing was important, and I'm willing to bet"—he raked Grey over with his eyes—"now that I see who we're meeting with, that this little meeting could have waited."

"I don't think so," Harland said. "Have a seat. We need to talk."

"What's on your mind?" Zane asked as he settled into one of the chairs. "Or maybe I can read your minds. You called me down here to tell me that Jakarta is no good for me and I need to get rid of her—right?"

"I wasn't going to put it like that," Harland said.

"But that's the gist of it. You feel that she is damaging my career, that this trouble that she had in the past is going to come up and ruin my chances, and you think I'd be better off without her here. Is that basically it?" Zane sighed in exasperation. "Look, let me save us all some time."

"You're going to listen to what I have to say," Harland snapped. "I have been nothing but supportive of you since this whole campaign began. You owe me the courtesy of listening to me now."

Zane leaned back into the chair, conceding the point. "All right, Harland, what is it?"

"I think Jakarta is a lovely young woman," Harland began. "I don't have any problems with her personally."

"Nor do I," Grey chimed in.

"But politically, she is a liability," Harland continued. "And you have to at least be honest enough to admit that."

"I know that there are people who are small-minded enough to see a problem for me in Jakarta's past," Zane said.

"Then you also have to know that some of those people are in the media," Grey said. "And whether or not they personally have any problem with Jakarta, they will smell a story and run with it."

"They don't ever have to find out," Zane insisted.

"Now you're being naive," Grey said. "Just like we found out, they'll find out. We just got hold of it faster."

"Because somebody chose to look for it," Zane said. "And who was that somebody, Gerard? You?"

"I had nothing to do with finding the information," Grey said.

"Why should I believe that?" Zane asked. "You had everything to do with convincing Jakarta she should leave."

"And I still think she should," Grey said. "I stand by that. But I didn't dig any information out, it was brought to me."

"By whom?" Zane demanded.

"That doesn't matter," Grey said. "The point is right now that information is in friendly hands, but there's no guarantee that it's always going to be that way."

"Look, Zane, we're not telling you to break up with her or that you can't ever see her again," Harland said. "Neither of us would say that. We're all men here, we understand how these things work. But I am saying to you that she needs to not be here now. The election is in five weeks. Surely you can do without her for five weeks. If you need companionship, that can be arranged in such a way that does not compromise your entire campaign effort."

"You say we're all men here, and we understand, but I think maybe you don't. You don't understand how much she means to me. You seem to think it's just about sex; that she's some kind of campaign plaything for me, some sort of pressure releaser. It's not like that at all. I love this woman, and I want her with me. I don't believe her troubles are going to be a political liability for me. But even if I'm wrong, that will be something I'm willing to deal with." Zane stood. "I respect you both, but this is outside of the campaign. We're talking about my life here. And I don't need your input for that. Now if you'll excuse me, I'm going to go home and spend some time with my woman."

Zane left the office without waiting for a response.

"You know that's trouble coming," Gerard said matter-of-factly to Harland.

"Yeah, I think you might be right," Harland replied.

When Zane arrived at their apartment, he found Jakarta still wrapped in the cotton robe, sitting on the couch with her knees hugged to her chest.

"What is it? What's happened?" He immediately picked up on the air of trouble in the room.

"I shouldn't have come back here." Jakarta's voice was muffled. "It's too hard."

"Baby, what are you talking about? I thought you understood I need you to be here."

"Maybe it's more trouble than it's worth," Jakarta muttered.

Zane suddenly understood. "Who's been talking to you? Was it Whitney?"

Jakarta shook her head. "It doesn't matter who—what matters is I don't want to be the cause of you losing this election."

Zane sat next to her and put his hand on her shoulder. "Jakarta, I want you here. That's all that should matter."

"Sometimes men don't know what's best for them," Jakarta said mechanically. "Sometimes the women who love them have to make the hard choices."

Zane's eyes narrowed as he studied her closely. "It was Naz," he said finally.

Jakarta's head jerked up. "What makes you say that?"

"Because that's the kind of thing Naz would say . . . it's the kind of thing she always says." Zane's expression grew hard. "Naz was here, today? And she got to you?"

Jakarta shook her head. "Don't be mad at her. She means well . . . she's got your best interests at heart."

"My best interests?" Zane snapped. "Nazimoba Monroe Reeves always thinks she knows best, but she's going to have to accept that I'm a grown man, capable of making my own decisions." He stood and stalked toward the door. "This is enough. She's gone too far now. She had no right to dump on you, and I'm going to tell her so."

Jakarta looked worried. "Zane, don't do that. She already hates me, that would only make it worse."

"I'm sorry, baby, but this is bigger than you. Mama's got to learn to respect my choices." Zane left the apartment, on his way to Hammond.

He fumed all the way to his mother's house, so by the time he arrived he was in a fine simmering rage. He found Naz and Nita sitting in their rockers on the veranda. He stood at the foot of the stairs.

"Zane? This is a surprise," Nita greeted him.

"Hi, Aunt Nita. I bet it's not a surprise to you, is it, Mama?" Zane glared at her.

"I don't know what you're talking about." Naz looked away.

"Yes, you do. You took a little road trip today, didn't you?" Zane stood stone still. "Down to New Orleans, right?"

Nita looked over at her sister. "What is he talking about, Naz?"

"She knows," Zane said flatly. "You had no right, Mama. You were so far off base you're not even in the ballpark anymore."

"I did what had to be done," Naz said haughtily. "That girl is nothing but trouble for you. She needs to go."

Nita gasped. "Naz! You didn't go down there to harass Jakarta, did you?"

"You say harass; I say talk to. She needed to understand what's at stake."

Zane's fiber-thin thread of control snapped. "It was not for you to say, Mama. I'm a grown man, I can make my own decisions. And I've decided I want Jakarta to be with me. You think it's a mistake . . . maybe, but it's my mistake to make. You cannot run my life."

"You know I have only your best interests at heart," Naz said defensively.

"I know that's what you say," Zane said. "But you need to back off."

"See? Look at the effect that woman is having on you already. You've never talked to me like this," Naz whined. "Can't you see what she's doing to you?"

"Let me tell you what I see. I see you still treating me like I'm a kid, incapable of making intelligent choices. And this is not about Jakarta. This little incident is just the straw that broke the camel's back, but this has been going on for as long as I can remember. I've tried to ignore it and excuse it, but this stunt today was just too much." Zane's tone was hard. "I swear, Mama, don't make me choose between you. . . . You won't like how it turns out. Jakarta is here to stay, and you can either accept that or not—your choice. But I don't want to hear it ever again." Zane spun on his heel and headed back to his car. "Good night, Aunt Nita," he called before he climbed in and sped away.

"Naz, what have you done?" Nita said after he'd left.

Chapter 19

Jakarta had decided to keep a low profile during the remaining weeks of the campaign. She still questioned the political wisdom of coming back with him, but she had no more doubts about the personal rightness of that choice. Even though Zane had become deeply embroiled in his campaign, and quality time for the two of them was rare, Jakarta had the confidence of knowing that he loved her. She saw her role in the campaign as giving him someplace where he could just let down his guard and be himself.

She still traveled all over the state with him, but seldom came to the campaign appearances. Life on the Zane Train was a little tense for her. Harland and Kennedy had made an uneasy peace with her presence. Elaina apparently had decided as long as Jakarta stayed behind the scenes, it would be okay. Whitney, however, was getting less and less subtle about her feelings toward Jakarta.

The whole team was gathered in Zane and Jakarta's hotel suite during a Baton Rouge campaign stop, planning their strategy.

"We're closing in on Primus," Elaina announced, holding the latest polling data she'd received. "We're still about five points behind, but last week we were eight points behind, so we're gaining ground." The group applauded that news.

"That's great," Zane said. "What do we need to do to close that gap?"

"Primus is going to be hard to beat in Baton Rouge," Elaina said. "He's very well known and very popular here. But I think we can do it. If we focus on our message, we can reach the people."

Whitney said, "We need to focus on Zane. The message is only part of the equation. The rest of it is Zane. He's the drawing card here. Look, if we put out this same message delivered by candidate Joe Blow, it wouldn't have the same resonance it's going to have when it's delivered by Zane. We need him up front and out there as much as possible." She cut her eyes at Jakarta, who although not participating in the meeting, was in the suite. "And we need to make sure that Zane is out there alone," Whitney said pointedly.

"And why is that, Whit?" Zane asked.

"We've got that whole eligible bachelor devoted to community service thing that we started, and you don't want to endanger that image by showing up with your *girlfriend.*" She sneered the word.

Jakarta's head whipped around to face Whitney. "You know what, Whitney—"

"We hear you, Whitney." Elaina cut the argument off before it got started. "Everybody hears you loud and clear. Let's try and focus now. Primus wants a debate, which is a good sign because he wouldn't even consider debating us unless he saw us as a threat."

"Fine," Zane said. "Tell him to bring it on."

Elaina hesitated. "I'm not so sure. He must want something specific. Maybe some kind of ambush he's got planned. Until I get a better handle on their strategy, I'm not prepared to agree to a debate just yet. I think we need to stay on our message, stay on point, and keep hammering away at it."

"Okay," Zane said. "So what's up for tomorrow?"

Elaina checked her schedule. "Tomorrow, you're being interviewed by the local CBS affiliate, and after that you have an interview with the political reporter from the *Baton Rouge Post,* and then tomorrow night there's a joint fund-raising appearance with the governor."

"Wow, the governor's out stumping too, huh?" Zane was impressed.

"It's important to him that the Senate seat remain Democratic," Elaina said. "He's going to do everything he can to help."

"Got it." Zane nodded. "I'm ready."

The team dispersed and left Zane and Jakarta alone in the suite.

"Sounds like you've got a long busy day tomorrow," she observed.

"Yeah, it is going to be pretty long." Zane paused. "Won't you come with me?"

"Oh, Zane." She shook her head. "We've been through all this before."

"I know, Jakarta, but none of these are really public appearances."

"Not public appearances?" Jakarta looked at him as if he had lost his mind. "You're going to be interviewed on television, interviewed for a newspaper, and appear at a fund-raising dinner. How are those things not public?"

"Okay, the dinner, maybe—so I won't ask you to go to that. But the interviews aren't public appearances . . . not really."

"Zane!"

"No, really. I'm not asking you to appear on camera with me, just be in the studio—in the wings—while I'm being interviewed. Same with the newspaper guy. You don't have to participate in the interview, just be somewhere nearby." Zane stuck out his bottom lip in an intentionally childish pout. "I miss you during the day. I get tired of being by myself or with the staff. It would be nice to have you with me."

"Aw, Zane, you're a pro at this stuff. Me being there is not going to have any impact, one way or another." Jakarta started to leave the suite's sitting room, heading toward the bathroom.

"Jakarta, please," Zane called to her. "Just go with me tomorrow."

Jakarta felt herself weakening. "Okay," she said finally, "if that's what you want. I'll go."

"Good," Zane said triumphantly. He walked over to her and kissed her lightly. "I've got to go now. Kennedy wants me to come to the local party office and chat with some of the volunteers he's rounded up."

"That's fine, honey," she said, returning his kiss. "If I'm sleeping when you get in, please wake me up."

He gave her a lewd and lascivious smile. "Count on it," he said. With a jaunty nod of his head, he left the hotel suite.

The meeting with the volunteers had gone very well. Zane was impressed by the people Kennedy had recruited, and humbled that they all seemed very committed to getting him elected. *I never quite get used to the support I get from strangers,* he thought.

He was alone in a small office in the party headquarters, going over briefing notes for the next day. He didn't want to have to do any work when he returned to the suite. He was concentrating on the notes when he heard the door open. He looked up and smiled at Whitney as she came into the office.

"What's up, Whit? I thought I was the only one left here tonight."

"Well, it's just you and me," she said. "Kennedy told me you might still be here. Do you have a moment? I'd like to talk to you."

"Sure," he said amiably, "have a seat. What's on your mind?"

"I don't really know how to say this, Zane—" she began as she settled in the chair.

"That's really rare," he interrupted. "Whitney Gramm, state-renowned media strategist, at a loss for words?"

"Don't tease right now, Zane, this is kind of important."

Immediately, his levity evaporated. "I'm sorry, Whit. What is it?"

"It's about your image," she said after a pause. "I'm worried about the kind of image you're projecting to the voters."

"Tell me what you mean."

"Well, you are very professional. You're the perfect candidate. You're handsome, strong, well dressed, and well spoken."

"Why, thank you, Ms. Gramm." Zane blushed a bit. "But none of that seems to present a problem."

Whitney raised her hand. "Let me finish. You are exactly what the voters want. I'm worried about Jakarta."

Zane cocked his head curiously at her. "Oh? And why is that?"

"Because she is not what the voters expect their senator to be involved with."

"I beg your pardon?"

"Face it, Zane, the voters have certain expectations

of the people they select to represent them." She ticked her points off on her fingers. "They expect you to be honest, they expect you to be responsible, and they expect you to be surrounded by good people."

"Are you saying Jakarta is not a good person?"

"I don't know Jakarta well enough to say that. What I'm saying is we're not even talking about her personality. We're talking image here. I'm in the media business. Image is everything."

Zane shook his head. "You're losing me, Whitney."

"Only because you're determined to be obtuse," she said. "Stop thinking like a man and start thinking like a politician. With those locks—she's even got seashells laced into her hair—and that whole unconventional, ethnic, bohemian vibe she's got going on, she is not the appropriate partner for you."

Zane struggled to remain calm. "Are you talking politically or personally?"

"I don't know how many times I have to say this or how many people I have to say it to, but at this level of the game there is no difference between political and personal. Everything you do and every choice you make is going to affect your political career. What I'm saying to you now is that Jakarta is a bad choice. You could do so much better."

Zane whistled as he listened to her. "You're way out of line, Whitney."

"Well, since I'm already out of line, I'm going to step even further and say to you that I have always felt," and Whitney's voice softened noticeably, "that you and I could be the ultimate Louisiana power couple. With our looks and smarts, we would be perfectly matched. Our strengths complement each other. I can take you so much further than you ever envisioned going. We would be so much better a match than you and Jakarta."

Zane sat in shocked silence for several moments, floored by Whitney's declaration. *I have to tread lightly here,* he thought. *I want to try and save our working relationship.*

"Whitney," he began, "I have the utmost respect for you as a media professional. Your instincts for my campaign have been right on, so far. And I do believe you have my best interests at heart—"

Whitney was quick to interrupt him before he could continue any further. "All those things are true. I do have your best interests at heart."

"I know," Zane conceded. "But this is too much. This campaign is not my whole life. Win or lose, I still have a life outside of campaigning and politicking. What you're talking about as far as Jakarta is concerned is a life partner for me. I am considering spending the rest of my life with her. Not just the rest of my career."

"Don't you see what I'm offering you, Zane?" Whitney tried again. "We could have it all. The life and career you have only dreamed of."

"Whitney," he said gently, "the life I have dreamed of is with Jakarta—politics aside."

She stood up and put her hands on her hips. "So, you're going to let that nappy-headed bohemian ruin your career, is what you're saying to me."

"What I'm saying to you is that I'm not going to tolerate you talking about my woman for another moment. And what you're going to have to keep in mind is that I am the candidate and you are the aide. You're working for me. Now, I'm going to choose to believe that you came to me in the spirit of trying to help this campaign, and I'm going to choose to ignore the things you've said about the woman I love. But, Whitney," and he fixed her with a steely gaze, "don't ever make the mistake of crossing that line again. Now if you'll excuse me . . ." He turned his attention back to the notes he'd been reading when she entered, dismissing her.

Infuriated and humiliated, Whitney could only turn and stalk out of the office. She held on to a shred of her dignity by restraining her urge to slam the door when she left.

We'll see about this, she thought. *You think your life and career are separate things? Yeah, we'll just see about that.*

After he heard Whitney leave, Zane dropped the pretense of work. He leaned back in the chair, both drained and stunned from the encounter. *I knew she didn't like Jakarta, but this?* He shook his head, thinking. *I don't know if Ms. Gramm is going to be able to continue working on this campaign. How are we going to work together ever again?* Zane could find no answers.

"I'm through with campaigns and politics for the night," he declared. He reached for his cell phone and called Jakarta at the hotel, desperately needing some normalcy.

"Hi, baby," he said when she answered.

"Hey, Zane." She sounded pleased to hear from him. "Where are you? Is the meeting still going on?"

"Nah. I was just trying to get through some reading I needed to do before I came back to the suite."

"What is it?" Jakarta's voice revealed her concern. "What's happened?"

"What makes you think something's happened?"

"I can hear it in your voice. Now tell me what's wrong," she insisted.

Zane was both impressed and pleased that she was so keyed in to his emotions. "Everything's fine now, baby."

"I don't believe everything's fine. But I'm here if you need me," she promised.

"You don't know how much I'm counting on that," he said. "I'll be there soon."

"I'll be waiting."

He disconnected the call with a smile on his face. The sound of her voice and the power of her concern reenergized him as he knew it would. He stood and turned off the lights in the office. With a spring in his step, he left the campaign for the night.

As she sat in her car, Whitney toyed with the over-size envelope for several minutes, flipping it up one side and down the other, hefting the weight of it, listening to the pages within shift with every movement.

"I'm doing the right thing," she repeated to herself. "It might hurt Zane in the short run—but in the long term, he'll see that this woman is not right for him. He will see that his career means more to him than she does. And then he'll thank me." She tried the words on again in her head, to see if the fit felt right. "It's the right thing to do," she decided finally. She started the car and pulled away from the curb, on her way to keep the appointment she'd set.

"Why are you doing this, Whitney?" The man across the table from her narrowed his eyes suspiciously. "As much time and effort as you've put into this man's campaign, why would you be trying to sabotage it now?"

Whitney and her counterpart from the Primus campaign, Peter Valley, were seated in a secluded corner of an out-of-the-way restaurant, far from the usual haunts of Baton Rouge's political crowd. It had taken some doing, but Whitney had managed to convince Peter that the meeting would be worth his time.

Now, after he had read through the file she had on Jakarta, Peter was trying to figure out Whitney's angle.

"I am not trying to sabotage it," Whitney said haughtily, "I am trying to save it. Not just this man's campaign, but his career. Nobody seems to see the threat this Jakarta is to his political future but me. So if I'm the only one who's willing to save him, then so be it. Do you want this information or not?"

"I don't think John would appreciate these kinds of dirty tricks. I've been working on John Primus's campaigns for years, ever since he first ran for city council in Baton Rouge, and he's always tried to stay above the dirty tricks."

"I understand that, Pete. That's why I called you and not John. Because I've known you for many years too, and you've never really been above the dirty tricks, have you?" She leaned across the table closer to him. "John has tied your hands sometimes, but dirty tricks are a staple of the business for you—isn't that right?"

Pete grinned. "Well, takes one to know one," he said.

"So listen, here's the information that I have. If it gets out to a couple of our media contacts, they'll take it from there."

"I don't understand why you think this is going to work," he said. "I haven't seen this woman around him in weeks. He's been appearing solo as far as I remember."

"Yeah." Whitney nodded. "She's been lying low, but leave that to me. I'll get her back out front. And then . . ."

"And then I'll know what to do," Pete said. "You know your boy's going to lose the election because of this."

"You thought my boy was going to lose the election anyway," Whitney pointed out. "Why do you care if it's because of this or because of something else?"

Pete nodded. "You've got a good point. We have you beat anyway . . . we don't have to resort to dirty tricks to win this election."

"So consider it a favor to me," Whitney said dismissively. "And just for the record, I don't think you have us beat. You've seen the polling data; we're closing in. Without something to stop the 'Zane Train' you'll be looking for a job in a few weeks."

Pete shrugged, conceding her point.

"So do we have a deal then?" she demanded.

"Yeah." He shook the hand she extended. "I don't really understand why you're doing this, but yeah, we have a deal."

"I understand why I'm doing this, Pete," she said. "That's the only thing that matters."

Chapter 20

The next day as Jakarta had promised, she went with
Zane as he began his round of interviews. His first
scheduled interview was to take place live during a
morning news show called *Wake Up, Baton Rouge*.
They had to be at the studio by 5:30 A.M.

"Why did I agree to do this again?" Jakarta groused
as she stumbled through the hotel suite trying to get
dressed. "I've never even seen five-thirty in the morning."

"It'll be great," Zane enthused. "Wait until you get
your first breath of early morning air. You'll never want
to sleep late again." He was already dressed—his stan-
dard politician uniform of dark jacket, pale shirt, and,
since it was early morning television, he'd opted for a
brightly patterned tie.

"You know what? I think one of your campaign
promises should be to round up all the morning people
and have them shot at dawn," Jakarta grumbled, from
the bathroom. "Who is up this early watching TV anyway?"

Zane laughed. "Baby, there's a whole 'nother world that exists before ten A.M. You might find you like it."

Finally dressed in a pair of cream linen slacks and a bright orange blouse with an African mask design, Jakarta emerged. "I seriously doubt it," she said.

"You look great," Zane said. "Come on, let's go."

"Are there even cabs available this time of the morning?" Jakarta teased as she followed him out of the suite.

In her capacity as media specialist, Whitney was at the television station early, waiting for Zane. She wasn't sure how he would react to her. *I probably overplayed my hand yesterday,* she thought. But until something happened to change things, she was going to do her job, just like normal. She had spent the night mulling over strategies to get Jakarta back in the public eye so that her exposure plan would work. Whitney was growing frustrated by her inability to concoct a convincing scenario, when Zane and Jakarta entered the studio.

Fabulous, she purred. *They're going to make this easy for me.* She took a deep breath, squared her shoulders, and hurried across the studio to greet them.

"Good morning, Zane. Good morning, Jakarta," she said.

"Good morning, Whitney." Zane's greeting was chilly.

Picking up on the undercurrent, Whitney went on the offensive. "Jakarta, I'm sure Zane told you about our conversation last night. Let me just say before we go any further that I was way out of line, and I apologize. Sometimes I get blinded by political ambition, and I lose sight of what's really important. I shouldn't have said anything, and I was wrong."

Jakarta gave her a blank look. "Actually, Zane didn't

mention anything to me. I guess he didn't feel that it was important enough to bring it up."

"Oh," Whitney said. "Then everything's fine, right?"

Zane scowled at her. "Everything's going to be fine, Whit. My concern right now is getting through this interview."

"Well, I'm really glad to see you, Jakarta," Whitney said. "The reporter wanted to have you participate in the interview as well."

Jakarta shook her head. "Nope. I don't do interviews. This is Zane's show, not mine."

"No, you don't understand. The reporter won't be asking you any questions," Whitney was quick to clarify. "They do a featurette kind of thing before the actual interview. Sort of a getting to know the candidate. It's just a few minutes of videotape that leads into the interview. For those few minutes of tape, they want to have you in there so people can start to get a sense of what Zane is like off of the campaign trail."

"I thought it was your position that I needed to stay in the background," Jakarta said suspiciously.

"Well, now I think that we have to have balance," Whitney hedged. "It's important that the voters see Zane as a responsible man, capable of committing to a relationship."

"What!" Jakarta snapped. "That completely conflicts with the eligible bachelor line you've been dishing out for weeks now. What are you up to, Whitney?"

"Honest, I'm not up to anything. I think that eligible bachelor might have been a mistake because it makes Zane seem frivolous, and we don't want the voters to think of him as some kind of playboy. So maybe it's time for us to present another side of Zane. It will help balance out the frivolous playboy image."

"I'm not prepared to be interviewed," Jakarta said.

"I'm not dressed for it, and I just intended to sit in the background."

"But that's all you have to do," Whitney promised. "The cameraman is going to take some video of Zane interacting with people. If you'll just be in the background, that will be enough for now. We're going to ease you into the public's vision again. We don't have to jump all the way out there at once."

Jakarta looked at Zane quizzically. "What do you want me to do?"

"Whitney might have a point," Zane said slowly. "Up until very recently I had always trusted her judgment."

"I seriously overstepped, Zane," Whitney apologized profusely. "Please, let's just act like it never happened. You know I only want what's best for you."

"So you think what's best is for Jakarta to be visible again?" Zane questioned.

"Just a little bit," Whitney clarified. "We don't want to make this the Jakarta/Zane show. But she is an important part of your life and the voters need to know that."

He looked at her skeptically, not completely prepared to let go of the memory of the things she'd said just the night before.

"I am glad to see that you're coming to accept this relationship," he said. "Jakarta and I will talk about her appearing on the tape, and we'll make a decision."

"Okay, that's fine," Whitney said. "Whatever you think is best. I'll go check with the anchorwoman and see when they want to get started with the interview." Whitney disappeared through a nearby doorway.

Zane led Jakarta to a pair of chairs set up in the back of the studio.

"What do you think?" he asked.

"I think Whitney's up to something. I don't trust her as far as I can throw her," Jakarta said flatly.

"But what could it be?" Zane wondered.

"I don't know, and I don't want to find out."

"But she has a point. You are very important to me, and the voters need to know that. And up until a few weeks ago, you were always in the background while I gave speeches. I don't see any harm in going back to that again." Zane grinned. "And look at it this way: when I do my big acceptance speech, you have to be somewhere nearby, and we don't want to just spring you on them."

She chuckled. "Acceptance, huh? You're sure that's the way it's going to go?"

"Absolutely," he said.

"So do you want me to do this?"

Zane shrugged. "All they're asking you to do is be a face in the crowd . . . a presence in the background. I don't see anything wrong with that."

"All right," she said, "if that's what you want me to do. Now suppose you do something for me? Suppose you tell me what Whitney is apologizing for? What happened last night?"

Zane sighed and looked away. "It was nothing. She said some things she shouldn't have, that's all."

"Some things about me, I assume."

"It doesn't matter. She was out of line, I told her so, and she apologized. It's over and done with."

"Why won't you tell me?" Jakarta asked.

"Because it's not important. It would take more effort than it deserves." Zane lifted her hand to his lips and kissed it. "Believe me, it's not an issue."

"So you've forgiven her?"

"I've decided to ignore it, and I want you to do the same. Whitney is very good at her job. If she gets a little overzealous sometimes, it's probably because of all the passion she pours into her work."

"Well, just so she is not trying to pour her passion into you," Jakarta said shortly.

When Whitney returned with the videographer, Zane let her know about their decision. "As long as you're sure," she said. "Let's set up the shots."

The videographer led Zane and Jakarta to a conference room. There were already a few people from the station's staff assembled there.

"Stand there at the head of the table," the videographer instructed Zane, "and just talk to these people. Miss," he addressed Jakarta, "you can just have a seat in that chair to his immediate right. There's not going to be any audio for this piece, so you all can talk about whatever you want. I just need a few minutes of Zane with an audience that we can run before the interview."

Zane nodded. "Let me know when you're ready," he said. He and Jakarta moved to their designated places. Zane removed his jacket and hung it over the back of the chair.

The videographer tweaked a few knobs on his camera and adjusted the light levels in the room. "Okay, let's get started."

Zane stood at the head on the conference table and leaned forward, his palms pressed on the tabletop. "So, I know why I'm here at five forty-five in the morning; what on earth are you all doing here?" He smiled broadly.

The staff members assembled around the table laughed. Jakarta, from her spot at his right, smiled up at him.

After a few minutes of chitchat, the videographer shut off the camera. "That's great. I've got what I need. Thanks, everybody." He turned to Zane. "I'm going to run this on down to production. I think your interview is at six-thirty."

"Yes, it is." Whitney reappeared just as the videographer was leaving.

"Where'd you run off to?" Zane asked. "You could have been in the shot too."

"I just had a little something to take care of. Besides, I really don't need to be on camera. People know who I am, that I work for you. Having me in the shot would make it look too staged."

"Yeah," Jakarta said sarcastically, "we certainly wouldn't want it to look staged."

By the time they'd finished with the preliminary videotaping, it was nearing time to begin Zane's interview. Whitney escorted them to the studio set where he'd be interviewed. The set consisted of two blue barrel chairs, a small table, and a large artificial plant. The backdrop was a pale blue wall. The reporter who would be conducting the interview was already on the set, making notations on index cards.

Whitney handled the introductions. "Zane Reeves, I'd like to introduce Nanette Ivens. Nanette, this is our next senator, Zane Reeves."

Zane smiled and shook hands with a well-coiffed blond woman, whose age he estimated to be around twenty-six. "Nice to meet you," he said.

"You too. Thanks for coming in so early." Nanette smiled.

"No problem," he assured her, studiously ignoring Jakarta's eye-roll in the background.

Zane and Nanette took their seats, and a crewman came over and attached Zane's microphone. "We'll come out of commercial right to you, Nan," the crewman said. "Then you're on."

"Good morning." Nan spoke in carefully modulated

tones into the camera. "This morning we'll be talking to Mr. Zane Reeves, Democratic candidate for the recently vacated seat of Senator Reid. Thank you for joining us, Zane," she said.

Zane nodded. "Thank you for asking me."

After a few general questions about Zane's stance on issues and the campaign, Nan asked, "How is your love life these days, Mr. Eligible Bachelor? We hear that you may be just about off the market."

Zane froze for a moment, and then struggled not to overreact to her question. "You know, having a love life on the campaign trail is pretty hard business," he answered lightly.

"But we understand you're making it work," she persisted. "So who is that exotic mystery woman you've been seen around Louisiana with?"

The question blindsided Zane. "I don't know if exotic mystery woman is what I'd call her." He chuckled nervously. "She's a very good friend of mine who has been very supportive during this campaign. And she fully understands and supports my views. Particularly my stance on pay parity in the workplace." Zane quickly deflected the topic from Jakarta back to the issues. Nan did not pursue the discussion on Jakarta; instead she picked up on his parity talk. The interview went on a few more minutes with no more bombshells.

"Well, that's all for today." Nan turned back to the camera. "Thank you for joining us this morning on *Wake Up, Baton Rouge.* Have a great day." When the red light went off on the camera, she turned to Zane. "Thanks a lot, that was a great interview."

"What was that business about my love life?" Zane demanded.

"Aw, c'mon, Zane." She shrugged. "Inquiring minds want to know."

He shook his head, snatched the microphone off, and left the set in disgust.

"I thought you handled it well," Jakarta said when he reached her side.

"It shouldn't have had to be handled at all," he snapped. "That was wrong."

"Well, sometimes things don't go as we planned," Whitney interjected. "You've got that interview with the *Post* reporter coming up. You're having lunch with him."

"Yeah, okay," Zane said, irritated. He still had a bitter taste in his mouth from the television interview. "Hope this one goes a little better."

"It will, I'm sure of it," Whitney said. "You've got a few hours before the lunch meeting; you feel like hanging around the statehouse building and meeting a few voters? I've got some 'Reeves for Senate' brochures in my briefcase; you could pass some out and shake a few hands."

Zane smiled, knowing contact with the voters always rejuvenated him. "That's an excellent idea." He turned to Jakarta. "Want to help?"

Jakarta nodded. "Sure, why not?"

After a few hours of glad-handing, talking with voters, and passing out brochures, Zane felt much better about the morning's adventure. As they headed to the restaurant where they would meet the *Post* reporter for lunch, Zane was relaxed and confident again.

The lunch and the interview were uneventful. Jakarta was able to stay in the background as she had planned, and Zane was able to focus on the issues as he had planned. By the end of the day, as they returned to the suite so Zane could get ready for the fund-raising dinner he had to attend, the experience at the television station had been all but forgotten.

"You should come to dinner with me," he said to

Jakarta once they were in the suite. "There's no media, and I don't really have to give a speech. Just a bunch of fat cats with money to donate."

"I don't know . . . I don't really feel like going," Jakarta said.

"Aw, c'mon. You've been hanging out with me all day—don't break up the team now."

She sighed. "Sure. I guess I have to dress up?"

He nodded. "Yeah, it's kinda dressy."

"Well, then, give me a few minutes, and I'll join you."

"Hurry," he called, "this shindig starts at six and it's after five now."

"Don't rush me," Jakarta teased. "I'm doing good considering I haven't had my nap today and I've been up and running since four this morning."

Zane laughed. "Welcome to my world."

A short time later, Jakarta and Zane headed out, Zane decked out in a black suit, a cream-colored shirt, and a red power tie, Jakarta looking elegant in a black cocktail dress with her locks gathered on top of her head and held there with a tortoiseshell clip.

Their destination was the ballroom of the hotel where the fund-raising dinner was being held. Zane was wrong in his estimation that there would be no media. He had underestimated the drawing power of the governor. The media were out in full force. Paparazzi and legitimate news media took pictures of Zane and Jakarta as they entered the ballroom and more pictures of them as they sat together at the table.

The evening was very routine. Zane and the governor both gave brief remarks, and the donors all opened their checkbooks.

It was nearly eleven o'clock when Jakarta decided

she was exhausted. She leaned over and said to Zane, "I'm going up to the suite. I'm pretty wiped out."

"That's fine, baby. Thanks for coming with me. I'll be up later."

"Take your time," she said. "Do what you have to do. I'm just going to get into bed."

Not quite ready to kiss him in public, Jakarta squeezed his hand and left the ballroom, heading back to their suite. When she arrived, she turned on the TV for company as she changed into her pajamas. She heard the opening theme music for a tabloid show called *Exposé* wafting into the bathroom as she washed her face.

"So who is the mystery woman standing on the arm of leading Senate candidate Zane Reeves?" the voice from the TV said. "And what's her dark secret?"

"What!" Jakarta dropped the washcloth to the floor and rushed to sit in front of the TV. When she got there she was stunned to see images of herself and Zane flashing on the TV. Some from the beginning of the campaign, but some from earlier that day. Jakarta's eyes widened in horror as she saw a snippet of the video she and Zane had shot earlier in the TV station's conference room.

"You may have seen him posing as one of the year's most eligible bachelors, but U.S. Senate candidate Zane Reeves, top contender to fill the seat of retiring Senator Reid, is not nearly as much a bachelor as you may think. During the campaign season, he has been seen many times with a mysterious young woman by his side."

Still pictures of Zane and Jakarta at the state capitol passing out brochures were shown.

"Exposé wanted to know, who is this woman who has caught the eye of the candidate?"

Jakarta's horror grew as she saw the pictures of them arriving at the banquet that evening.

How the hell do they do that? she thought. *That was just a few hours ago.* She jumped up from the bed and paced the room anxiously. "This is horrible," she repeated over and over again. "This is horrible."

"We're not sure exactly who the mystery woman is yet," the voice from the TV continued, "but leave it to *Exposé*—we'll get all the inside information." The story ended and a commercial appeared.

"Oh, my God," Jakarta breathed. "That means there's going to be more."

She wanted to talk to Zane right away, but he was still downstairs at the fund-raiser. "Oh, no," she moaned, "this is going to be bad."

In her own hotel room, Whitney was gleeful. "Damn." She giggled. "It happened faster than I could have dreamed." She congratulated herself. "And it's going to be a multipart story? It'll start with this little trashy tabloid show, but before the week is out the affiliates will be all over it. It's just a matter of time, Little Miss Jakarta . . . it's just a matter of time."

When Zane got into the suite that night, he found Jakarta sitting on the edge of the bed with a look of panic on her face.

"What is it, baby?" he said. "What's happened?"

"The absolute worst thing we imagined," she said in a whisper. "Somebody's doing a story on me."

"What?"

The phone rang, interrupting their conversation. "What?" Zane barked into the phone.

"Did you see it?" Elaina yelled into his ear. "What the hell is going on?"

"No, I didn't see it," Zane answered. "Jakarta was just telling me about it. You tell me what's going on."

"It's *Exposé*—some trashy tabloid show. They're doing a story on Jakarta."

"How do they know to do a story on Jakarta?" Zane demanded.

"I don't know, but you damn well better believe I'm going to be finding out. I'll get back with you." Elaina hung up the phone.

"That was Elaina," Zane said. "She's ticked."

"Me too," Jakarta assured him.

"Well, what was it? What did the show say?"

"It wasn't so much what they said, it's what they insinuated. That I'm some sort of mystery to be solved, and that they'll be on the case keeping everybody posted."

Zane sat down heavily next to her. "You've got to be kidding."

"Do I look like I'm kidding?" Jakarta said, agitated. "I've got to find out how this happened."

"I don't know if it matters how it happened," she said. "What matters is, what are we going to do about it now?"

"Let's just wait and see what develops," he said. "It might not be as bad as we think."

Jakarta shook her head. "Trust me, Zane, it's going to be worse."

Chapter 21

As Whitney had so gleefully predicted, the next few days bought a barrage of media attention. The more Zane tried to deflect the story, the bigger it became. Before long, Jakarta was the topic of conversations at water coolers all over the state. As *Exposé* had promised, they uncovered all of Jakarta's past troubles, putting the worst spin possible on both her hospitalization and her arrest.

The story was generating so much heat, Jakarta was reluctant to leave the apartment. There were reporters out front, and she wasn't up to facing them and their microphones and their probing questions—again. The presence of so many reporters shot her back to ten years before when the hearings had been going on. Back then, as now, she had tried to avoid the reporters and the microphones, but Dr. Sullivan had done no such thing, she remembered.

I wonder if he's heard about the story coming up again. I'll bet he's loving it—he's probably in Detroit giving interviews every day. What a son of a bitch.

The thought of Sullivan reminded her yet again of the way the media could skew and distort a story. She remembered feeling like a hunted animal when the story had happened the first time around, and she wondered if it would get that bad again.

And if it's that bad for me, she thought, *I wonder how it will be for Zane. Do I really have a right to ask him to go through this?*

She pondered that question for a few moments, and could find no answers. She decided to call the campaign office so she could talk with Zane about the situation.

"Reeves for Senate," a chipper volunteer answered the phones in the office.

"Is Zane in please?" Jakarta asked.

"Who's calling?" the volunteer asked.

Jakarta hesitated, not wanting to give her name, unsure of what kind of reception she would get. "This is Jakarta," she said finally, hoping that she could count on the volunteer to maintain her friendly demeanor.

"Oh, hi, Ms. Raven," the volunteer said, never skipping a beat. "Mr. Reeves is not in right now. Can I connect you with Ms. Winters?"

"Elaina's there?" Jakarta asked.

"Yes, she's in her office. Do you want to talk to her?"

"Yes, please, that would be great," Jakarta said.

"Elaina Winters." She answered the phone with crisp efficiency, and more than a little irritation.

"Hi, Elaina, this is Jakarta. Do you have a couple of minutes?"

"Sure, Jakarta." Elaina's tone softened. "I'm surprised to hear from you. What's up?"

"Elaina, I've been thinking an awful lot about what's been going on, you know, with the story and all."

"Yeah, I imagine you would," Elaina agreed. "I'm so sorry you're having to live through this again, it's got to be hell on you."

"It's no picnic," Jakarta admitted, "but it's not me that I'm worried about. I'm worried about how it's going to affect Zane."

"What do you mean?"

"Come on, Elaina, we're both women of the world. You know as well as I do that all this negative publicity is not going to help Zane's campaign."

"I can't deny that," Elaina said. "But I think that we can spin past this story. I don't think it's going to be the defining moment of the campaign."

"Do you really not think that or are you just saying that because you don't want to hurt my feelings?" Jakarta asked.

"I'm not going to lie to you, Jakarta, this is bad. But it's not your fault," Elaina insisted, "and I don't want you to feel guilty about this."

"Oh, please. How could I not feel guilty?" Jakarta said. "And how can it not be my fault?"

"This happened ten years ago," Elaina pointed out. "Before Zane even knew you. Anybody with half a brain can see that it has no relevance to what's going on now."

"My concern is the mass electorate might not have half a brain," Jakarta said. "I've been thinking the best way for this story to end is for me to leave again. If I head back to Detroit, just until the election is over, then the story will go away with me."

Elaina was quiet for a few moments. "I don't think that's such a good idea, Jakarta," she said finally.

"Why not?" Jakarta demanded. "It just seems so obvious to me—if I'm gone, the problem's gone."

"Zane loves you," Elaina said, "and if you're gone,

then Zane's going to be gone too. He's not going to let this chase you out of town. He will come after you."

"You can get him to stay, Elaina," Jakarta said. "You can explain to him how important it is to his campaign that he's here."

"I don't think so," Elaina replied. "I tried that when he went after you before, and he was not hearing it then. And unless I'm a blind woman, you two have gotten even closer now. He won't be trying to hear it again."

"But, Elaina, you and I both know it's for his own good. He has to focus on the campaign, and the best way for him to do that is for me to get out of his hair, and out of the public's line of sight."

"Jakarta, if you leave, Zane is only going to be focused on you. The campaign will go to hell in a handbasket until he gets you back down here. So on a personal level, it's not going to help him at all for you to go. Even if you don't believe that, let me tell you what I think about the political consequences of you leaving." Elaina took a deep breath. "If you leave, it will look as if the story were true. It will look as if you ran because you couldn't take the heat. And then that will reflect even worse on Zane than what we're going through now. I think we have to tough this out. I know it's uncomfortable for you; I know it brings back unpleasant memories for you, but we're all going to have to tough this out. Running away is not going to be your answer. Not now."

Jakarta was silent, hearing in Elaina's words the same wisdom that her sisters had been giving her for years.

"You don't think I should leave," Jakarta said quietly.

"I absolutely do not. I don't think it would be good

personally for Zane, and I don't think it would be good politically for him. The best thing for us to do now is just ride out this storm."

Jakarta sighed. "Thank you, Elaina," she said. "I trust your judgment implicitly."

"Good, then you'll stop all this talk of leaving and toughen up. Politics is a hard game and it's not for the weak at heart."

"Yeah, I'm coming to see that," Jakarta said. "Thanks again, Elaina." She hung up the phone, went to the French doors, and looked out past the courtyard to the street. She could see two news trucks parked on the quiet street and knew that the reporters were still waiting for her.

Okay, I won't leave town, but I'm not leaving this apartment right now either, she decided. *I'm not going to face those people without Zane by my side.*

The sound of a key in the door caused Jakarta to turn. Her eyes narrowed when the door opened.

"What do you want now, Miss Naz?" she asked. "Come to gloat a little?"

Naz shook her head. "I've come to get the truth. You told me a while back that I only knew half the story. I want to hear the other half."

"Why?" Jakarta demanded. "You made up your mind about me a long time ago. What difference could it make now?"

Naz took a deep breath. "I trust my son's instincts, and he believes in you. I want to believe in you too." She took a step closer to Jakarta. "Please, give me a chance to be on your side."

Jakarta studied her long and hard, trying to gauge the older woman's sincerity. After a long tense moment, Jakarta motioned to the dining table. "Pull up a chair. It's a long story."

Jakarta proceeded to pour out her story, much as she had done weeks before in Detroit with Zane. And Naz listened quietly, her horror and pity showing on her face. When Jakarta had finished, Naz got up from her chair and circled the table to hug her.

"I don't know what to say," Naz breathed. "I had no idea. Oh, God, what you've been through." Naz shook her head sadly. "And now you're having to go through it again. Oh, Jakarta, I'm so sorry."

Jakarta struggled to control the tears that threatened to spill out. Naz's motherly touch reminded Jakarta of her own mother, and reminded her of how much she missed a mother's concern.

"Please forgive me," Naz said. "I had no idea. I was so wrong about you."

Jakarta gave up trying not to cry and let the tears go. "But you weren't wrong about the election," she sniffled. "Zane is probably going to lose because of me."

"That's not important anymore," Naz said gently. "What's important is that you know this horrible incident is not who you are. And it's important that you know I was wrong to judge you, and wrong not to trust Zane. I only pray you two can forgive a foolish old woman."

They hugged and cried together then. And when Zane came home later that evening, he found the two most important women in his life snuggled next to each other asleep on the couch.

I can't wait to hear what that's all about, he thought.

Chapter 22

As the story grew, Elaina became more and more livid. She canceled all their campaign stops for the next few days and called everyone together at the New Orleans headquarters for an emergency strategy session.

"We've got to do something about this," she said.

Zane shook his head. "I disagree. I don't think we do anything. I think we ignore it and let it go away. The more we talk about it, the more juice we give this story."

"It's not going to go away," Elaina said. "It's been four days now, and the networks are starting to talk about it."

"National networks?" Jakarta was stunned.

"Yes. Zane is hugely prominent, and a lot of people have been watching this race across the country. This has now become an enormous story. We cannot ignore it." Elaina was firm.

"But what can we say?" Jakarta asked. "It's all true. We can't deny it."

"But maybe we can spin it," Elaina said. "We have to try and put the best face on this."

Zane glared across the room at Whitney, who had so far been silent. "Why don't you tell us how they found out about this, Whit?"

"Me? Why do you think I know?"

"Don't even try it." He was disdainful. "You and I both know where the media got that story."

"Zane . . ." Whitney's voice had a pleading tone. "I'm on your side. I've always been on your side. I don't pretend to have been a friend of Jakarta's, but I'm all for you. I wouldn't do anything that would hurt you," she said, fully believing her words.

"Well, then, how did they find out?" he demanded.

"It could have been any number of ways, but that's not what's important here. What we need to focus on is what we're going to do about it now."

"And what do you suggest, Whitney?" Zane said caustically.

"You're not going to want to hear my suggestion."

"Try me."

"I think Jakarta should go away again for a while."

Zane snorted. "So you want to hide her."

"I wouldn't think of it as hiding her, but we have to take the heat off of her, and that might be the best way to do it," Whitney said.

Jakarta had sat quietly long enough. "Oh, that is the biggest bunch of bull I have ever heard," she snapped. "Do you really think for one instant that I don't know where this story came from? Do you think that you're fooling anybody?"

Whitney bristled angrily. "What exactly are you accusing me of?"

"You know exactly what I'm accusing you of. More importantly, you know exactly what you've done."

"And what is it that you think I've done?"

"I think it's obvious. I'm accusing you of sabotaging

Zane's campaign. I'm accusing you of wanting to get at me so badly that you're willing to sacrifice Zane. I told him months ago that you were a barracuda and you needed to be removed from our team."

"I don't see this as being productive," Elaina interjected. "I don't know if it matters where it came from. What matters is what we're going to do about it."

"Of course it matters where it came from," Jakarta insisted. "Because if we don't identify this source and stop this leak, there's no reason to believe it won't happen again, and again, and again."

Zane nodded. "Jakarta's right. Whitney, I don't trust you anymore. You don't belong here . . . you should go now."

"You are firing me?" Whitney was indignant.

"Yes, I am. It's time for you to move on. Party's over for you."

"I'm not going anywhere," Whitney said. "I'm going to see this through until the end."

"What is the 'this' that you're referring to?" Jakarta sneered. "You want to see how Zane crumbles now?"

"Look, witch—" Whitney jumped up and stepped toward her.

Jakarta stood. "Oh, you don't want to bring it to me."

"No, no, no!" Elaina jumped up and placed herself between them. "This is not the kind of campaign I'm running."

"Look," Zane inserted, "everybody calm down. Here's the bottom line. Whitney, I believe you have betrayed me, but even if you didn't, I think you did. So I don't trust you anymore. And I can't work with people I don't trust. So you'll have to go."

"You need me," Whitney said.

"No, Whitney, I don't. I need people around me that I trust and believe in. You are no longer one of those people. Get out."

"Now?" Whitney looked dumbfounded.

"Right this instant. I don't want you listening to another thing that my campaign supporters have to say. You don't deserve it."

"You are dead wrong about me."

Zane shook his head. "I don't think so. Now get out," he repeated.

Whitney looked around the room, hoping to find an ally. No one met her glance.

"Why are you people so blind?" she said. "Can't you see what's at stake here? Zane could be president one day. He just has to have the right people around him. That's all I'm concerned about . . . making sure he's got the right people around him."

"You are no longer one of those people," Zane said forcefully. "Now do I have to call the police to have you removed?"

Banished, Whitney stormed out of the headquarters. This time, salvaging her dignity was not nearly as important to her as the ear-shattering slam she left in her wake.

Zane released a breath he hadn't been aware of holding when he heard Whitney finally leave.

"What if you're wrong about her, Zane?" Elaina asked.

"I'm not wrong about her," Zane declared, "but even if I am, it doesn't matter anymore, I don't trust her. I'm through talking about Whitney—what are we going to do now?"

Elaina took a deep breath and refocused on the story. "I think you have to address it. I think you have to tackle it head-on. Because it's not going away. And the more you try to ignore it, the bigger a story it seems to be. Deal with it and make it end."

"Deal with it how?" Zane asked.

"Primus has been itching for a debate with you for a while now. Let's do it," Elaina said. "We can have some control over the venue and how the message gets out."

"You think it's time to debate him?"

"Well, Zane, he's been one of the loudest voices questioning your judgment of character because of your association with Jakarta. I think he's going to have to be neutralized, and I think that can be done in the debate."

"Okay," Zane agreed. "Set it up."

At their apartment that night, Jakarta was apologetic. "I don't know how to say this, Zane, but I'm so sorry for what has happened."

"It's not your fault," he said tersely.

"It's obviously my fault. If we were not together, you wouldn't have to deal with this."

"If we were not together, I wouldn't have most of the joy in my life," he said. "I wouldn't trade the time we've had together for anything. Not any election, or anything else. Stop trying to own this problem," he said. "This is a problem that was exploited by Whitney. She knew how much the public would relish a story with lurid details. So maybe it's a problem with the public. What kind of society are we living in where candidates are judged by the past problems of their friends? It just pisses me off—this isn't about me, this isn't about the issues, this isn't about anything but the public's need to hear dirt on people."

"I still feel like if I had stayed in Detroit, at least until the campaign was over with, you wouldn't have to deal with this."

"Baby, if it wasn't this, it would be something else. As it is, I'm glad you're here."

"Are you sure a debate is the best way to deal with this?"

"Yes. There are some things that need to be said, and I'm ready to say them."

"Okay, I'll be there."

"You will?" he asked.

"I wouldn't be anywhere else, ever again," she assured him.

Elaina managed to schedule the debate for two days later. There was only a week left before the special election would be held, and the story about Jakarta was consuming the news. It was the only thing about the campaign that anybody ever talked about anymore. Their opponent made it a point whenever he could to attach significance to the Jakarta story by saying it was clearly an indication of Zane's ability to judge character. Primus wondered aloud how the voters could trust someone who counted as his love a woman who had wrongfully accused a prominent psychiatrist of abuse and then attacked him when she wasn't able to make those charges stick. Elaina knew that if they didn't have this debate soon and start to diffuse these charges, Zane's election hopes were dead in the water.

Jakarta was in regular contact with her sisters. As Elaina had warned them, the story had attracted the attention of the networks, and since Jakarta was from Detroit, the Detroit press was following the story closely as well. She talked to at least one of her sisters every day, and some days she talked to all of them. They were steadfast in their support of her and had offered to go to the media and tell the truth.

"This story they're spreading is just a lie," Paris said to her during one of their group conversations. "They can't be allowed to keep spreading these lies about you. Let us go and tell them the truth."

Jakarta declined. "I love you for wanting to do that, but Zane doesn't want us to handle it this way."

"What does he think we should do?" Paris asked.

"From Zane's point of view, it doesn't matter whether the story is true or not. Zane's position is that the story itself doesn't matter."

"That's pretty idealist," Sydney said.

"I agree with you this time, Syd," Jakarta said, "but it's Zane's campaign and he has to follow his convictions."

"So let us know if you need anything," Savannah offered.

"And if you need us to make sure the truth gets out, we can do that too," Paris chimed in.

"It's okay. What you're doing right now, being there for me, is what I need. Thank you."

As the debate neared, Zane grew more and more intense. Jakarta understood the fighting instinct that she saw in him, because it was hers as well.

"It's going to be okay, baby," she assured him many times.

"They have no right to put us through this," he said, indignant. "No political office is worth this sort of drama."

"You will do us both proud," she said. "I know that. I have complete confidence in you." She pulled him to her and held him close. "Whatever happens we will always have each other. Remember telling me that we have each other and nothing is ever going to be stronger than the two of us together? Do you remember that?"

"I remember."

"You were right then, and I am right now. We can do this, and we'll do it together."

* * *

On the night of the debate, Zane and Jakarta arrived at the venue hand in hand. The debate was being held in the auditorium of the local community college. The auditorium was already packed when they arrived. Normally, a debate like this would not have generated this sort of interest, but everyone was aware of the titillating details of Jakarta's story and wanted to be on hand to see what would happen.

Elaina met Zane at the door. "Whitney's here," she told him.

"It's a public place," Zane said dismissively. "She can be wherever she wants."

"I'm still not convinced she did this thing you've accused her of," Elaina said.

"It doesn't matter. All that matters now is this debate."

"Are you ready?" she asked.

"Yes, I am," he said confidently.

"Let me give you the logistics." She quickly briefed him on where he would sit and what to expect. "And remember, this is a live telecast," she finished.

"I'd like Jakarta to be near the front," he said.

Elaina looked concerned. "Are you two sure about that?" Her look traveled between Jakarta and Zane.

"Yes," Jakarta said firmly. "We've talked about it and I want to be in the front. I want people to know who I am, and I want people to know that I'm not afraid."

"Okay." Elaina nodded. "You two are calling this shot. Let me go make the arrangements."

"You ready, baby?" Jakarta said to him as she adjusted the knot on the silk tie he was wearing.

"Absolutely."

Elaina came back. "It's time. Jakarta, come with me." Jakarta turned to Zane and hugged him tightly, not wanting to kiss him and leave a lipstick print behind. "I love you," she said.

"I know."

Zane took a deep, steadying breath and took his place on the stage. The debate stage was set with two podiums of equal height that the candidates would stand behind. The commentator would be across the stage from them, facing the candidates, his back to the audience. Each candidate would have three minutes to make an opening statement and then the commentator would read selected questions from the audience for the candidates to answer. The stage was festooned with red, white, and blue bunting. The flags of Louisiana and the United States of America stood on poles at the back corner of the stage. There were lush ferns on the floor in front of the podium, further dressing the stage.

Before the broadcast started, Zane crossed the stage to greet his opponent, John Primus. Primus was a fit, robust-looking middle-aged white man. He had a full head of white hair carefully coiffed for tonight's appearance. He was not as tall as Zane, but he had a commanding presence. He radiated the confidence of a career politician who was in his comfort zone.

"Good luck tonight, John." Zane extended his hand.

"And to you too, Zane," John said. "I hope you know this has all just been politics for me. I don't have anything personally against you or your girl."

Zane stared at him coldly. "It hasn't been all politics for me, or for Jakarta. That's because I'm not the politician that you are. But I'm learning."

John smiled dumbly, not fully processing the jab Zane had just lobbed at him.

The floor director for the broadcast approached them. "Take your places please, gentlemen. We're thirty seconds from the start."

Zane went and stood behind his podium. He closed his eyes for a moment and gathered his thoughts. When the music signaling the start of the broadcast swelled throughout the auditorium, Zane was ready.

"Good evening, ladies and gentlemen," the commentator said directly into the camera. "Thank you for joining us for this live broadcast of the debate in the Louisiana U.S. Senate race. This special election, one of the most hotly contested in Louisiana's history, is being waged between Orleans Parish Assistant Prosecutor Zane Reeves, and the state representative from Baton Rouge, John Primus. Each man will have an opportunity to address you directly, and then will take questions. We'll be going alphabetically tonight, which means"—the commentator turned in the direction of John—"we're starting with you, Representative Primus."

John nodded and smiled. "Thank you." Primus used his three minutes to remind the voters of his outstanding record in the House and to talk about his family values. He ended his speech with a thinly veiled reference to the controversy.

"Character is important these days," he said. "It is what defines us; it is what defines a good man in our society. Not just the character of the man, but the character of the people around him. My grandmama used to say to me, 'Birds of a feather flock together,' and I've always believed that to be true. When you think about this decision you have before you, don't just consider the record, consider the man. Consider who you want to represent you in Washington. Thank you."

Overly enthusiastic applause from Primus supporters filled the auditorium. When they had quieted down, the commentator turned to Zane.

"And now, for your opening statement please, Assistant Prosecutor Reeves."

Zane looked into the audience, trying to find Jakarta. Once he found her, he took a moment to lock eyes with her. She returned his gaze, and mouthed the words "I love you" to him. Energized, Zane began.

Chapter 23

"Ladies and gentlemen, I believe my opponent is exactly right," Zane said. "I believe you can judge a man by the company he keeps. But I also believe something else. I believe that in this campaign or any campaign, the focus has to be the issues of the day. People who attempt to hold public office in our society these days open themselves up for public ridicule or scandal. This should not be. Politics should be a noble profession. We should support, not destroy, those people who are willing to step into public life.

"These last few days, you've heard much about a situation that happened a decade ago to a woman whom I hold very dear. It doesn't matter at this point what the truth is, although believe me, you haven't heard the truth from these stories you've been fed. What matters is, why did you even want to know? Will knowing the sordid details of Jakarta's situation help you to know whether or not you are for pay parity for men and women? Will knowing the details about Jakarta's incident help you decide whether or not your family deserves to breathe the air that can be cleaned only if

Washington leaders insist on strict environmental controls on the oil refineries in the gulf? Sure, we all like to be entertained. And sure, sometimes titillating details are most certainly entertaining. But when the rubber meets the road, the question that you have to ask yourself when it comes to this election or any election is, 'Will this candidate improve my family's life?' If you believe that a candidate can do that, then that's the person you should support.

"Politicians deserve to have private lives too. Even politicians who are actively seeking office. If we as a society do not respect that, if we as a society do not respect the privacy of the men and women who put themselves out in front of the firing squad for the honor and privilege of representing us, then people will stop trying to serve, and we will not have the level of representation that we deserve. We owe it to ourselves as a society and we owe it to our politicians as individuals to respect their privacy. There's a line between your right to know and my right to be left alone."

The auditorium was quiet for a long, tense moment. The silence reverberated through the audience. But then Jakarta began to clap. A solitary sound at first, but soon her clapping was joined by a few others, and then a few more, and then the whole auditorium burst into wild applause, acknowledging the bold and brave speech that Zane had just delivered.

Jakarta felt tears well in her eyes as she applauded for him. "Bravo," she called, "bravo!"

It was several long minutes before the audience could be quieted enough for the debate to continue. What would come next didn't matter. Zane had done what he set out to do.

*   *   *

"You were magnificent," Jakarta said to him once they had returned to their apartment. "You were eloquent and intelligent and passionate. How could anybody not vote for you?" She helped him shrug out of the suit jacket he'd worn on TV.

"You wouldn't be a little biased, now, would you?" he said.

"Maybe, but that doesn't change the fact that you were amazing tonight. And it really touched me."

Zane's eyes grew dark with need. "Did it touch you here?" he asked as he placed his hand at the base of her throat.

Jakarta's breath quickened at the warmth of his palm. "Absolutely," she said.

"And did it touch you here?" With his index finger, he drew a line from the base of her throat to the V of her shirt and came to a rest between her breasts.

She nodded. "There too."

He backed her up against the wall of the dining area and pressed his body against her. "And did it touch you there?" His voice was a low, husky whisper.

Jakarta lifted her arms and wrapped her hands around his neck, pulling his mouth to hers. "It touched me everywhere," she said softly against his lips.

He slid his tongue into her mouth, and she accepted the warm wetness of it, tasting and suckling it. He pressed her farther against the wall, grinding the bulge of his manhood against her through their clothes.

"Now," he breathed urgently into her ear. "I want you now."

She unfastened his pants and slid them and his briefs over his trim hips down to the floor. At the same time, he was insistently lifting the hem of her dress. He ripped the waistband of the lace panties she wore in his urgency to remove the obstacle. Jakarta gasped as she felt the fabric rend around her.

Zane bent slightly at the knees and wrapped his arms around Jakarta's legs and bottom. With ease, he lifted her from the floor. Her back against the wall, Jakarta wrapped her legs around his waist and urged him home.

Zane entered her quickly with one solid thrust. They shuddered together for a moment and were still, trying to gain some sense of equilibrium and control. Zane held her close to him, and with her arms and legs wrapped around him, he was as much her prisoner as she was his. They moved together, a timeless, ageless ballet of passion and need, fulfillment and want. Their need to become one body, one flesh was a rejection of the world that scrutinized them. This was Zane and Jakarta releasing the pressure, a declaration of their privacy in the most intimate fashion possible.

Zane kissed her as he thrust into her, reveling in the sensation that Jakarta alone roused in him. Their passion mounted as their movement grew faster and more insistent. Jakarta reached the mountaintop first. As she unconsciously clawed at his back, hanging on to him with every ounce of strength she had left, her body tensed and contracted, sending dynamic waves of orgasmic pleasure coursing through her body. She yelled his name as though the power of the universe could be found in that one word. Zane felt her release against his body and gratefully surrendered all pretense of control. The sensation that rocked through him caused his knees to buckle, and he barely managed to hold them both up. He felt his seed shoot from his body and spread into hers. The intensity of the moment was clouded only by a sudden realization.

"Oh, baby, we forgot to use a condom," he muttered.

Only now beginning to gather her wits as she rested her head against his shoulder, Jakarta could only shrug.

"But what if—" he began.

"If 'if' happens," she said, "then we'll deal with it. And if we have to deal with it, I hope it's a little boy who looks just like you."

Zane kissed her again deeply before he lowered her to the floor. "I hope it's a little girl who looks like you," he whispered.

The last two days before the election were intense. Jakarta threw herself into the campaigning as fiercely as Zane did. She was passing out flyers, walking the neighborhoods, and working the phone banks. Some people who recognized her were supportive and encouraging. Most of the feedback Zane's team had received from his debate performance had been positive.

"But I don't really care what the people think," Zane said. "I said what needed to be said, let the chips fall where they may."

It was full-court press right up until the polls closed on Election Day. Finally they had done all they could do and all that was left to be done was to wait. Zane, Jakarta, Elaina, Harland, Kennedy, Naz, Nita, and the volunteers all gathered at the party headquarters on Election Night awaiting the results.

The headquarters had been festively decorated; the volunteers were anticipating a victory party. There were balloons and confetti held close to the ceiling with netting that would be released at the appropriate time by a tug of the rope in the corner. Brightly colored banners and ZANE REEVES FOR SENATE posters filled the space even more than usual. Naz and Nita had been put in charge of food, so there were finger sandwiches and popcorn and desserts and soda and beignets and coffee available for the celebrants. It was going to be a long night of returns and they all settled in to wait.

"It was a good race, Zane," Harland said, "and I think you stand a good chance to win."

"Well, whatever happens, I believe we ran as hard as we could," Zane said.

"Do you think the story about me hurt in the end?" Jakarta asked Harland.

"I think that if that story hadn't happened, the voters never would have had the chance to truly see Zane's character," Harland replied, "so maybe it was all worth it in the end."

Elaina was on the phone constantly speaking to her contact at the board of elections, trying to get advance information on the results before they were released to the media.

"They've counted the votes in four percent of the precincts," she called, "and Primus is ahead sixty to forty percent." That announcement was met with a chorus of boos.

"Never fear," Harland called out, "that's only four percent, and that's the four percent out in the swamps."

The volunteers laughed.

"So how are you feeling, Zane?" Jakarta asked him as they shared a muffaletta sandwich.

"I'm tired," he said, "and I'm glad that it's over, whichever way it goes."

Kennedy came over to them. "Have you thought about what you're going to say to the volunteers?" he asked.

"Yes, I have," Zane answered. "When do you want me to address them?"

"The media people will be here soon, and it might be nice if you had a word with the volunteers before the press got here," Kennedy replied. "That might make it more intimate."

"Good suggestion," Zane agreed. "Why don't we gather them up and I'll do that?"

Kennedy nodded and left to see to it.

Zane walked to the podium set up at the front of the room where he would give either his acceptance or his concession speech later in the evening.

"Hey, y'all," he called out, attracting the crowd's attention. "Let me take a few minutes before it gets too crazy in here to express my gratitude." He paused and reached for Jakarta's hand, pulling her to the front with him. "Or should I say, 'our' gratitude? This campaign has been a real series of ups and downs for all of us. Jakarta and I really appreciate your support. It has meant more than you'll ever know. Whatever happens tonight, I know that I have made friends that I will keep for the rest of my life and I know that you all are the best. Thank you for everything you've done."

The volunteers applauded wildly and began to chant: "Zane! Zane! Zane!"

Zane and Jakarta left the podium and went into the audience shaking hands and accepting hugs of support.

"They're up to twenty percent of the precincts counted," Elaina yelled from her spot at the phone. "It's Primus fifty-seven, Zane forty-three. We're closing in on him!"

The crowd bellowed their approval.

"We're getting closer." Jakarta hugged him. "We might just pull this off after all."

Zane was surprisingly serene about it all. "I'm not even sure I care anymore," he said to her quietly. "It's been such a difficult fight, I'm not sure how I feel about winning."

"Don't let them hear you say that," Jakarta teased. "These people have worked too hard to get you in here for you to be acting like you don't even want to win."

Zane smiled at her. "Still being my campaign conscience, huh?"

"Beloved, some things will never change. Whether you're campaigning or not, I'm always going to be your conscience."

He hugged her. "Some things, beloved, never should change."

Naz and Nita emerged from behind the food tables to join them. "This is quite a party," Nita observed. "Looks like everybody in New Orleans is here."

"Everybody who matters anyway," Naz inserted. She reached for Jakarta's hand. "I hope you know how sorry I am for my behavior, and how happy I am that you didn't let me chase you away."

"Miss Naz, you were just protecting your son. I understand that." Jakarta squeezed her hand. "No more apologies are necessary. I just hope you know how much I love him and how committed I am to making him happy."

Naz hugged her fiercely. "You are everything Zane will ever need."

Nita hugged Jakarta next. "See? I told you she'd come around. She's always been as stubborn as a mule."

Naz shot her sister a withering look that reduced them all to laughter.

Ted Johnson, the media specialist who'd been called in at the last minute to replace Whitney, approached Zane. "The media will be arriving soon. I'm going to have them start to set up their equipment up front. They're going to be doing live cut-ins from here, so they're going to want to talk to you periodically."

"That's great, Ted. I understand. Thank you by the way for stepping in at the eleventh hour to help out."

"Glad to be of service," he said. Nodding at Jakarta, Naz, and Nita, Ted left to attend to his responsibilities.

"Sixty-two percent of the precincts counted," Elaina announced, "and we've closed the gap even further. It's

Primus fifty-five, Zane forty-five, and they haven't counted New Orleans yet!"

A noticeable sense of victory permeated the crowd.

"New Orleans is our stronghold," Harland told Jakarta. "If New Orleans is still out, then you can believe our numbers are about to improve."

"This is all so exciting," Jakarta said.

At that moment, Zane's cell phone rang. With a curious look on his face—"Hell, everybody I know is here"—Zane answered the phone. A smile spread across his face. "Of course, she's right here, hold on. Jakarta, it's for you."

Jakarta looked at him quizzically. "Huh?" She accepted the phone.

"Girl, we had to know what was going on, we could not wait another moment!"

Jakarta laughed, thrilled. "You guys! Who's on the phone?"

"I'm here," Savannah said.

"Me too," Paris chirped in.

"I'm here too," Sydney said.

"A conference call? You guys conference-called me long-distance to a cell phone?" Jakarta asked.

"Hey, we had to know what was happening," Paris said.

"So give," Sydney chimed in. "What's the status?"

"The last count we just got a few minutes ago had Zane down by ten points. But that's okay, we started out the evening down by twenty. We're closing in on them, and they haven't counted the votes in New Orleans yet. That's Zane's parish. We're gonna own New Orleans."

"So it looks like he might pull it off?" Savannah said.

"I don't know," Jakarta answered, "but it's looking pretty good so far."

"This is so cool," Paris enthused. "When will it be finished?"

"I'm not sure. The media is setting up here now, so I guess it can't be too much longer."

"Well, we're just going to stay on the phone until we hear," Sydney declared.

"It could take a long time," Jakarta warned.

"So? We don't have anything else to do," Savannah said.

"I love you guys. You are the best!" Jakarta beamed with happiness.

"That's what everybody tells us." Paris laughed.

Zane had gone with Ted to greet the members of the media. Jakarta, still talking into the cell phone, worked her way through the crowd to the front of the room and took a seat in the front row facing the podium.

The room was fairly humming with energy. The final returns were expected any moment now. Elaina was still on the phone, trying to get the information. As Zane chitchatted with the media, he felt amazingly calm. He wasn't sure yet whether he'd be giving the acceptance speech or the concession speech, but he knew that whatever happened, his life would never again be the same because of this campaign experience.

He was looking at Jakarta's animated face as she giggled with her sisters on the phone. He was struck by a wave of love for her. *This woman has changed my life,* he realized. He was about to walk over to her when Elaina came up to him.

"You look grim, Elaina. What's happened?"

"Come over here." She led him to a relatively private corner of the crowded room. "The final count's in."

"And I take it we lost," Zane said, looking at her face.

"I'm sorry, Zane, it got so close. The final count was fifty-two to forty-eight. We're going to request a recount, but—"

"But those numbers will probably stand," he said matter-of-factly.

"Yeah, I think so," Elaina said sadly. "You gave it a good run, Zane. You were an excellent candidate."

"And you were an excellent campaign manager."

"When you get ready to do this again," she said to him, "call me."

"Do this again?" He laughed. "What makes you think—"

"Because you're a good man, Zane Reeves," she said. "And you can't keep the good ones down. Go on, it's time. Make your speech."

He hugged her. "Thank you."

He went in search of Ted. "It's time," Zane told him. "I'm ready to give my speech."

"It's a concession speech," Ted guessed.

"Yeah, but it's okay."

Ted nodded. "I'll gather them up."

A few moments later, Zane stood behind a phalanx of microphones with television lights blazing on him. From her seat in the front row between Naz and Nita, Jakarta could sense his mood. *We lost,* she thought to herself.

"What is it, J? You got quiet. What's going on?" Sydney's voice rang through the phone.

"Zane's about to give a speech."

"Well, hold the phone up so we can hear it," Savannah commanded. Jakarta lifted the phone toward the front.

"Good evening, ladies and gentlemen," Zane began. "Thank you all again for being here. At this time, I'd like to take the opportunity to congratulate our next U.S. senator, John Primus."

Wails and moans of disappointment rolled through the room.

"No, no, no—it's okay." Zane held his hand up to calm the crowd. "John is a good man, he'll make a fine senator for us all. It's time now for the good people of Louisiana to come together behind their choice. I'd like to go on record as saying if there is anything that I can do to be of service to Senator-elect Primus, I'm ready to help."

"Zane! Zane! Zane! Zane!" The crowd renewed their chant from earlier.

"Thank you all so much. It was a hard-fought battle, and we've done a good thing for Louisiana politics, and don't you ever forget it. We've made campaigns focus more on the issues and less on the people. If every campaign takes our crusade a little further, before long all campaigns will be just about the issues and not about personalities."

The crowd cheered wildly. Zane looked out at Jakarta's face. He felt her love and support. For a moment, the crowded room fell away and it was just the two of them, sharing a private moment of understanding and support.

Suddenly Zane's attention snapped back to the cameras. "This campaign has meant a lot to me for a lot of reasons," he said. "And let me reintroduce you to one of the biggest reasons this campaign has been so significant for me. Jakarta, would you come here please?"

Jakarta looked stunned for a moment and started to shake her head.

"Please, honey, come up here," Zane urged.

"Go on!" her sisters were screaming through the cell phone. Naz and Nita nudged her gently from either side.

Jakarta rose and crossed the few feet between them to stand by her side.

"Jakarta," he addressed her directly, "having you with me has been the only thing that has kept me sane throughout this whole experience. I didn't realize how much you meant to me until now." He ignored the sea of microphones, cameras, and people, and focused his attention exclusively on Jakarta. "I know we lost this election. But I will consider myself having won the biggest prize of my life if you would consent to marry me."

A collective gasp raced through the room, Jakarta included. There was no sound for a few moments.

"Answer him!" a tinny voice drifted up from the cell phone she held in her hand.

As if she were coming out of a trance, Jakarta's face burst into a smile. "Yes!" she said, loudly and clearly, "a thousand times yes!"

The audience cheered more loudly than they had at any point during the evening. Naz and Nita hugged each other, happy tears streaming down their faces. Someone pulled the release rope, and hundreds of red, white, and blue balloons and tons of confetti cascaded down around them. Zane opened his arms, and Jakarta walked into them. And then, before the entire state of Louisiana on live TV, they kissed—a kiss intimate and private, full of promise and hope, a kiss that united them emotionally as surely as the marriage ceremony later would unite them legally.

"I love you," he said when the kiss ended.

She looked deeply into his eyes. "I love you, too."

As if suddenly realizing that they were not alone in the room, Zane turned his attention back to the crowd.

"Looks like I won after all," he said.

Dear Reader,

Does the public's right to know outweigh a public figure's right to privacy? It's a question that becomes more and more relevant as we search for the boundaries between privacy and legitimate information. Jakarta and Zane had to face this very complicated question, and I believe the power of their love got them through. *Passion's Destiny* pits love against politics . . . and as it should, love wins out.

I hope you had half as much fun with Jakarta and Zane as I did. I truly enjoyed the time I've spent with them, and it was wonderful for me to visit again with Jakarta's sisters. Savannah, Sydney, Paris, and Jakarta are fascinating to me; I love waiting to see what they're going to do. I'm going to be hanging out with Paris for a while next. She strikes me as a sista with a story to tell. I can hardly wait! I hope you'll join me.

All best wishes,
Crystal Wilson-Harris

ABOUT THE AUTHOR

Romance novelist Crystal Wilson-Harris is an associate professor of developmental English at Sinclair Community College in her hometown of Dayton, Ohio.

Crystal enjoys spending time with her family and volunteering in various community service organizations. Her other interests include jazz, cyberspace, auto racing (watching, not driving—yet), a not-so-secret affinity for all things *Star Trek* (*Next Generation* only, please), and an almost obsessive love for home-improvement/decorating programs.

Despite a schedule that has her juggling a full-time job, two kids, a dog, a cat, and a new husband, she is currently hard at work on her next book, the third in her series *The Raven Sisters—Women of Destiny*.

Crystal loves to hear from other lovers of great romance. She invites you to contact her via e-mail at CrystalWH@netzero.net or snail mail at P.O. Box 60702, Dayton, Ohio 45406.

DO YOU KNOW AN ARABESQUE MAN?

CHARLES HORTON, JR.
ARABESQUE MAN 2002

featured on the cover of

One Sure Thing by Celeste O. Norfleet / Published Sept. 2003

Arabesque Man 2001 — PAUL HANEY
Holding Out for a Hero by Deirdre Savoy / Published Sept 2002

Arabesque Man 2000 — EDMAN REID
Love Lessons by Leslie Esdaile / Published Sept 2001

Arabesque Man 1999 — HAROLD JACKSON
Endless Love by Carmen Green / Published Sept 2000

WILL YOUR "ARABESQUE" MAN BE NEXT?

ONE GRAND PRIZE WINNER WILL WIN:
- 2 Day Trip to New York City
- Professional NYC Photo Shoot
- Picture on the Cover of an Arabesque Romance Novel
- Prize Pack & Profile on Arabesque Website and Newsletter
- $250.00

YOU WIN TOO!
- The Nominator of the Grand Prize Winner Receives a Prize Pack & Profile on Arabesque Website
- $250.00

To Enter: Simply complete the following items to enter your "Arabesque Man": (1) Compose an original essay that describes in 75 words or less why you think your nominee should win. (2) Include two recent photographs of him (head shot and one full length shot). Write the following information for both you and your nominee on the back of each photo: name, address, telephone number and the nominee's age, height, weight, and clothing sizes. (3) Include signature and date of nominee granting permission to nominator to enter photographs in contest. (4) Include a proof of purchase from an Arabesque romance novel—write the book title, author, ISBN number, and purchase location and price on a 3-1/2 x 5'' card. (5) Entrants should keep a copy of all submissions. Submissions will not be returned and will be destroyed after the judging.

ARABESQUE regrets that no return or acknowledgment of receipt can be made because of the anticipated volume of responses. Arabesque is not responsible for late, lost, incomplete, inaccurate or misdirected entries. The Grand Prize Trip includes round trip air transportation from a major airport nearest the winner's home, 2-day (1-night) hotel accommodations and ground transportation between the airport, hotel and Arabesque offices in New York. The Grand Prize Winner will be required to sign and return an affidavit of eligibility and publicity and liability release in order to receive the prize. The Grand Prize Winner will receive no additional compensation for the use of his image on an Arabesque novel, Website, or for any other promotional purpose. The entries will be judged by a panel of BET Arabesque personnel whose decisions regarding the winner and all other matters pertaining to the Contest are final and binding. By entering this Contest, entrants agree to comply with all rules and regulations. Contest ends October 31, 2003. Entries must be postmarked by October 31, 2003, and received no later than November 6, 2003.

SEND ENTRIES TO: The Arabesque Man Cover Model Contest, BET Books, One BET Plaza, 1235 W Street, NE, Washington, DC 20018. Open to legal residents of the U.S., 21 years of age or older. Illegible entries will be disqualified. Limit one entry per envelope. Odds of winning depend, in part, on the number of entries received. Void in Puerto Rico and where prohibited by law.

ARABESQUE

BET BOOKS

The Arabesque At Your Service Series

Four superb romances with engaging characters and dynamic story lines featuring heroes whose destiny is intertwined with women of equal courage who confront their passionate—and unpredictable—futures.

__TOP-SECRET RENDEZVOUS – _Air Force_

by Linda Hudson-Smith   1-58314-397-1 $6.99US/$9.99CAN
Sparks fly when officer Hailey Douglas meets Air Force Major Zurich Kingdom. Military code forbids fraternization between an officer and an NCO, so the pair find themselves involved in a top-secret rendezvous.

__COURAGE UNDER FIRE – _Army_

by Candice Poarch   1-58314-350-5 $6.99US/$9.99CAN
Nurse Arlene Taft is assigned to care for the seriously injured Colonel Neal Allen. She remembers him as an obnoxious young neighbor at her father's military base, but now he looks nothing like she remembers. Will time give them courage under fire?

__THE GLORY OF LOVE – _Navy_

by Kim Louise   1-58314-411-0 $6.99US/$9.99CAN
When pilot Roxanne Allgood is kidnapped, Navy Seal Col. Haughton Storm sets out on a mission to find the only person who has ever mattered to him—a lost love he hasn't seen in ten years.

__FLYING HIGH – _Marines_

by Gwynne Forster   1-58314-427-7 $6.99US/$9.99CAN
Colonel Nelson Wainwright must recover from his injuries if he is to attain his goal of becoming a four-star general. Audrey Powers, a specialist in sports medicine, enters his world to get him back on track. Will their love find a way to endure his rise to the top?

Now Available in Bookstores!

Visit our website at **www.arabesquebooks.com**.

Arabesque Romances
by *Roberta Gayle*

__Moonrise $4.99US/$5.99CAN
   0-7860-0268-9

__Sunshine and Shadows $4.99US/$5.99CAN
   0-7860-0136-4

__Something Old, Something New $4.99US/$6.50CAN
   1-58314-018-2

__Mad About You $5.99US/$7.99CAN
   1-58314-108-1

__Nothing But the Truth $5.99US/$7.99CAN
   1-58314-209-6

__Coming Home $6.99US/$9.99CAN
   1-58314-282-7

__The Holiday Wife $6.99US/$9.99CAN
   1-58314-425-0